Victoria Fox

Glittering Fortunes

MILLS & BOON

Mills & Boon, an imprint of Harlequin (UK) Limited,
Eton House, 18-24 Paradise Road, Richmond, Surrey TW9 1SR

© Victoria Fox 2013

ISBN: 978 0 263 91028 5

097-09013

Harlequin (UK) policy is to use papers that are natural, renewable and recyclable products and made from wood grown in sustainable forests. The logging and manufacturing processes conform to the legal environmental regulations of the country of origin.

Printed and bound by
CPI Group (UK) Ltd, Croydon, CR0 4YY

For Kate Wilde

ACKNOWLEDGEMENTS

Love and thanks to Sally Williamson, Jenny Hutton, Donna Condon, Ian Grutchfield, Ali Wilkinson and all at MIRA/Mills & Boon, for turning a hot date into a romance.

Also to Maddy Milburn, who works so hard for my books; to Cesca Major for what makes a hero; and to Alice Usherwood for letting me borrow her beautiful name.

PART ONE

CHAPTER ONE

IT WAS A fine day to be on the sea. Summertime in England and the sky was wide and cornflower-blue, golden sunshine twinkling on the water, and on the shore the small Cornish town of Lustell Cove sat pretty as a drawing.

Olivia Lark sensed the wave at her back and began to paddle, working her arms as the rush gathered pace and she braced herself for the leap. On a surge she lifted on to the board, the motion of the swell carrying her for an electrifying instant before her footing slipped out from beneath her and she toppled into the water. For seconds she was submerged in a whoosh of salty-fresh silence before surfacing, half gasping, half laughing, into the day, and feeling, as she always did, on the receiving end of a cosmic punchline. Despite a mouthful of chalky Atlantic and the noose of seaweed wrapped around her ankle, out on the water she felt happiest of all.

She splashed into land, the board tucked under one arm and the other lifted to squeeze the briny dregs from her chestnut hair. On the beach, bronzed bodies basked in the heat on pink towels, a rainbow of parasols fluttered lazily in the breeze and chased an arc around the horseshoe inlet. Holidaymakers licked strawberry ice cream and patted castles out of gritty, grainy buckets, while on the water black shapes paddled, bobbing on the sway, counting to the ultimate wave.

Swiftly she showered and dressed, tying her hair in a loose, damp ponytail, and made her way across the sand. She couldn't put it off for ever.

The Blue Paradise surf shack was a timber cabin bordered by cut-out palms. Out front a heap of kayaks were knotted together, haphazard driftwood stumbling a path to the entrance. She almost collided with a group of girls on their way out.

'Oops,' she backed up to let them pass, 'sorry!'

Slinky as panthers in their wetsuits, tossing manes and tinkling laughter, the girls were like glossy creatures from another planet. Olivia couldn't help wondering if, in her younger years, she had enjoyed access to mascara, a hairdryer, a *wardrobe*—words that through her teens had taken on the exotic overtones of a far-flung spice market—she might have earned access to that kind of magazine-friendly femininity. As it was there seemed to be an awful lot of effort that went into it (seldom was the day she staggered into the morning with so much as a perfunctory glance in the mirror), time that could be better spent doing other things, like sticking your head out of a car window, or running at cows through a mud sludge, or daydreaming about the guy you fancied, or having a lie-in, or painting a picture, or making lists about all the things you really ought to spend your time doing, which wasn't any of the above.

Even as a child, playing Teatime at Tiffany's (horrid little conferences she had endured as a six-year-old; Tiffany Price pouring air out of the spout and asking if anyone took milk, which had troubled Olivia's young mind deeply because how could there be milk if there were no actual *tea*?) had never held the same allure as whatever adventure the boys were having—building dens, firing catapults, hunting the beach for gold. She had scrambled into their fold by way of initiation: Oli who could climb a tree quick as a monkey, who picked up spiders in her bare hands, who drew her own comic books with a blunt pencil and who always had grass stains on her knees.

Taking a breath, she stepped inside.

'Hey, Addy.'

She propped her board by the door. The shop was gleaming with drowsy afternoon glow, its shelves stacked with reef gear, trunks and bikinis, racks and wax. On the wall hung an impressive model of a Great White, tail whipping and teeth bared.

Addy Gold was in his usual position at the counter, thumbing through his phone with his top off, a string of beads at his neck and wrists. Illuminated in a shaft of sunlight, his six-pack glistening above the peeled-down skin of his wetsuit, Olivia half expected a burst of choral music to accompany the sight.

'Hey,' he mumbled, glancing up from important business to give her a fleeting, if somewhat confused, smile. 'Back already?'

'It's been a year.'

'Has it?'

His indifference stung. 'Yeah, well, London didn't work out.'

That was the understatement of the century. It was hard to believe she was back at Lustell Cove, her childhood home: scene of angst-ridden school years at Taverick Manor, endless lazy Saturdays paddling the water and stolen kisses after dark with Theo Randall from the tennis club, who had always smelled faintly of Aertex. At twenty-two Olivia had graduated from a local art course, London had seemed like the next logical step and so she'd headed to the city to Become A Painter (how ridiculous that sounded!), envisaging days spent floating about museums discussing abstract expressionism and sipping free wine. Instead she'd spent the next year trading an Aix-en-Provence atelier for an Archway bedsit, and camping with a tortured writer who never bought loo roll and who was in possession of so much body hair it was like showering after a gorilla. Wading ankle-deep through unsold drawings had soon become depressing and, following a series of short-lived bar jobs, the last of which had culminated in Olivia telling an aggressively sexist customer to fuck off, her bank account had finally run dry and she'd been forced to admit defeat.

'No kidding,' he droned.

She smiled brightly. 'So did I miss much?'

'Nah.' Addy yawned, stretching so his chest opened before her like a casket of treasure. 'The cove's dead. Nothing exciting ever happens round here.'

'It will now I'm back. I can't spend the *entire* summer sitting under my mother's caravan roof, you know.' If it could be called that: parts of Florence Lark's ancient Pemberton Static were tacked down with masking tape.

'Guess you'll be looking for a job?'

'It's why I'm here.' She consulted the noticeboard. 'Anything good come up?'

'Dunno—haven't checked it in ages.'

Every opening at the cove advertised at the Blue Paradise and the display was thick with flyers requesting bar staff, shop help, grape pickers at the Quillets Vineyard or muck shovellers at the Barley Nook stables... The list went on. Olivia had taken most as holiday earners when she was still in training bras.

'Suppose I should,' Addy commented boredly. 'New horizons and all that.'

Her head snapped up. 'You're leaving?'

'Maybe. I'm antsy. You know how I get. I need more out of life than sitting round here chatting up girls... It's samey after a while, you know?'

She forced a smile. Was Addy aware of how she felt? Maybe. But then he could have the pick of any girl he wanted, and she was just his friend. She could make him laugh. She could surf with him in the rain. She could help him with his English homework because he had a fear of any book that was longer than fifty pages. What she couldn't be was a six-foot blonde with legs that went on for miles.

Even though Olivia had known him since the beginning of time, the Addy fire burst before her now just as brilliant and dangerous as the first day she'd seen it. She'd been six and he'd been nine, and Addy's little sister a regular at Tiffany's tea parties. Olivia would spy him outside with his friends playing Gun Tower Home! and would long to flee the dinky dining room and china pots filled with nothing, and tear through the brambles till her dress ripped. Of course the boys had tried everything to shrug her off: locking her in the Creepy Shed, vowing that she had to be slave, racing on their bikes so she couldn't keep up, setting up dares they never thought she'd meet… But Olivia was determined, and once she had accepted the ultimate challenge of sprinting across the field owned by Farmer Nancarrow, a shadowy, mysterious, darkly enticing character who had become in the children's eyes more myth than man—he would shoot anyone who trespassed on his land and then cook them for supper!—they had finally accepted her as marginally all right for a girl.

It was a lifetime ago, and yet still only yesterday.

Olivia had hoped that seeing Addy again might have prompted an epiphany, a realisation that all these years he had tricked her into seeing what wasn't there, believing what wasn't true. But with Addy, just with Addy, always with Addy, it returned to the same. Olivia wasn't stupid, but he made her crazy. She was solid; he turned her to mush. She was level-headed; with him she went wonky. Her love for him could be traced back to twelve, eleven, ten, maybe before, when they had made hide-outs in the ferns and she'd started noticing his eyes were blue, not grey, and her mum would pack them fish-finger sandwiches, and each time Olivia gave him a sketch, of him, of her, of the swinging tyre they had rigged above his parents' lake, folded tight and slipped into his pocket, it had felt like losing a tiny piece of her heart.

'There's tons of stuff on here,' she said, without conviction.

'No offence, Oli, but I'm aiming higher than the cove. I haven't bothered with that waster pinboard.' Addy scratched his chin. 'I'm thinking *big*.'

Olivia almost didn't see it.

A leaf of paper obscured by a yachting brochure, but where its edges escaped it bore the unmistakeable crest she remembered from her youth:

Usherwood Estate
seeks able & enthusiastic gardener
Summer hours at competitive rates—
please enquire

She frowned. As the stately residence of the former Lord and Lady Lomax, grand old Usherwood was a fairytale castle of turrets and wings, towers and acreage, a majestic relic of a forgotten time. The Lomax couple had perished in a plane crash thirteen years ago, and their sons, at that time only teenagers, had inherited. Cato, the eldest, was notorious, a Hollywood A-lister who had bolted after the tragedy, never to return. The youngest had stayed at the ancestral home, and was by all accounts a recluse.

'Hey, Humpty, check this out!'

The voice was so upper class it sounded like there was a bag of marbles rolling around in its mouth. Olivia turned. A strut of city boys had located a window mannequin in a state of undress and one of them was making an obscene gesture at her nether regions. Lustell Cove attracted the *Made in Chelsea* set. With its lush, wild panoramas matched by higgledy-piggledy streets dotted with quaint Cornish cottages and tea shops, it was far enough from the capital to feel exclusive to the seriously wealthy, while its hot beach culture ensured it was anything but a stuffy hideaway.

'Too funny, Ruffers, too funny.' Humpty was sporting a pair of Hawaiian-print boardshorts despite Olivia's suspicion he had never done anything in the water save a breaststroke—and that only if it promised not to get his hair wet.

'D'you surf?' asked Addy, not especially interested. Olivia saw his eyes scan the gathering for a hot blonde with a trust fund—she knew him too well.

'My dad's got a Maxus,' Humpty replied, tossing his coiffed arrangement in the direction of the marina, which was bobbing with sleek white speedboats. His entourage of Hooray Henrys guffawed their approval. 'Who needs a plank of wood?'

'Can I help you, then?' said Addy. 'You know, with anything *surf*-related?'

One of them asked: 'Dude, do you know the Lomaxes?'

Addy returned his attention to his phone. 'Not if you mean Cato,' he bristled. 'Far as I know he hasn't been back here in, like, for ever.'

'The house is pretty creepy, huh,' said Humpty.

'Is it true it's, like, the biggest house in England?' enquired Ruffers.

'I heard they've got champagne fountains in the gardens,' said another.

'And Cato keeps a monkey in the cellar,' put in Humpty, 'to bring him things. I read about it. Someone saw it swinging about in a gold waistcoat.'

There followed an inventory of increasingly extravagant fictions. Everyone was so busy talking that they didn't notice when Olivia unpinned the Usherwood flyer and fed it discreetly into the back pocket of her jeans. She slipped outside.

The sun had vanished, casting the bay in shade. Olivia folded her arms against the rash of goosebumps prickling across her skin. High on the hill loomed the vast silhouette of the Usherwood Estate, staining the horizon like a great inkblot.

She stepped on to the beach. The sand was cool and silky between her toes and she padded across the inlet, away from Usherwood and back into sunshine.

CHAPTER TWO

'OH, BABY, YES! Keep going, stud—you are truly the best in the world!'

With each brutal thrust Susanna Denver's back was scraping painfully against the knobs on her lover's gold-plated washroom cabinet, but then space was always going to be at a premium at thirty-five thousand feet above the Atlantic.

'Keep it dirty,' Cato growled, his breath ragged in her ear. 'You know I love it when you talk filth, you scandalous harpy.'

Susanna clamped her thighs around his waist and reached down to clasp the most famous backside in America (recently initiated into the Hollywood Hall of Fame after an Award-nominated nude scene). Sharp crimson nails dug into his flesh.

'Harder!' she squealed, bucking a touch too fervently so that behind her a decorative tap flicked on and she found her ass being sprayed with water. 'Faster!'

'Not wet enough already?' Cato snarled in that impossibly attractive English accent, which made Susanna think of black-and-white World War II movies where everyone went about smoking pipes and talking about submarines.

'Always for you, baby,' she gasped, 'always for you!'

Cato slipped a hand between her legs, dousing her in the liquid heat.

'Say my name,' he croaked, 'say it!'

'Ca-to!' she managed, the word severed in two as he thrust into her, his black shock of hair abrasive against her chest and his face buried in her tits.

'Say my full name—my full name, goddamnit!'

'Lord Cato! Fuck me, Lord Cato, fuck me, fuck me, fuck me!'

Lord Cato did as he was told, seconds later coming so fiercely that Susanna's ass was slamming in and out of the porcelain bowl and Cato had water coursing down his legs and into the nest of suit pants pooled at his ankles.

'You're a rampant little nympho, aren't you?' he choked afterwards, fighting to catch his breath. 'Be a good girl and run along, I could murder a gin on the rocks.'

Back in her seat on the Lomax private jet, Susanna patted her hair and checked her reflection in a crystal compact. Her lipstick was smudged—Cato preferred there to be a prime blowjob on the menu; it was one of his foibles—she fixed it and smiled with satisfaction. Looking back at her wasn't just the face of Susanna

Denver, romcom queen who commanded ten million a movie—oh, no, it was the face of a future Lady of the Manor! She couldn't suppress the mewl of excitement that escaped when she thought of it. Surely it was only a matter of time before Cato proposed, and what would she say? She would say *Yes, yes, yes!* as fiercely as she had five minutes before with his cock driving through her like a steel truncheon.

It was several minutes before Cato joined her (he always needed the bathroom after sex: another eccentricity). He picked up his Tanqueray and balanced the tumbler in the palm of his hand. The dark hair on his knuckles was a stark contrast to the clean, ice-cracked liquid, and on his pinkie he wore a fat gold signet.

'Everything all right, darling?' Susanna asked, giving him her most winning smile. She had considered that he might have asked her to marry him on the jet—after all, he spent most of his life on the darned thing—but obviously he had something far more romantic planned for when they got to Cornwall. She couldn't wait to see the mansion: it looked like Charles Dickens lived there, as if they'd have a chimney sweep, and a maid who wore a doily on her head! It was too sweet for words.

'Fine,' Cato barked. She went to rub his shoulders but he batted her off. 'If you must know, I'd rather turn this filly around and be touching down in LA in an hour's time, not bloody Heathrow.' He swigged the gin in one.

'Oh, darling,' she comforted, 'it'll be gorgeous when we get there…'

'Will it? It's England, Mole; it rains all the time.'

How Susanna wished he wouldn't call her that. It was an endearment—she had a freckle birthmark on the small of her back—but all the same it made her sound like a soggy, twitchy little thing emerging blindly from the ground. Cato had taken to introducing her as Mole in new company, which she absolutely had to put a stop to.

'I don't mind a bit of rain,' said Susanna, flipping open her magazine.

'You're not cut out for it,' Cato retorted.

'I can be. I will be.' She wanted to add *when we're married*, but didn't.

A muscle twitched at his temple. 'If Charles did the right thing and moved on I'd be a damn sight happier. Usherwood *is* mine, after all. I'm the eldest; it's *my* inheritance. Still,' Cato swirled the glass, 'I can't apologise for being a trans-Atlantic man. Career calls—not that my brother would know the first thing about that.'

Susanna flushed with pleasure. She loved it when Cato talked about claiming the estate full-time. Things were going impossibly well for him in LA right now, but come next year he would be ready to divide his time between the two—and she would be right there alongside him as the next Lady Lomax. She couldn't wait.

'Another,' Cato commanded one of his staff, holding aloft the empty glass. 'Why he insists on being such a miserable bastard is well and truly beyond me.'

Susanna craned to see. 'Go easy on him, baby, he hasn't been with us long…'

Cato shot her one of his *your-stupidity-never-ceases-*

to-amaze-me looks. 'I'm not talking about that cretin,' he snipped. 'I'm referring to Charles. Naturally.'

The gin landed, accompanied by a miniature offering of salted nuts.

'Just because Mummy and Daddy got lost in the fucking Bermuda Triangle'—Cato said 'fucking' like 'fahking'—'I mean, let's get over it, shall we?' He chucked the nuts into his mouth like a shot of Tequila and appeared to swallow without chewing. Susanna found him urgently sexy. With his splintering eyes and jet-black mane, so brutish and carnivorous, he possessed the kind of unreconstructed maleness that had women worldwide longing to experience the Lomax magic. Once she was his wife, Susanna Denver alone would achieve that privilege.

'These are stale,' Cato complained of the nuts, but continued to pulverise them nonetheless.

'Try and relax, sweetheart...'

Cato loosened his tie. 'I *am* relaxed. Just don't talk to me about my brother.'

'I'm not.'

'You brought him up. And now look! I'm in a terrible mood thanks to you.'

Susanna had learned early on in their acquaintance that Cato was not a man with whom to be argued. She knew better than to raise the issue of Charles (like the prince!), but privately thought their relationship was bound to be strained what with the family history being so raw. Cato rarely talked about the accident, only in garbled bursts when he was blind drunk on Courvoisier.

Thirteen years ago, Richmond and Beatrice Lomax had taken a single-engine plane for a day flight over the Bahamas—at nine a.m. they had departed; by twelve they had abandoned radio signal. Their plane was lost, the bodies never found. To this day their deaths remained unclassified.

'Put him from your mind,' she calmed him. 'Shall I rub your shoulders?'

Cato scowled.

Susanna couldn't help but suspect there was more to the brotherly rivalry than met the eye. Reading between the lines it seemed that Charles, the youngest, had always been the favoured son—and Cato resented him for it. Funny how such petty jealousies could wind their way into adulthood. Perhaps Susanna could be the peace-maker, encourage the men to see what was really im-portant. Once she and Cato moved into Usherwood on a permanent basis she saw no reason why Charles should have to be evicted. Where would the poor mite go?

On cue Cato pronounced: 'Charles is in for a terrific surprise when I tell him I'm taking over. He never could handle the place; it's falling apart around his bloody ears. What Usherwood needs is a *real* man to take care of it.' Buoyed by the thought, he turned to Susanna and awarded her an indulgent smile. 'A bit like you, Mole.'

Susanna took his hand. 'Indeed,' she purred demurely, in the way English ladies surely did when they were soon-to-be-heirs to great stateliness and fortune.

Cato downed the drink, exhaling heavily through his nostrils like a bull with a ring through its nose. He closed his eyes. When he opened them he said, 'I think I'll have your mouth wrapped around my cock one more time before we land,' as though he were considering which route they would take into the southwest once they hit the roads tomorrow (Susanna suffered from jetlag and preferred a night at Claridge's before entertaining an onward journey). She had selected a vintage burgundy Bentley for the trip and might even don a floral head-scarf, if the weather was clement.

England's fields appeared like patchwork in the window, a quilt of greens and yellows stitched together by thorn and thistle: Land of Hope and Glory.

Susanna sighed the sigh of the devoted. She couldn't wait to be introduced to her new home. And once Cato proposed, everything would be just perfect.

CHAPTER THREE

CHARLIE LOMAX STOPPED at the stream to let his dogs drink. He wiped his dark brow, the material of his T-shirt damp with sweat and sticking across his shoulders. It was a scorching day, thick with heat, the only sounds the steady babble and the hounds' lapping tongues as they attacked the water in loud, contented gulps.

He squinted up at Usherwood House. One hand was raised to counter the glare, and the skin where his sleeve drew back was pale compared with the tan on his forearms. The earthy, musty pocket of his underarm was a hot, secret shadow.

The dogs clambered to their feet for a vigorous shake, their fur releasing a shower of glittering drops. Comet, the setter, pricked his ears in anticipation of his master's next move: tail bright, eyes alert. Retriever Sigmund panted happily.

Russet sunshine bounced off the stonework, drawing-room windows rippled in the haze. Charlie could picture its quiet interior, shafts of light seeping through dusky glass. A sheet of verdant lawn rolled up to the entrance, studded with flower beds that flaunted summer colour despite their neglect. Mottled figurines hid behind oaks like ghosts, a head or a hand missing, moss-covered and cool in the shade.

It was habit to see everything that was wrong with the place: the dappled paintwork, the peeling façade, and at the porch a stippled, stagnant fountain whose cherubic statuette sang a soundless, fossilised tune. But on days like today, lemon sunbeams bathing the house, the old monkey puzzle rising proud in the orchard and the flat grey sea beyond with its white horses flirting on the waves, it was possible to imagine an inch of its former glory. When Charlie would return for yearned-for ex-eats, the car pulling up alongside his mother's classic Auburn, gravel crunching under the tyres and the smell of buttered crumpets soaking into the purple evening, those were the times he remembered. That was what Usherwood meant to him.

He climbed the ditch, put his fingers out so a soft, soggy muzzle came in curiosity to his touch, and with it the hot lick of an abrasive tongue.

Through the Usherwood doors the great hall echoed, high windows illuminating a mist of dust particles that drifted into the vaults. Above the sooty inglenook a portrait of Richmond and Beatrice was suspended, its frame a tarnished copper. The dogs skated muddy-pawed through to the library, tails thumping as they waited for Charlie to catch up.

'Oh, you scamps!' Barbara Bewlis-Teet, housekeeper since his parents' day, came in from the kitchen. She shook her head at the dirt the dogs had brought with them. 'Mr Lomax, you'd let those mutts rule the roost given half the chance!'

Charlie ran a hand through his raven hair. It had grown longish around his ears and he hadn't shaved in a week, giving him a rugged, piratical appearance. His eyes were panther-black. The bridge of his nose had been split years before in a cricket match, and the residual scar made him look more fearsome than he was.

'They're all right.' He pulled off his boots, thick with caked-on mud.

Affection made Barbara want to reach out and touch him, the boy she had once known—but she couldn't, because Mr Lomax was untouchable.

How she wanted to rewrite the story whose beginning and end could be found in the landscapes of his face: the concentrated, permanent frown; the dark angle where his jaw met his neck; the fierce brushstrokes of his cheekbones. There was Charlie before the tragedy, a dimly recalled child with a clever smile and a skill for putting things together—cameras, watch mechanisms, telescopes—to see how they worked; and Charlie afterwards, wilted at the Harrow gates, at thirteen so young, too young, for the education that sometimes what was taken apart could never be reassembled. She had driven through the night to collect him in her Morris MINI, doing away with the nonsense of a chauffeured car. Cato had left for the South of France, done with his final year, a hard-boiled show-off whom nothing seemed to touch. Barbara wasn't sure when Cato had returned to Usherwood, if he even had, to join the mourners and to console the younger brother who had needed him.

'Tea's ready,' she said gently, wiping her hands on her apron. 'Shall I bring it through?' It was four p.m. sharp and the time-worn set patiently waited, citrus steam rising from the delicate chipped cups Barbara still insisted on using; a splash of milk in a porcelain mug, a silver basin of sugar and a plate of powdery gingerbreads. So long as Mr Lomax cared about Usherwood's standards, so must she.

'I'll be at my desk.'

'Of course.' She nodded. 'And shall I light a fire?'

'No, I'll manage.'

Barbara was used to his economy with words. He didn't give himself away, not to just anyone. He was twenty-six this winter, and to all intents and purposes had removed himself from the world. He was a distant rock battered by storms, a locked door in a darkened corridor, a half remembered song.

After what had happened, how could it be different?

'Very well,' she said softly. 'Will that be all?'

'Yes,' Mr Lomax replied, 'that's all.'

It was cool in the library; cellar draughts seeping through the floorboards, the damp in the walls making everything chill despite the heat of the day. Charlie dragged on a frayed Guernsey and lit the flames. His hands were broad and work-roughened, the flesh stained and splintered, chapped by outdoor grind. Sparks burst and crackled and he spread his fingers to warm them in the orange, spitting glow.

He settled at the morning's post. Red warnings glared through envelopes, demands for payment and threatened court action. Sigmund padded over and absent-mindedly Charlie scratched the retriever's head. The dog put both paws on his lap, resting his chops and gazing up at his master forlornly.

The books told a sorry story. Usherwood was in dire straits and despite Charlie's initiatives—selling off his mother's art collection; opening the outbuildings; renting the south field as a campsite—it scarcely touched the sides. Each cheque was engulfed by a rising tide of demands. The drive needed resurfacing, the greenhouse was suffering a leak, the roof in the old maid's lodgings begged a restoration, the arch on the chapel was collapsing… He couldn't keep up. Maintaining the occupied quarters was bad enough. They'd had neither heating nor hot water for over a month, and Charlie had taken to bathing early morning in the bitter spinney stream.

Of course he was meant to be rich. This was a mansion, after all—palatial, exquisite, the finest example of Jacobean architecture in the West Country—and its inhabitant aristocracy, heir to great fortune. But the upkeep had sapped every penny of that fortune. Huge chambers slept unused, locked away, spaces once bright and vital now relegated to the graveyard. Piece by piece the house was shutting down. It reminded Charlie of a night when he was eight, camping in the trunk of the withered oak with a blanket up by his ears. The house had seemed an advent calendar of golden windows, his father passing through to extinguish one light at a time until nothing was left but the stain of dark upon dark, the shell of a house sliced out of the night.

Amid a nest of paperwork, a red blinking caught his attention.

One message pending:

'Can't stop, old bean,' came a familiar, hated voice. *'Susanna's been hankering after a taste of the Cornish Riviera and you know me—never one to disappoint a lady. We arrive tomorrow. Tidy the place up, won't you? Oh, and do spare us by getting those rotten hounds on a leash; Susanna won't like them a bit.'* He was about to ring off, before a parting: *'Tell the girls to whip up something nice. Susanna wants British; you know the thing. Tarts. Shortbread.'*

The line went dead.

Charlie listened to it a second time before hitting delete. His knuckles cracked.

Cato Lomax.

Movie star, icon, Casanova—but the world didn't know him as Charlie did. His Cato was narcissistic, decadent, reckless, wicked; the grubby-palmed boy who had terrorised him, pushing him from the apple tree so he knocked his front teeth grey, dunking his head in the glacial lake one vicious winter, bolting him in the stuffy leather trunk they had taken to Harrow and feeding in a sack of crawling beetles, trapping him in the secret passage that ran between the pantry and the sword room...

And then, when they were adults, taking from him the one thing Charlie could never forgive him for. People said it hadn't been Cato's fault, but Charlie knew better.

Acid clutched his heart when he thought of that furious, thundery night… Cato's tail lights disappearing down the Usherwood drive, rain slashing the windows, a red torch bleeding into darkness…

The very last time he had seen her.

The manslaughter charge had been dropped. Nothing more said about it. That was what money could do—it could buy justice, as rotten and corrupt as it came.

But by Charlie's judgement, his brother could never be forgiven.

Whenever he read about Cato in the papers, posing with a new actress girlfriend, he swallowed fury like a knot of wire. Despite it all Cato still imagined himself to be emperor of Usherwood. By virtue of his age the true and righteous Lord Lomax, winging in whenever it suited to boast his heritage to a Plasticine army of Americans. Cato had no clue about the place or what it needed; all he cared for was his reputation and the social currency Usherwood awarded. Being gentry wasn't about playing polo and hanging pheasants; it was about a birthright that had been passed through generations, this wounded house that Charlie toiled for night and day because he *felt* it in his soul, his true devotion and his true belonging.

He went to the window and released the catch, grounding himself against the approaching storm.

That was it, then: the prodigal son returned.

Cato's imminent arrival slid over the surrounding hills like an army on the mount. The air outside was fragrant. A cabbage white fluttered on to the sill, twitching its wings. Somewhere in the grounds a nightingale sang.

CHAPTER FOUR

OLIVIA SHOULD HAVE known that the car wouldn't start. For most of the year Florence Lark had been using the battered green-and-white Deux Chevaux as an elaborate planter, filling it with sorrel and sage, parsley and peppermint, basil and bay. Olivia wasn't sure if this arrangement was intentional or if her mother had just neglected to unpack the allotment spoils one day and things had grown from there.

'Take the bicycle,' Flo said from her position on the caravan steps, where she was busy peeling apples into a basin. She was an attractive woman with a stream of honey-blonde hair, bright blue eyes and the skin of a seventeen-year-old. 'It's a glorious afternoon; you could do with getting some country air back into you. I can't imagine how you put up with The Smoke for so long. I never could.'

'It was only a year.' Olivia had a brief, strange pang

for the Archway bedsit, and the top decks of buses she'd see sailing past her window as she ate breakfast.

'Well, a year's long enough.'

'I'm not staying, you know.' She yanked the pushbike from its moorings amid a hillock of grass. A slick of oil smeared blackly across her dress and she wiped it with the back of her hand. 'This is just a stopgap.'

'Hmm, you say that now…'

'I'll be saying the same in a month.'

'But you love the cove!'

'Nothing ever happens here, Mum. It's full of the people who never left.'

Her mother pulled a face. 'Like Adrian Gold?'

Olivia glanced away. 'Maybe.'

'You're drastically out of his league.'

'You would say that.'

'And you'll never see it, of course.' Flo sighed. 'There he is sailing about with a string of airheads in bikinis without a brain cell to speak of between them…'

Olivia rolled her eyes. So much for the sisterhood that had been drummed into her since birth—and anyway, what was wrong with wearing a bikini and being hot and having Addy Gold lusting after you? All her life she had been steered away from the tricks that helped a girl look nice, and suddenly she felt pissed off, as if she'd been robbed of her only shot, which was ridiculous because it was hardly as if a stick of gloss and a spritz of Dior would have made all the difference. Or would it? *Natural is beautiful*, her mother insisted, and besides, stuff like high heels and make-up were Crimes Against Women. They were *alternative*, remember? But alternative was fine when you were forty and wore moccasins and smoked damp roll-ups, and not when you were sixteen and just wanted to go on a date without having to explain why your shoes were made of hay (that was an exaggeration—but only just).

Olivia saddled up. Thanks to this conversation she felt every inch the grumpy adolescent: how did coming home always achieve that?

'Wish me luck,' she muttered, before she could mutter anything else.

'Don't let that Lomax give you any trouble,' counselled her mother. 'He's meant to be downright insufferable. Any nonsense and you tell him what for.'

In finding her feet on the pedals Olivia almost toppled sideways. It was ages since she'd ridden and the squeaky brakes and cranky gears did little to bolster the confidence. Flo gave her a push and she teetered off down the path.

Olivia might find herself pining for the city, but even she couldn't deny how free she felt flying down Lustell Steep with the wind in her hair, up on the handlebars, sheer momentum carrying her. She could taste the ocean and hear the swooping cries of seagulls as they wheeled overhead. Over the mount she passed the church. Sweet buds nestled in hedgerows and the back-end of a hare darted into the mossy verge.

This was the way she used to come in the holidays, racing against her best friend Beth to reach the old bench first. Past the weathered seat there was a gap in the border, big enough for two girls to squeeze through. They called the field beyond the Hush-Hush—perhaps because it had been quiet as a lake on the day they'd found it, or perhaps because they'd sworn to keep its discovery a secret. In the hot months it was bright with corn and rape, kernels you could pick off in juice-stained fingers and pop their oily pods in your mouth. In winter it was rough with earth and churned up like the sea in a gale. This was where her mother had taken them when she'd first bought the 2CV, picking them up from school with a tray of eggs laid out on the rear shelf, pink and smooth as pebbles and lined up neatly in rows like a cinema for bald people. Flo had driven fast as a rocket across the field and the car had gone bouncing and bounding and leaping over the ridges, Olivia and Beth in the back, clutching each other and laughing till they cried, shrieking, 'Slow down!' even if they hadn't wanted her to, and when they stopped they were amazed to see the shells still intact.

'There you go,' Florence had triumphed. 'Best set of wheels on the market.'

That was before Olivia found out that Farmer Nancarrow owned the Hush-Hush land. She had never told the boys this, but once, ages ago, she had seen him kissing her mother at a barn dance, a dark, dusky giant of a man, and she had hid in the wings of the stage, wide-eyed and watching.

* * *

By the time she reached the foot of the Usherwood drive, the sun was lowering in the sky and early evening shadows were lengthening across the plots.

At the entrance a sign announced the house, faded with age and leaning to one side. Across the cattle grid the route opened up and Olivia rode faster, the track galloping away beneath her wheels. All her life the estate had been a distant wonder, perpetually beyond reach, the untouchable palace of the aristocracy. She'd been ten when Lord and Lady Lomax had died, and supposed she must have come once or twice when she was little, but the memories became eclipsed by their grim successors: TV crews descending; reporters on the streets; the canvas of shocked, sad faces as the cove had digested the news. People like that—rich, glamorous, exceptional people—didn't just disappear. For months afterwards, Olivia had imagined divers scouring the ocean depths, finding nothing except a diamond bracelet winking on the seabed.

She had been too young then to appreciate what it must have been like for the children left behind. Losing her own father at six had at least spared her the pain of a proper understanding, the significance of it too big, too serious, to process. Even when Flo had held her close and told her Dad was never coming back, Olivia had secretly known that he would. He'd show up one day and surprise them. *Got you, monkey!* A game; like when he'd chase her round the garden and throw her over his head, forcing her to squeal her delight. But as the weeks turned into months and the seasons unfurled, so did the realisation that her mother had been right. Grief assailed her gradually; there had been no ambush. The Lomax boys had been ambushed.

Through a canopy of trees Usherwood at last came into view. It was beautiful and sad and majestic all at the same time. The entrance was arched, the exterior dotted with dozens of bay windows that gazed enquiringly back at her. Curvilinear gables, peaked like the spade suit in a deck of playing cards, adorned the ridges like icing. Close up, telltale signs of decay blushingly revealed themselves: chalky efflorescence on a renovated chimney, a weathered ox-eye on a central facade, twisted pillars pockmarked by age… Yet nothing could rob the mansion of its splendour.

The drive widened into an oval expanse of gravel, stones grinding beneath her tread, and Olivia climbed off to wheel the rest of the way.

She spotted a man up a ladder, his back to her. From what she could see he was fixing a gutter. She pictured how she must look, a stranger with a cloud of auburn hair and thistle scratches on her legs, pushing a bike whose pannier was stuffed with a beach towel and a crumpled sketchbook.

Two dogs bounded over, hindquarters bowed in excitement, their tails going frantically. She made a fuss of them, patting their flanks and scuffing their ears.

'Hello,' she called. 'Hello there!' She gave a pointless little wave, like someone on the deck of a ferry.

The labourer swore. He sucked the tip of his finger

where he'd splintered it, or bashed it with a hammer, or whatever it was he was doing up there, and turned.

'Can I help you?' he hollered down irritably. His voice was very deep, and low, like a shout thrown back from the distant end of a tunnel.

Olivia couldn't see his face, just a big black shape where he obscured the melting sun. 'I'm, er, looking for a job,' she replied uncertainly. 'I saw the ad at the beach; you're after someone to help with the gardens? I hope I'm in time…'

The man thought for a moment before climbing down. She could practically *see* his bad mood, sense it like a squall on the water when she was out on her board and the weather was changing. As he came nearer she was dwarfed by his size. He had a tousle of coal-black hair and his shoulders were treble the width of hers. He was so tall she barely came up to his chin. His eyes were darker than three a.m.

'I'm Olivia,' she started. 'Olivia Lark.'

His eyes narrowed. 'I know.'

She took in his paint-splashed work trousers and faded checked shirt. He had a clever, angular face, catching the sun on one side. His eyelashes were long. Sooty. She wondered if he had helped out on her mother's allotment.

'Could I speak to the owner?'

His frown deepened.

'Or if now's a bad time…?'

He continued assessing her in that peculiarly pene-trating way. She had never been on the receiving end of such stark, unapologetic scrutiny.

'The thing is,' she forged on, 'I'm an artist. That sounds massively wanky, but it's the truth so I might as well be truthful, and the other truth is that I'm unemployed and I need to make money so that I can move back to London and get on with things.' Why was she babbling? She never babbled. His frown became more of a scowl. 'So I'm back for the summer, and I'm hardworking, and reliable, and I wouldn't ask to be paid too much. I'm good with plants and stuff—and I cook a bit…though actually,' she retracted it, 'not very well; as a matter of fact I had a complete catastrophe with a macaroni cheese the other day. You should have seen it! All burned on the top and chewy as bootlaces…' She trailed off. His expression was stony.

'I don't like macaroni cheese,' he said eventually.

'Whoever doesn't like macaroni cheese?'

'I just told you: I don't.'

There was a long, difficult silence that he appeared entirely untroubled by. Olivia's patience expired. What the hell was his problem? No wonder the house was going under with people like this charged with greeting outsiders.

'I'm sorry I've interrupted,' she said, prim as a debutante as she turned on her heel. 'I'll come back tomorrow.'

'Don't.'

Flabbergasted by his rudeness, she raged, 'Bloody hell, you're rude. You could've just—'

'Now will do.'

He rubbed the stubble on his jaw. He was sexy, in a

prehistoric sort of way. There was something very raw about him, like one of her pictures when she'd only done the most ragged outline in pencil. The top of his nose was cracked out of shape.

'I'm looking to open the ornamentals at the end of the season,' he said. 'I've drawn up the plans, and I dare say you'll be cheaper than a hired hand. It'll be hard work and I won't be paying more than I have to. Believe it or not, we're in need of money ourselves, so that's one thing we already have in common.'

She expected him to smile but he didn't.

He named his price, concluding indifferently: 'Take it or leave it.'

Olivia agreed before he could change his mind. 'But shouldn't I speak to Mr Lomax? I mean, I don't know who *you* are, but—'

'I am Mr Lomax.'

'Oh.'

She looked away, embarrassed, as if he'd just taken all his clothes off in front of her. There were shades of Cato, maybe: a coarser, unpolished version. She had always envisaged the other brother as the hunchback in the attic, warty and stooped and living on a diet of pickled onions. The reality was rather different.

One thing was for sure: arrogance ran in the family.

'Well,' she said stiffly, 'you could have said—'

'Remember I didn't ask you to be here. You asked me.'

She blinked. 'All right.'

'Be aware that this house owes you nothing except

your pay. My brother doesn't live here, so if that was your motivation you can leave right away.'

'It wasn't,' she clarified hastily. 'I don't even fancy him!'

Her statement sounded impossibly stupid in the quiet that followed.

'I'm Charlie,' he gave her eventually. 'Don't bother with Mr Lomax or sir or anything like that. Just Charlie.'

'OK. When do you want me to start?'

'Not now, I'm expecting people.'

'Right. So…'

'So leave?'

Olivia bit back the smart retort he'd been begging for since she'd arrived. Did this man have absolutely no social graces? Deliberately he had put her on the back foot, watching her squirm because that was exactly the kind of enjoyment a person in his position preferred. She supposed life must become tiresome when you were king of all you surveyed, lord of a privileged, proud dominion that sprawled as far as the eye could see. Commoners like her were just a passing opportunity for entertainment. Wasn't Mr Lomax—sorry, *Charlie*—meant to be an advocate for the upper classes? It went to show that all the huff and puff of an absurdly expensive education couldn't buy manners. And anyway, Lomax or no Lomax, she wasn't sure she could ever altogether trust someone who didn't like pasta and cheese.

'Monday morning,' he directed, 'eight o'clock. Don't be late.'

He returned to the ladder, gazed up at the darkening

sky, dusted his hands off and lifted it from the stones. Olivia watched him disappear inside the house, the dogs behind. She stood feeling like a prize lemon and hoping against hope that the gardens were miles away from Charlie Lomax… The other side of the county would be fine.

She scooped up her bike, running through all the things she wished she'd said. It was his opener that had thrown her. How could he have any idea who she was?

Puzzled by it, she pushed off through the weeping, hanging boughs. The drive was shrouded in gloom, no faint shimmer of streetlights, no passing sweep of traffic, no distant drone of life, only the far-off crash of waves as they washed over the cliffs. A pair of early evening bats swooped between trees, their leather wings fluttering.

Olivia negotiated the twisting route, and was halfway to the road and lost in thoughts of her mother's roast pork supper with lashings of Granny Smith sauce, when, seemingly from nowhere, a monstrous car appeared around the corner. The last thing she saw was a pair of dumbstruck faces, bone-white in the burgeoning dusk, before she was thrown from her saddle and after that there was nothing.

CHAPTER FIVE

'DEAR GOD, WHAT in heaven's name was that?' There was a sickening crunch as the wheels bumped over something. Susanna's hands flew to her face. 'It's a ghost! We've hit a ghost! Did you see her? A girl! We've killed her!'

'Don't be insane, woman.' Cato stopped the vehicle and climbed out. 'Put those ruddy lights on, will you?' He'd said he didn't need them, knowing the place so well. Perhaps it was a deer. They had deer here, didn't they? Deer who rode bikes?

Susanna flicked on the headlamps to aid his investigation and patted her headscarf with fear. 'Should I come?' she called, praying they wouldn't be confronted with a corpse. Imagine the headlines! LORD & LADY LANGUISH BEHIND BARS.

'All right, all right, Mole,' came the impatient response. 'Are you with us, sweetheart? Ah, there you go. Bump on the head, that's all. What's your name?'

It sounded like it was in the land of the living, what-ever *it* was. Susanna joined him on the track, the engine purring behind her. Her heels click-clacked on the stones.

'Oh.' She was surprised to find Cato bending rather too willingly over a girl, who was youngish, early twen-ties at a guess, and who was rubbing a wild nest of curls. The girl wore a flummoxed look and Cato was rubbing her shoulder.

'Look what we've done, old thing,' purred Cato. 'Frightened the poor angel half to death! See if there's a blanket in the boot, would you? She must keep warm.'

I'm sure she'll manage fine with your arms clamped around her, Susanna thought uncharitably. And since when had he called her *old thing*?

The trunk offered up little more than a spare tyre and a leaking vat of windscreen wash. 'No luck!' she sang. 'Shall we get her in the car?'

'We'll have to try,' answered Cato. Goodness, how handsome he looked. Rugged and wild against the trees, his eyes glinting like a night-time beast's, but at the same time irresistibly polished and carrying the scent of safety, of warm hotel rooms, of expensive restaurants and the interiors of chauffeur-driven Mercedes. Part of Susanna felt bilious at Cato's attentions being lavished over another woman; part of her was madly turned on by it. Just wait until they were in their four-poster tonight.

'Shall I take her legs?' asked Susanna.

'She's not a blasted plank of wood!' Cato scoffed, turning to address the casualty with a far gentler: 'Are you able to walk?'

'I—I think so.' The girl had a very sweet English accent. How pretty was she? It was difficult to see.

'We'll take you up to the house,' decided Cato, helping her to her feet.

'I've just come from there.'

Cato's voice changed. 'Charles' girl, are you?'

'No! I—I came for a job. I've never been here before. But I have to get home; I told my mum I'd be back…'

'Come now, one step at a time.' Cato steered her towards the vehicle with gut-wrenching tenderness. When was the last time he had treated Susanna in such a way? She was overtaken by the desire to find the nearest main road and toss herself under a passing truck—see if that got him prioritising his attentions.

Once the girl was installed in front and the bike parked by a tree, Cato drove the rest of the way. Susanna was able to get a proper look at her before the interior bulbs faded. She was plain, which was a relief. Her hair was a mess and her skin could do with a California tan. She was wearing a blue dress, too short for those legs.

Relegated to the back seat, Susanna stared glumly out of the window, feeling miserably like a forgotten-about child. She tried to blot out her lover's ministrations as he chatted kindly to the girl, no doubt aware that a report of this type would do little for his precious PR. Right now she wanted nothing more than to run a very deep, very hot bath and sink into it with a glass of chilled Sancerre. It had been a long drive from Heathrow. Cato's mood— at least until now—had been frightful, and Susanna, usually adept in keeping her pecker up (as Cato would say) had in turn become tired and irritable. Couldn't they have taken a helicopter? It was infinitely more civilised.

Yet as they skirted the final corner, the Usherwood approach she had pictured so many times, the magical house at last appeared. Its details were tricky to decipher in the creeping dusk, but, oh, it was so definitely *there*, solid and timeless and noble, and when Susanna let the window down she was met by a fragrance of floras and honeysuckle, heat-soaked after a day in the sun, the quiet rush of a stream and the first faint glimmer of stars high above them in the lilac sky.

A single flare glowed downstairs. She wondered if they still used candlelight! It would be most charming if so.

Cato halted the vehicle, emerged from the driver's side and immediately bolted round the bonnet to assist their ward. Susanna tried to open her door but it wouldn't budge. She battered the window and Cato was forced to return to release an absurd child lock they'd had fitted— the humiliation!

'Good evening, my lord.' A large, flustered-looking maid came rushing out. She had a scribble of grey hair and a rubicund complexion, and Susanna was assailed by the unsavoury suspicion that she could have hidden her entire body behind one of the woman's haunches, like someone hiding behind a tree trunk.

Barbara. Unfortunately for the housekeeper, she was just as imagined.

'It's good to have you home,' offered Barbara, with a

half-bob. Seeing Susanna, she added warmly, 'I'm Mrs Bewlis-Teet, welcome to Usherwood.'

'Baps,' barked Cato by way of greeting (a private amusement: Barbara heard it as 'Babs'), 'regretfully we've had an accident. Bloody pothole back on that drive, Charles really ought to get it looked at; the damn thing's a liability. Threw me right off course—Olivia here almost went under the wheels!'

Susanna didn't think they had gone over any potholes.

Baps went to help. 'Oh, dear me, you must have had a terrible shock.'

'I'm fine!' said Olivia, who was pale as a sheet and clearly disorientated. Her arm was bleeding. 'Really, I'd like to go home.'

'Listen to Baps,' proclaimed Cato, 'she's a wise old goose.'

'But I'm OK.'

'There is to be no argument.'

'Please, if I could just—'

'Absolutely not—you're concussed: you haven't the faintest clue what you're saying.' Cato draped his arm across her shoulders. 'I won't let you out of my sight, little one.' His teeth flashed white. 'That's a promise.'

Susanna heaved her suitcase from the boot.

'This is Mole,' Cato tossed over his shoulder, before sliding through the door.

Susanna put her hand out. 'Susanna,' she said cordially.

Baps shook it, and curtseyed ever so slightly in a way that made Susanna's heart tremble with pleasure, for it had to be due to her imminent Usherwood status rather than her celebrity: Baps didn't look like the sort of woman who would have seen one of Susanna's movies, which were typically about twenty-something city cliques on the lookout for Mr Right; she looked like the sort of woman who thrashed through undergrowth with a walking cane and made blackberry jams from scratch.

Through the entrance it was huge and echoey. The great black hood of a fireplace was crackling embers, deep with smoke, and a massive staircase climbed through the floors. A catalogue of Cato's ancestors posed dourly: the men in breeches, boasting muskets and shotguns and earnest, humourless expressions; the women seated primly, their ringed fingers nestled in the fur of some lap-dwelling pet.

The light Susanna had seen on approach emanated from an adjoining room, from which she could detect the most delicious cooking aromas. The glow it provided cast sallow shadow across the largest oil portrait, a study of the former Lord and Lady Lomax. The couple eyed their guests on arrival, sombre faces flickering and jumping with every leap of the fire. The woman's expression could only be described as sad. The man's was blazing with latent savagery. Susanna shivered.

'We're saving electricity,' explained Baps, as she led the way. 'Heating too—despite the season it can get awfully draughty. I've made up the fire in your room, and there's a supply of blankets in the wardrobe. You get used to it after a while.'

Susanna followed, gazing up as she went so that she

almost tripped over the frayed burgundy rug that covered the flagstones. She tried to picture herself living here—if the rest of Usherwood were like this they would have to gut the whole thing! Beneath the supper smells lay the steeped, woody scent that old houses carried, not entirely unsavoury, and nothing one couldn't undo with the help of a few plug-in air fresheners (Vintage Rose was her favourite). How much would Cato permit her to spend? She could hear the wind whistling through the vaults: replacement windows were a must, as were new carpets, plenty more lighting, and a spread of fabrics and furnishings to brighten up the space. They would work from the bottom up, beginning with wallpapering the downstairs and covering up those ugly mahogany panels. How ancient it looked! The house was crying out for a woman's touch. It was easy to feel overwhelmed, but Susanna would attack it logically, as she did everything.

'Rotten scrape you've got there,' Cato was saying, his voice somehow louder in their new surroundings, ricocheting through the hollow caverns and reminding the house to whom it formally belonged. 'Bandages, if you please, Baps!'

In the kitchen a table for three had been laid, silver cutlery and goblets for wine, through which Cato's bungled efforts at winding the dressing blew like a storm. She wondered why they couldn't eat in the dining room, before deciding it too might be in drastic need of her attentions. One of Susanna's greatest incentives was the thought of hosting her infamous dinner parties here, sending out invitations, boasting the family glassware, the consummate queen of Usherwood.

Wait until her LA friends saw! They would be mad with jealousy.

'Oh, let her go, Cato,' Susanna said, wafting in. It was important she make her mark, show them all who was boss. 'Someone can drive her, can't they?'

'Do pipe down, Mole,' came Cato's peeved response.

Susanna dropped on to a hard wooden bench and plucked an emery board from her purse. She was attending to her manicure when another woman, a fraction younger than Baps and decidedly more attractive, emerged from the scullery. She was slim, naturally pretty and her fair hair was wound in a knot.

'I'm Caggie,' she introduced herself, 'house cook.' She put out a flour-caked hand, which Susanna deemed rather disrespectful. Weren't there rules about this sort of thing? When one met the Queen, for example, didn't one wait to be presented, instead of sticking one's grasping fingers out like a beggar clutching at coins?

'Hello,' said Susanna. She was accustomed to meeting new people and basking in the glow of her reflected celebrity—she *was* world-famous, after all—and was disturbed at how Caggie regarded her levelly, her green eyes spelling a challenge.

'Caggie's been here almost as long as me,' supplied Baps. 'She's really wonderful; you'll get to taste her best while you're over. She's been whipping up the most super treats ever since the boys were small.'

'I'm sure it'll be a far cry from the private chefs

of Beverly Hills,' said Caggie—a touch sarcastically, Susanna thought.

Was it her imagination, or did Cato's gaze flicker just a moment too long over their new addition? She refused to entertain it: Caggie had to be flirting with fifty, and must spend her life elbow-deep in lard and gravy. She was tired, that was all. And anyway, once she and Cato were married they would be cutting both the women loose. Susanna would learn to cook herself, thank you very much, and if she needed extra help she would simply fly in Kaspar from her favoured bistro on Rodeo.

'Back again so soon?'

Another voice joined them. It was serious as thunder. Susanna turned.

Oh my. Oh my, oh my.

She ought to rise to greet him but found herself rooted to the seat. This was Charles Lomax? It couldn't be. Where was the weedy boy Cato had conjured, trailing at his brother's heels with a snivelling nose? The vision before her could only be described as a man: categorically and formidably a man. He was wildly dark, darker than Cato, even, with thick, muscular shoulders and hard black eyes. His face was brutally beautiful, a passionate structure beneath the shadow of a beard. His hair was a liquid, livid sable. He carried the scent of damp forest glades and burning wood.

Olivia stood. The mangled attempt at a bandage spooled to the floor.

'Anyone would think you weren't pleased to see me,' Cato sneered.

'I wasn't talking to you,' said Charles.

Cato pushed back the bench with an alarming scrape and sprang to his feet, his palms spread wide on the wood. 'I hope you're pleased with yourself,' he spat. 'Letting the place go to rack and ruin, risking a young girl's life!'

The jet eyes landed on Olivia. 'What happened?'

'Nothing.' The girl spoke up. The wound had started to prickle with crimson and she clutched it to keep it hidden.

'I'll call for a taxi, shall I?' Baps retreated, pulling Caggie after her.

'We almost had a death on our hands,' Cato hissed, 'thanks to you and your lackadaisical attitude. Even after all these years do I *still* need to tell you how to run your affairs, old boy? Olivia here nearly wound up as road kill—if I hadn't been so deft at negotiating that canyon of potholes who knows what might have happened?'

Charles was unmoved. 'She looks all right to me.'

Susanna was gratified that, despite his brother's looks, the Lomax charm had all gone in Cato's direction.

'I'm Susanna,' she said, giving him her most winning smile.

He didn't take his glare from Cato's. 'Would it be too much to hope you might arrive, for once, without the usual dose of drama?'

'Please,' Cato swiped back. 'You've been thriving on drama for the past fifteen years.'

'There's only one of us who's thrived.'

'Is that so?'

'That's so.'

'Do get over it, Charles,' he blasted. 'The rest of us have.'

Baps appeared, fingers knotted nervously at her waist. 'A car is on its way.'

'Thank you.'

Charles' voice was shiveringly intense, deep and soft as the most exquisite of fucks, and Susanna was overcome with the desire to fling herself between the two brothers and have them each ravish her ferociously over the kitchen table, at the centre of which was a lamb casserole that was rapidly getting cold.

And then, something extraordinary happened. On Olivia's way past, he seized her wrist and brought it towards him. The speed and seamlessness of the movement was utterly spellbinding. Wordlessly he pressed a rag against her skin and wound the lint, quickly, once and then twice and then it was done. It was horrifically sexy.

Bewildered, mumbling her thanks, Olivia shot from the room.

Moments later the front door slammed.

'I'm going to bed,' said Cato.

'What about supper?' Baps objected. 'Aren't you hungry?'

Cato stopped at a level with Charles, the top of his head a fraction shorter than his brother's. 'I can't think why, but I seem to have lost my appetite.'

A thread could have divided the men's chests: Cato's lifted and fell with the hot breath of combat; Charles' was utterly still. The silent war raged on.

Cato broke it, lips curling round the bitter shape of a single word: 'Goodnight.'

Susanna gazed longingly at the casserole as her lover slipped from the room. A bowl of crispy golden potatoes sat next to it, sprinkled with rock salt and rosemary.

'Come along, Mole!' came a distant, urgent summons.

With a brief, apologetic glance at Charles, she scurried after it.

CHAPTER SIX

ON SATURDAY MORNING Olivia wobbled up the muddy track to the Barley Nook stables, sandals slipping off the backs of her feet so that her ankle kept catching on the greasy chain. Her denim shorts were baking hot, and beyond the paddocks the green line of the sea was desperately tantalising. She stopped at the crooked gate and wheeled on to the verge, jamming the bike over a crusted fold of earth before resting it against the hedge. To the south lay the avocado expanse of the Montgomerys' vineyard, where a pair of figures milled in floppy hats, their pastel edges blurred in the Cornish heat, fluid as a Monet watercolour. Up ahead a riding lesson was unfolding. Horses were circling the ring, the strident aroma of hide and manure vinegary and sweet.

Beth Merrill was in the stalls, grooming her beloved stallion Archie. Beth had been inseparable from her horse ever since she'd picked him up as a wild foal: crossing the grassland at the tip of Lustell Cove she had discovered him on the brink of death, tangled in barbed wire and severely dehydrated. Over time she had nursed him back to health, housing him at the stables and riding him every day.

Olivia waved excitedly, making her way over. The girls hugged.

'I want *all* the details,' Beth instructed, her green eyes sparkling. 'I mean everything. Right now. From the beginning.'

Olivia laughed. 'All right, give me a chance!'

'You're seriously working there?'

'As of Monday—but swear to God, I didn't know about the Cato thing.'

'Bollocks.'

'I didn't!'

'Everyone in town's going totally crazy. At first it was just a rumour, then Harriet Blease's sister's friend's boyfriend said he saw them in this massive car going through the Usherwood gates and the window was down and apparently Susanna Denver's had so many facelifts her chin's up by her ears.'

'She doesn't look *that* bad.'

'Well, go on then—spill!'

Olivia obliged, running through her first encounter with the Lomax family—she was still weirded out by the whole thing. Each time she recalled it she had to pinch herself, as if she had dreamed it, or it had happened to another person: the collision must have put her in a kind of stupor. She'd been led through the house by a movie star and his actress girlfriend, and it was only when she had returned to her own bed later that night that her brain had finally clicked into gear. Her mother's caravan had never felt so small.

Beth listened intently, as she always had to Olivia's adventures; a ten-year-old sitting cross-legged in the garden while she was showered with stories of monster quests and jungle riots, of pirate loot and buried treasure, and of how Addy had held Olivia's hand one day when they were out in the forest and they thought Gun Tower HQ was being attacked but it had turned out only to be a badger. Since the girls were little, they had been like sisters. Beth was the more cautious, sensible one, a tempering agency on Olivia's hot-headedness, where Olivia was reckless and fun, dragging her friend over walls and under fences, whispering secrets as they shared their first cigarette, pilfered from the locked tin box Flo kept under the sink. Seeing Beth at home was like no time at all had passed; they could have been those kids again, making potions with her mother's hemp shampoo or dragging their sledge through the snow. They had shared so much at Lustell Cove.

'Can I help, d'you think?' Beth asked, awestruck when she reached the end. Her hair had gone coppery in the sun and her skin was tanned. 'Since you've got the added bonus of visitors at the house? I could wash Cato's pants?'

'I'm not sure Cato wears any pants.'

'Have you seen?'

'No,' Olivia lifted an eyebrow, 'just an instinct. And

anyway, I don't know if Cato being there *is* a bonus. He and Charlie seem to really hate each other.'

'Ooh,' Beth teased, 'it's "Charlie", is it?'

'Shut up.'

'Is he still all tortured and moody?'

Olivia regarded her quizzically. 'Huh?'

'You remember—at Towerfield?'

Something faint glimmered at the edges of her memory. Before the Lomax boys were bundled off to Harrow they had attended the local prep. Cato had been way older, she couldn't recall him, but another boy in Addy's year, yes, possibly: shirt untucked, messy hair, the big polished car that used to drop him off at the gates...

'Silly question.' Beth's expression was wry. 'You wouldn't remember because you were so obsessed with Addy that you never even noticed anyone else.'

'I was not.'

'You were, too.'

'He didn't hang out with Addy. I'd have noticed if he had.'

'That's 'cause he didn't like Addy.'

'How would you know?'

'It might be an impossible concept for you to grasp,' Beth sighed, 'but not everyone does. It's just you who's got this massive blind spot.'

'All right, all right!' Olivia bristled. 'Anyway you should have seen him with Cato. They were at each other's throats, standing there yelling at each other. No,' she frowned, 'not yelling, it was more restrained than that—and kind of more intense for it. At one point I thought they were going to strangle each other!'

'Sexy!'

'Hmm.'

'Is it any wonder, though?' Beth resumed grooming her horse, taking the brush in long slow strokes across the animal's flank. 'Of course they can't stand to be in the same room, what with Cato shooting off the second their parents disappeared. Poor *Charlie*,' she grinned, 'got left behind to look after everything.'

'I suppose.'

'What age was he back then, thirteen?'

Olivia shrugged, trying to work it out in her head. Charlie would have left Towerfield at twelve, when the boys had gone into senior school. He would have been at Harrow a year before his parents vanished, and she guessed that the housekeeper had taken care of him after that. He definitely hadn't been at Towerfield when it happened because if he had then Addy would have talked about it; and she would remember Addy talking about it, if nothing else.

'It would have been bad for Cato, too,' Olivia argued. 'I expect running away was easier, maybe he just couldn't face things here.' Cato had been far nicer to her in their brief acquaintance, and she felt the need to defend him.

'Maybe.'

Olivia narrowed her eyes.

'Between you and me,' she confided, 'I can't help feeling the animosity's about more than the parents dying. Something else, something deeper…'

Beth leaned against the stable door. 'Here's an idea, Oli,' she suggested. 'How about you take this job for what it's worth—just like I and *every* other girl at Lustell Cove would—and not get in way over your head like you always do?'

'I have my head perfectly above water, thank you very much.'

Beth giggled. 'Only you could get run over by Cato Lomax in your first week back.'

'It was an accident! Besides he was lovely to me, very apologetic.'

'For fear you'd sue his arse—sorry, *ass*—all the way back to America?'

Olivia nudged her. 'Cynic.'

'Oh, great.' Beth groaned. 'Look who it is.'

With sinking hearts they spotted the Feeny twins making their way across the courtyard. Thomasina and Lavender had been in their form at Taverick Manor, and had stayed at the cove ever since, living off Daddy's pocket money. They were snotty, spoiled little madams, with upturned noses like piglets. One was riding a black stallion; the other a white mare, like a pair of evil chess queens.

'Hell-air!' called Thomasina, easing her beast to a stop. Olivia could tell it was Thomasina because her nose was slightly more piggy than Lavender's.

'Hey.' Olivia gave them the benefit of the doubt: perhaps they'd changed.

'Good to see you settling back into your old life,' commented Thomasina, peering snootily down at Olivia as if she were something growing mould in a petri dish. 'There must be *terrible* competition in London to look thin.'

They hadn't changed.

'Though I'd imagine Cato Lomax being back in town would be diet incentive enough for anyone,' she finished. Next to her, Lavender tittered.

'What do you want, Thomasina?'

'Ooh, well excuse *us*!' Lavender had the annoying habit of emphasising the final word in every single sentence she said. 'Is this conversation *private*?'

'Not any more.'

'What's it about,' she whined, '*boys*?'

'You must be finished, then,' put in Thomasina, thinking herself extremely clever. 'There can't be a great deal to talk about!'

The Feenys were insufferable—grade-A picture-perfect sorority bitches who nipped miserably at sticks of celery and slagged off anyone over a size 6. Ever since Olivia's very first day at Taverick they had treated her no better than the offerings their rat-like pooches occasionally left in the bottoms of their Aspinal tote bags. According to the Feenys, Olivia was the scruffball who didn't live in a proper house, who probably didn't wash and who came with un-brushed hair into a school her mother couldn't afford to send her to (she had got in on a scholarship).

Like most of the girls at Taverick Manor, Thomasina

and Lavender took everything for granted: the Pacific island they jetted to on holiday, the yacht Daddy bought to moor off the Napoli coast, the wardrobe of designer labels they'd get bored with after a week. Olivia and Beth were always going to be outcasts. Beth's family were working class and had only afforded her education because a distant Merrill cousin had died and left them a wad of cash—something Beth felt permanently guilty about: last year her father's business had gone down the pan, and nowadays her parents had barely two pennies to rub together—while Olivia's scholarship was, according to the Feeny brigade, a heinously unfair pass into a life of privilege which she had neither the faculties nor the finesse to appreciate.

'Actually, Olivia's working with the Lomaxes this summer,' Beth chipped in, giving her a jab with her elbow. 'Isn't that right, Oli?'

The twins were stricken.

'What do you mean?' panicked Thomasina.

Olivia put her hands in her pockets. 'Charlie Lomax hired me.'

Thomasina burst out laughing, a high-pitched, taunting sound she'd used to inflict on a blubbing Clarabel Maynard whenever she forgot her gym knickers, pushing her to the floor and triggering one of Clarabel's nose bleeds. Once Olivia had hauled Thomasina off and slammed her into the changing-room lockers. She'd earned detention for a week and Clarabel still hadn't spoken to her in the lunch queue.

'You expect us to believe that?' Thomasina carped.

'With Cato back at the house? Come *on*. At least think up something *semi*-realistic, Chopped Liver.'

Chopped Liver had been her school nickname. Olivia had the sudden sensation of never having left Lustell Cove at all, the past year of city life, new friends and new horizons, evaporated in a single toxic gust of Feeny breath.

'She's gardening for them,' elaborated Beth. 'Charlie offered it on the spot. She's already met Cato and Susanna.'

'He hired *you*?' quailed Lavender. Her horse performed a prissy circle, swishing its tail as if it too could scarcely grasp the outrageousness of this suggestion.

Thomasina was quiet. She was thinking more carefully about things.

'By the way,' she said mildly, 'I saw Addy yesterday.'

Beth rolled her eyes. 'Shut up, Thomasina.'

'He was talking about you.'

'Just go away, would you?'

'He said how happy he was that you were back.' Thomasina was all at once sweetness and light. 'Addy finds it hard to express his emotions—but then he *is* a guy, what can we expect? I think he's plucking up the courage to ask you out.'

'Good for him,' stepped in Beth, folding her arms. 'But if you don't mind, I've got a lesson to run and you're in the way.'

'I could put in a word,' offered Thomasina innocently. 'The trouble is, Olivia, I'm just not sure he's confident you *like* him. You've been friends for so long, he probably reckons that's all it is…'

Olivia had a recollection of her final term at Taverick, during which Addy had been discovered by Head Matron having frantic moonlight sex with one of the sixth formers in a broom cupboard. She remembered wanting nothing more than to wallow in a tepid bath of her own teardrops, and then possibly drown to death in them. To this day she was tortured by the idea that it could have been one of the Feenys.

'Well?' pressed Thomasina. '*Do* you like him?'

'Bye, you two!' called Beth.

'Seeing as you ran off to *London*.' Lavender caught up and joined the assault. 'Men are so sensitive, aren't they, *Tommy*?'

Thomasina nodded gravely. 'Leave it with us,' she said amiably. 'Who knows, maybe we could organise a double date? You and Addy, me and Cato…'

Lavender was wounded.

'You'll have to have the other one,' Thomasina explained snippily. 'Cato already has a girlfriend. You're not equipped to deal with that.'

'With what?' Beth spluttered. 'Stealing other people's boyfriends?'

Thomasina ignored her. 'Just think about it,' she finished, with a little quirk of the head. 'Promise?' She pulled the reins; Lavender followed suit. The girls turned on their steeds and sashayed off across the cobbles.

'Can you believe them?' Beth asked in wonder. 'As

if you're dumb enough to fall for that.' She peered sideways at Olivia. 'And you're definitely *not* dumb, right?'

'Thanks for the vote of confidence.'

'You won't like me saying this but Addy's just as bad as they are.'

'He is not!' she protested. 'You just don't get him like I do.'

'I get that all he's ever done is make you feel like shit. He's aware how you feel about him and he loves stringing you along.'

'You don't know that.'

'You're right, I don't. But I do trust my instincts and I've known you both long enough. I don't trust him, Oli, and neither should you.'

The first of Beth's students arrived at the gate.

'I've got to scram.' She crossed the yard, calling back, 'Catch up tonight? Come to mine. We'll have pizza and you can talk to me more about Cato's pants.'

Olivia smiled. 'Sure.'

'Don't do anything stupid in the meantime. The Feenys are full of it, and so is Addy. Forget them. You will forget them, won't you?'

'Already have. Thanks, Mum.'

Beth smiled sweetly. 'Always a pleasure.'

Olivia put her hand to Archie's muzzle. She sighed.

Beth was right: the Feenys were poison.

But not Addy—Addy was different. He wasn't like that. He was her friend, her partner in crime, her hero; he was the blond-haired soldier crashing through leaves in autumn, the boy who had taught her to surf.

Her head refused to believe a word that came out of the Feenys' mouths.

If only she were able to tell her heart the same.

CHAPTER SEVEN

CHARLIE LAID THE PAPER in the tray, tipping it gently so the thick-smelling solution washed across the undeveloped image. He liked how the photograph revealed itself piece by piece, an outline here, a detail there, silver greys that became stark blacks, and whites that stayed as pure and bright as the gloss beneath. Ever since his father had given him his old Minolta Maxxum, he'd been hooked. Years ago it had been the magic of bottling everything he saw. Now, it was what he didn't see that captivated: moments that slipped by too quickly the first time, things he'd missed—people he missed—contained on a sheet, for ever unchanged.

The darkroom was an extravagance he knew he ought to get rid of. Penny had encouraged him to build it after their first trip together; her hand in his as they had strolled the canals of Amsterdam, taken bicycles to the flower markets and marvelled at the brave, raucous colours. She'd been happy, her chin resting in the palm of her hand as they had lingered outside cafés and talked about the future.

You should do this properly, she'd told him when they returned, poring over stills he had captured of bridges, cathedral spires; a stray dog they had encountered on a street corner. He'd unveiled the room to her weeks later, holding his hands over her eyes as they had stumbled into the uncanny light; red glow bathing the benches and worktops in fire. They'd kissed, hard against the wall; papers swiped from surfaces, her knees hoisted up around his waist. Charlie had made urgent, passionate love to her against the cabinet, reels of negatives hanging between them like wilderness threads, the black-out curtain torn by a sweat-drenched hand so that his day's work had been flooded with frozen daylight. It was how her love had made him feel: as if every slate could be wiped, every book rewritten, every bad memory erased…

Except for the memory of her.

It had taken a blind leap to open up to Penny in the way that he had. He should have known better. To trust her had been foolish.

To this day he could not forgive himself for allowing Cato into their lives. Everything his brother touched turned to dust.

Charlie pegged the images and emerged into the chill cellar, closing the door behind him. Along the walls were the powder-covered graves of vintage wines and ports, dusty hollows where the bottles had been removed and sold, leaving only cobwebs behind. Above him neat rows of Hungerford bells lined the passage, a remnant of life below stairs, the labels faded and tarnished: HER LADYSHIP'S ROOM. GRAND STAIRCASE. LIBRARY.

What must it have been like in the servants' day, at the height of Usherwood's glory? Hard to conjure it now: the energy, the bustle, the rush and spill of household secrets. His father had told him a story once about how as a boy he had crept underground for the servants' Christmas party, had danced until he could no longer stand, and had to be carried to bed by a butler called Ashton. But by the time Charlie came along, servants were *only good for gossip, my boy*. No wonder the remaining few he could remember had been dismissed before Harrow.

Sigmund and Comet were panting at the top of the stairs, fur still damp from an afternoon on the moors. They wagged their tails when they saw him.

'Hullo, pups.'

'What's that God-awful *stink*?' The quiet of the afternoon was obliterated.

Cato stormed into the hall with a hand clamped over his nose and mouth. His brother had taken to just *appearing*, cropping up unexpectedly like a grim rabbit out of a hat. The house was so big that it was possible to forget he was there.

'Oh.' Cato landed on the dogs and said disgustedly, 'There's my answer.'

'They're animals.'

'Precisely my problem.'

'This is the countryside, not downtown Los Angeles.'

'Just because we're in the countryside doesn't mean we have to be *in* the countryside,' came the riposte. 'We might as well be rolling about in the bloody paddocks.' Cato was wearing several bulky jumpers to drive home the fact he was cold, and had irately suggested over lunch that he would organise a cash injection to land with the estate by morning. *Then we can get this wretched heating sorted at last!* This sort of sporadic, mood-dependent handout was typical. Charlie had endeavoured on several occasions to secure a long-term solution to the invading damp—Cato matching every pound Charlie put in, for example—but such temporary measures were part and parcel of his brother's warped sense of obligation: the sun had to be shining wherever Cato was, and everywhere else could languish in the rain.

'Susanna's awfully distressed over the beasts.' Cato took a cigar from a box he had positioned on the mantelpiece and lit it. He ejected a billow of smoke. 'She's allergic to your menagerie; I knew she would be.'

Charlie glanced out of the window. His brother's girlfriend was under a parasol, fanning herself against the thunder flies.

'I'm sure she'll survive,' he said.

'She's very sensitive. I may have to ask you to keep them outside.'

'And I may have to remind you that this is my home.'

'*Your* home?' Only Cato could lace two words with such a potent mix of spite and incredulity. 'I rather think you're just looking after it for me, old bean.'

It was a good job Barbara came in when she did, or

Charlie would have floored him. 'How many for sup-per?' she asked.

'We're heading out this evening,' mused Cato, pout-ing out a smoke ring, 'it's arranged. I suppose I ought to show Susanna what this backwater's got to offer.'

'Very well,' said Charlie. 'It'll just be me, then, Mrs B-T.'

'Oh, no, it won't. You're coming with us and you're bringing that girl with you. I'd say an evening out was the very least you could do.'

'Olivia?'

'Of course Olivia—whom else would I be talking about?'

Beyond Susanna's elegant pose Charlie spotted his new planter's distant shape in the Sundial Garden, crouched over the foxglove bulbs. He had recognised Olivia the moment she'd shown up—the girl who used to hang around the Towerfield gates on her bike, bare legs smeared with mud from where she'd charged through a puddle or fallen out of a tree. It had been years, but he remembered. Charlie had observed her some days, sit-ting in the shade while she waited for the school bell, scribbling in a book or making a chain out of daisies. He'd wanted to go and talk to her but he hadn't known what to say. She'd had a thing for the pretty boy—all the girls had, though he couldn't see why. Adrian Gold didn't play rugby in case it messed his hair up. He couldn't put up a tent. He didn't read books, or play music, or know how to tie a reef knot. He didn't get jokes the first time and once during a test he couldn't arrange the vowels in 'beautiful', which had struck Charlie as unfortunate because there was enough prettiness in the world but beauty was rarer to come by, and if Adrian was friends with Olivia Lark then he ought at least to know how to spell it.

'Do you really want her running to the papers,' Cato rampaged on, 'saying Charles Lomax all but finished her off with whatever health and safety transgression the pedants' contingent are creaming their frillies over these days? She might act like butter wouldn't melt, but believe me: they've all got an eye for the main chance. If you don't keep her happy it'll be your name on the line.'

'I would've thought that might have been yours.'

'Don't flaunt your ignorance, Charles.'

'I hired her. That's a line I don't wish to cross.'

'You might have hired her, but you very nearly did away with her.'

'Wasn't it you behind the wheel?' His temper swelled, bright and lethal. 'Forgive me if I'm sensing a pattern developing here—'

'If I could interrupt.' Barbara stepped between them, compelled to make the peace as she had done for the last twenty years. 'I spoke with Olivia this morning and she's adamant that no one's to blame. She'd like us to forget the episode, if possible.'

'Go away, Baps,' said Cato.

The housekeeper dutifully retreated.

'Do you get a kick out of being so vile all the damn time?' demanded Charlie.

'Ah, look at her.' Cato came to stand next to him at the glass.

At first Charlie thought he was talking about Susanna. He wasn't.

'Such a pretty little thing,' said Cato, 'and so nice to have a bit of flesh to bite into. Susanna's a minx but it's all bone and sinew.'

'Keep away from her, Cato. I mean it.'

Cato smirked. He puffed a bit more on the cigar.

'Come on, Charles.' He winked. 'You know me better than that.'

CHAPTER EIGHT

SAFFRON ON THE SEA was the only restaurant in the British Isles to boast three coveted Gastronomy Stars. Despite this accolade it was entirely unpretentious, a simply festooned yacht moored in a quiet creek between two cliffs. In the summer it caught the moonlight perfectly as patrons feasted on its bulb-strewn deck, and in winter its cosy wooden interior was intimate and seductive.

Ex-model Serendipity Swain, a ravishing six-foot brunette, owned the restaurant with her husband Finn Avalon, a rock musician who had enjoyed modest fame in the nineties. The couple had started coming to Cornwall as a bolthole from their London lives, before the cove slipped under their skin and they decided to set up here permanently. A mixture of brilliantly selected chefs and star-sprinkled clientele ensured the business had grown from a pet project to a goliath in *haute cuisine*.

Serendipity greeted them at the bow, cinnamon hair

teased by the breeze and her elegant trouser suit rippling against the ocean backdrop. The sea was as still as silk, bubbles of conversation streaming from the deck and the waves lapping gently.

'Cato, this is an absolute pleasure.'

'Serendipity, *hi*.' He kissed her elaborately on both cheeks.

As Finn led the group to their table, a mercifully secluded spot roped off at the stern, heads turned to discreetly assess the newcomers, by nature of the restaurant too moneyed or too proud to surrender themselves fully to a blatant examination.

Susanna was beside herself, settling at the table and fingering the arrangement of wild flowers at its centre. In a moment, she would describe it as charming.

'Isn't this charming?' she enthused. Charlie was learning she would happily apply the adjective to anything so long as she was surrounded by English accents.

'Indeed it is, Mole.'

'Cato, please—' she objected, before he pulled her close and planted a very public kiss on her cheek, which made her start simpering all over again.

Charlie flipped open the menu. Saffron on the Sea was strictly *fruits de mer*. When Serendipity returned he ordered local Lustell oysters, enough for everyone, followed by hot shellfish with chilli and lemon, and a great deal of wine.

Next to him, Olivia looked as if she was moments away from tossing herself into the water and swimming for the shore. Cato had invited her, and despite her objec-

tions she'd been all but manhandled into the car. Saying
no to Cato was like trying to reason with a shark.

'It must be extra special for you, Olivia,' commented
Susanna, as she twirled the stem of a glass between two
fingers. When their waiter arrived with a bottle she covered the flute with a dainty palm. 'I can't imagine you
get out to places like this very much. You must be quite
overwhelmed!'

Olivia spread her napkin on her lap, seemed to change
her mind about it, and replaced it in a bundle on the
table. 'Yes,' she replied, taking a swig of Chablis before
Charlie had a chance to taste it. 'It's a far cry from KFC.'

Susanna frowned.

'How *are* you finding work on the estate?' she asked.

'Oh, I love it.' Olivia's voice warmed to the theme.
'I studied landscaping as part of my design course and
I've missed being outside all day so it suits me well. It's
pretty cool to plant something and watch it grow—good
for the soul, I think.'

Susanna wasn't listening. 'I haven't seen much im-
provement to those shabby lawns,' she commented, 'but
I suppose these things take time, don't they?'

'Right now it's a salvage operation,' said Charlie, indi-
cating to the sommelier to pour. 'Once the ground's recovered we should start seeing results. At this rate, we'll
be able to open to the public quicker than I thought.'

'The public?' Susanna cringed, as if he had suggested
unveiling a sewage tank in the rose garden. Cato pla-
cated her with an imperceptible shake of the head: no,
that wouldn't be happening, not on his watch.

'Well,' Susanna shredded a seeded plait with her fingertips and declined the offer of butter, 'it wouldn't be for me. I can only stand an hour in the heat before my skin comes out in the most outrageous rash. Isn't that right, Cato, darling?'

'You're a delicate flower, my dear.'

'I can't imagine it,' said Olivia, tucking into a bread roll. 'Me, I couldn't be cooped up for any length of time. When I was in London it did my head in being trapped indoors all day... I surf, so I'm used to the fresh air.'

'You surf?'

'What's wrong with that?'

'Well, nothing, I suppose.' Susanna considered it. 'Only it's not very ladylike.'

Cato's eyes were flashing. 'I think it's rather sexy. I say, perhaps we should get you out on a surfboard, Mole.'

'Over my dead body!'

'You should try sometime,' offered Olivia. 'I'll teach you, if you like.'

Susanna went to pour scorn on the suggestion before Cato supplied wolfishly:

'You can teach me.'

'I think she offered to teach *me*,' Susanna huffed, snapping a grissini in two.

The oysters arrived, a majestic array of rocky shells, bolstered by wedges of sunshine lemon, their flesh pearlescent in the candlelight and doused in sweet shallot.

Cato seized a mollusc and threw it back. 'Go on, girl,'

he encouraged Susanna, who took a suspicious sniff. 'Down the hatch!'

'These look awfully slimy,' she observed. 'Are they alive?'

Olivia lifted hers and it vanished down her throat. 'Not any more.'

Susanna was horrified. Olivia laughed, and put her elbows on the table.

Charlie stole a glance at her. She was unembellished in a plain dress, her auburn hair loose, and she wore no make-up. In the shimmering light her cheeks were soft as apricots, and her eyes were the colour of the sea. Around her neck was a delicate gold locket.

He had kept the picture. He didn't know where it was now—gathering dust in a box with all his old school stuff, probably. Remembering it felt strange, deceitful somehow, as she sat beside him.

The summer before he left for Harrow, Adrian and his gang had been in the common room, scrapping over a piece of paper, pointing at it and laughing. There had been some disagreement over its contents, a round of jostling and teasing, before the pretty boy capitulated and tossed it in the bin. Charlie had retrieved it after they'd gone, flattening it and smoothing down the creases. Straight away he had recognised the OL initials in the bottom right-hand corner.

It had been the most wonderful drawing. A map of Lustell Cove done in sharp, determined pencil, incorporating the beach and the Steep, the moors and the cliffs, with three big fat Xs scratched in red crayon at the foot of the bluff, where a sailboat was coming in to land, armed with treasure-seeking pirates. What had struck him wasn't just how good it was, how talented the artist, but with what care it had been done. She had done it for Adrian, and he had thrown it away.

Susanna was attempting to sip her oyster from its shell. She looked like a mother bird returning to the nest, a regurgitated worm dangling from her mouth.

'Suck it up, Mole, come on now!'

In a slurp it vanished. Susanna shuddered.

'She's trying to like them,' explained Cato. 'There's the most terrific pressure to serve them at dinner parties.'

Susanna smacked the table with her hand. 'That's it!' she cried.

'What in heaven's—?'

'We'll have a party,' she announced. 'At Usherwood! We'll invite everybody! Get the gang down from London, I'll do the place up, get designers in—caterers too; it'll be the society event of the decade! Oh, can we, Cato, can we?'

Cato stroked his chin. 'I don't know about that, Mole…'

'The town could come,' she said recklessly, turned to Charlie for support, whose face was distraught. 'Lustell Cove. Let's see what your precious public makes of that! Oh, it'll be wonderful. You know how easily bored I get when I'm not working. It would be a treat for me to plan something like this, a pet project—'

'Let's not get carried away…'

'It's not happening.'

The force of Charlie's interjection plunged the table into silence. It was definite as a slammed door. Cato and Susanna might have opened every aspect of their lives to the masses but that didn't mean he had to. The gathering wouldn't be for the cove, or even the couple's friends. It would inevitably drag an army of paparazzi and press attention with it: presumably that was the point.

Cato assumed everyone wanted the limelight. Charlie didn't.

But predictably, his brother's veto spurred Cato to a decision.

'Let's consider it, Charles—this might just be a fine idea.' Next to him, Susanna clapped her hands together and released a squeal. 'Since when has the old place hosted anything on that scale, hmm? It'd be good for the image.'

'I don't care about the image. It's not reality TV, it's a family home.'

'Precisely. So this must be a family decision.'

The men stared each other down.

'And as the eldest,' continued Cato, 'I think you'll find it falls to me.'

'You're never here,' lashed Charlie, 'so how can it?'

Susanna went to dispel the fracas. 'Ooh, look!' she exclaimed, as a dish of razor clams and langoustines arrived at the table. 'Aren't they pretty? I do love pink.' A light bulb went on above her head. 'We could have a pink theme—not Barbie pink; prawn pink! Crab pink! Lobster pink! All seafoods pink, inspired by—'

'Olivia, what do you think?' Cato turned to their guest.

'About the pink?'

'About the party.'

'It's not for me to say.'

'Of course it is,' said Cato impatiently, 'if I've just asked you. Keep up.'

'Well, I—'

'It's not my job to keep your girlfriend entertained,' interrupted Charlie.

Cato drew a sharp intake of breath. 'Neither was it mine to entertain yours,' he returned. 'Strange how she didn't seem to object.'

The table fell into a long and excruciating quiet.

Eventually, Charlie spoke. 'You forget yourself.'

He pushed his chair back. Without another word he threw a stash of bank notes into the middle of the table, pulled on his jacket and walked away.

His brother's voice chased him from behind, ripe with evil glee.

'Not to worry, darling,' Cato said. 'We'll send out invitations later this week. Never mind the decade, it'll be the party of the century—just you wait and see.'

CHAPTER NINE

SUSANNA WOKE AT one a.m. with the most formidable stomach cramps, her belly growling and gurgling as if it were about to explode. Cato's side of the bed was empty, the blankets pushed back and the imprint of his body fresh on the sheets.

As she staggered to the bathroom, all she could see were those horrid slithery oysters grinning back at her. She retched over the porcelain bowl. Why oh why did she insist on trying them? After a weak bout of spitting and weeping, she crawled on all fours back into the bedroom, a pitiful shadow, and slid beneath the covers.

It was utterly freezing. Had Cato left a window open? Susanna forced herself to investigate, her nightdress shining white as she staggered to the panes, imagining how she might look from miles away: a lonely ghost belonging to some bygone era, Victorian perhaps. The drapes were musty and thick, and when she drew them the grounds of the estate gleamed before her, impossibly still and as quiet as a painting. A river of star-glow spilled across the lawns, snaking between giant trees whose hulking frames were black as crows. The cherub in his pond, youth everlasting, sang a silent song to the sky. An owl hooted in the distance, a low, melancholy call.

Darting back to bed, she pressed a hand to her forehead. It was clammy and hot. The four-poster was lumpy, pockets of air and knotted springs in the fabric beneath, as if she were lying on a slab of her own distressed intestines. She gripped the sheets up to her chin and watched the door hopefully, waiting for Cato to return. Perhaps he could fix her a sparkling water: carbon was the thing for nausea.

Several minutes passed. Susanna's teeth chattered with cold. Through the curtains a milky ribbon of moonlight threaded into the room, the world outside so quiet it was deafening, and she cursed the damp walls and draughty windows that made everything so damn Baltic the whole time—oh, to be in her condo in Malibu, sunbathing by the pool! Though she hadn't broached the subject with Cato, she couldn't understand why he didn't just sell off one of his cars—he scarcely drove the Porsche, for instance—and solve Usherwood's heating problem once and for all. Did his conflict with Charles really run that deep? Was his refusal to help more than a proud conceit; was it that as far as he was concerned, the sooner Charles froze to death in here the sooner he could step in and reign supreme?

She'd had no idea that Usherwood was in such a state.

Cato holding back when he could so easily make a difference spoke volumes. Susanna remembered a drunken litany he had delivered last year.

The golden boy isn't so golden now, is he? If Daddy could see what a failure he's become, then he'd come running. He'd come begging me *for the money: he'd pay* me *some attention, then, wouldn't he?*

It was a shame there had been such a spectacular falling-out over supper. Cato had been in a black mood when they'd returned, tossing her to the floor, unbuckling his trousers and demanding sex. Any other time she would have been desperately turned on by it, but tonight she had felt too queasy.

She hoped he wasn't sulking. She vowed to compensate for it with an early morning blowjob, provided her gag reflex had settled by then.

With any luck the party would get things back on track, Susanna decided, and as she envisaged the revelry, the paupers' gasps as they were led into the ballroom (which despite its raggedness was clearly where they had to have it) and the creativity she could unleash on the decorating process, she instantly felt better. Parties brought people together, didn't they? Perhaps Cato and Charlie could use it as a bridge over their troubles, rendering Susanna not just a consummate hostess but also a saintly peacemaker, like Jesus, or the Pope, or a far younger and hotter Mother Teresa.

She was considering how this unification might also prompt Cato into the long-awaited proposal when she heard a short, high-pitched yelp coming from the far reaches of the house. Or had it come from outside? She couldn't tell.

Her heart thundered in her chest. It came again, this time a prolonged whinny.

What was that?

Susanna gripped the bed-sheets. She listened for it, and where first there was silence she began to detect a thin moaning sound, high and reedy, almost a wail.

Her eyes were big as saucers. Her psychic in LA had promised her that this month would be spiritually fertile. Was she tuning into the desperate, drowning cries of a poor servant girl as she sobbed through the house of the dead?

Susanna gasped. Her eyes darted to the clock at her bedside, half expecting it to leap up and fling itself in her face because who was to say this wasn't a poltergeist? Her ears searched for the sound, honing it to a pinpoint then just when she'd captured it away it would fly, offering up a moment's respite before resuming its grisly song.

Perhaps it was the wind, a pesky current whistling through the deserted wings.

Perhaps it was a television, or a radio—? No, it was closer than that.

Perhaps it was a creaky floorboard…

That some heinous phantom was stepping on!

Her chest was about to blow open with all the blood that was hammering through it. She watched the door, convinced the handle was about to turn. Tentatively she extracted herself from the bed, the pains in her stomach all but eclipsed in the shadow of her fear. Her hand was like snow in the darkness, reaching for the door, disembodied as if it didn't belong to her at all.

On the landing she backed up, forced to choke on her scream when a dour life-sized painting of one of Cato's grandfathers assailed her vision from the top of the stairs. She crept down the passage, the yowling getting closer. The hall flickered uncertainly, a rich wood smell where the old panels seeped their age; and the framed ancestry of Lomaxes-past lined the walls, expressions shifting and melting in the gloom. Barefoot she padded among their watchful stares, the spectre at the feast.

A ticking clock matched her steps. By the time she reached the winding steps she dared not look behind her.

Here she could tune in to it more cleanly. It was a definite, protracted sigh, punctuated by an occasional whimper, and as Susanna tiptoed closer she swore the pattern was getting faster, the wailing higher, breaking momentarily into a screech, before a series of great sobs erupted, one after the other, an agony of ecstasy...

Abruptly, it stopped.

So did she. A chill prickled up the back of her neck and she knew then, *absolutely knew,* that she wasn't alone. Her lips went dry and she gulped, swallowing the lump in her throat like a ball of cotton wool.

Too afraid to turn for fear of meeting the presence at her shoulder, Susanna reversed down the corridor, hands flailing behind her, fingertips exploring the unseen, and when she met the rough wood of her bedroom door she whipped it open and dived inside, slamming it shut and flinging herself into the safety of the bed.

It was ages before she got any sleep. Some time later she was distantly aware of Cato climbing in beside her, and bewilderedly she reached for him, content to encounter his solid, reassuring bulk. Only then did she drift into dreams.

CHAPTER TEN

THE MORNING AFTER Saffron on the Sea, Olivia arrived at Usherwood early. The calm, quiet hours she spent in the gardens were a far cry from the hectic pace of city life, squashed in on the rush-hour tube or queuing for sandwiches in a café on Holborn, and while she was still hoping to get enough cash together by the end of the month to put down a deposit on a flat, she had to admit that being back at the cove was making her happy. With every day that passed she felt herself growing calmer, more centred and more like her old self—and she'd started drawing again.

'Something's got you inspired,' Florence had commented at the weekend as Olivia had torn yet another page from her sketchbook. 'Or should I say someone?'

'Whatever, Mum.'

'I'm just saying...'

'Well, don't.'

The last thing she needed was another lecture about Addy. It was so annoying!

Why did everyone feel the need to get involved in her love life? No wonder she hadn't brought home either of the guys she'd dated in London, if this was the kind of interrogation they'd face. She ignored the voice that suggested it was because one had been a stoner who spent his entire time 'gaming' with nine-year-olds in Japan, while the other's name had been Nimrod—he was Jewish, though, to be fair.

There was a mountain of weeding to be done and Olivia wanted to plant the geranium seeds before lunch. Her mother had given her a box of vegetable roots from the allotment and made her swear to ask Mr Lomax about them. *All that space and he hasn't got room for potatoes?* Florence had wedged the crate into her pannier.

Olivia wasn't sure *what* Charlie had room for in his life. He was perpetually indifferent. He never spoke to her. He never looked at her. He never touched her. Not that she wanted him to touch her, but just little things, like when he came to check on her progress and she held out a bulb, plump as a miniature gourd and gritty with soil, and he would never take it from her. Or if Barbara gave her a cup of tea to bring to him and he would never accept it directly, just keep on with whatever he was doing and wait for Olivia to leave it there, offering only a curt and dismissive, 'Thank you.' Or when she'd tripped one day in the Sundial Garden, putting out her hands to break her fall, and he could easily have caught her, but he hadn't.

He seemed to go out of his way to escape having any kind of contact with her. If she had been the sensitive type, it might have upset her, but it wasn't her business to dwell on the reasons for his withdrawal and so she didn't bother taking it to heart. She didn't like him, so there was only so far she could bring herself to care.

'Breakfast!' Barbara's call travelled across from the house.

Olivia dusted off her knees, waving over the top of the wall to indicate that she'd heard. The orange bricks were mapped with vines that were brittle with age and perishing in the heat—climbing rose and wisteria and clematis, once upon a time—and the soil beds were crusted with earth, their borders collapsing. Beaten gravel paths ran towards a central kidney-shaped plot that years ago would have bragged an abundance of colour, azaleas, rhododendrons, fragrant lavender, but now was obscured in a burst of overgrown shrubs. It was more a wilderness than a garden, yet all it took was a bud pushing through the dirt, a swallow coming to rest on the dappled stone bath and beating its wings in a puddle of rain, or the sun setting behind the towering oak and throwing it into a heavenly blaze, to reassure Olivia that everything was salvageable. There was still life here, if you knew where to look.

She crossed to the house, aromas of black coffee and smoky bacon seeping into the morning. In the hall Sigmund was gulping noisily at a bowl of water, sandy paw prints dotted across the stones from where he'd been down on the beach. She glanced around for Charlie but couldn't see him.

'I hope you're hungry,' said Barbara as she entered the kitchen. Caggie was at the window buttering doorstop slabs of toast, and smiled when she saw her.

'Starving.'

'You'd better be. We had a delivery from Ben Nancarrow this morning—sausages, eggs, milk, you name it.' Barbara poured the coffee. 'He dropped by earlier, called it "a token of my admiration". Cato always did know how to attract attention.'

Olivia's tummy grumbled. After last night's fall-out the evening had wound quickly to a close, with Cato angrily bolting his seafood and Olivia finding she couldn't eat a thing. Susanna had chattered merrily about her plans for the party, prompting Cato to leap up and order a bottle of the establishment's finest champagne, which he'd proceeded to quaff almost entirely himself.

'This looks delicious,' she exclaimed as Caggie deposited a plate in front of her. It was piled high with creamy scrambled eggs, herby mushrooms and crispy potato cakes, thick, salty rashers and sausages that popped with greasy flavour.

Susanna drifted in. She was bereft of make-up, a turban wound elaborately round her head. Immediately she put a hand to her mouth, her shoulders heaving.

'Goodness, are you all right?' asked Barbara.

Tightly she nodded. She was wearing a floating peach robe, and on her feet were dainty slippers with furry baubles on the front. Olivia had caught the end of one of her movies last year, a fluffy chick-flick about an eternal bridesmaid, and knew her friends would die to know she was sitting down to breakfast with its leading lady.

'I'm seriously unwell,' Susanna croaked, sinking into a chair.

Barbara was alarmed. 'Do you need a doctor?'

'I need caffeine.'

'Here.' Barbara was quick to oblige. 'Have you a temperature?'

'Something I ate,' Susanna managed, casting a sickened squint at Olivia's breakfast and turning a deeper shade of green. 'I had to cut off a call to my agent, I felt so appalling. Just some dry toast, please, Mrs Bewlis-Teet.'

'Right away.'

'I hope it wasn't something I cooked,' offered Caggie.

Susanna glanced at her sharply.

'You poor thing,' said Olivia sympathetically. 'Was it the seafood?'

Susanna checked the other women were otherwise occupied. She leaned in.

'You do realise this house is haunted?' she whispered hoarsely.

Olivia blinked. 'No. I didn't realise that.'

'I heard her. Last night. A woman, crying out.' She shuddered. 'I was beside myself with fear. I don't think I can sleep another night in this place.'

'Old houses make all sorts of noises,' comforted Olivia. 'I expect it was the wind. Buildings like this throw sound all over the place.'

'Whatever it was, it's left me with the most piercing headache. That's how I know this was a supernatural intervention.'

Olivia spiked a mushroom and put it in her mouth.

'My psychic,' Susanna went on, 'she says I'm a vessel for these things.'

'A vessel?'

'The headache's brought on by exhaustion. I've been working though the night, you see, connecting with the spirits.' She straightened as Barbara returned with the toast. Alone again, she hissed, '*Unfinished business*, that's what these energies are about. They simply cannot rest until the past has been rectified, until they've claimed their dues, and it takes somebody like me to facilitate that.'

'Wow. That's quite a responsibility.'

'You're telling me. Usherwood is swimming in it. She'll be back.'

'Who?'

'The *ghost*, of course.'

'How about some fresh air?' Caggie dropped down opposite with a plate and a mug of tea. 'A brisk walk might do you good.'

'I'm too fragile to venture outside on my own.'

'I'm sure the dogs will go with you.'

'*The dogs?*' Susanna echoed disgustedly.

'Where's Cato?' Olivia asked.

Caggie said, 'Still in bed, I should think.'

Susanna pursed her lips. 'That's right,' she muttered.

'And *I* should know, since *I'm* the one who left him there.'

After a feeble endeavour with the crusts, she retreated to her chambers. Olivia joined Caggie at the sink to help with the washing up.

'Do you believe in ghosts?' she asked. 'Susanna thinks she heard some strange sounds in the night.'

Caggie smiled. 'No,' she replied. 'I do believe in night-time noises, but more often than not they're in the land of the *very* much alive.'

Olivia took the back route out to the gardens, through the drawing room and on to the covered porch, from where the geometric lines of the greenhouse could be seen through the arches, glinting in the sun. The door to the library was ajar and she went to it, recalling her mother's allotment offering, and tapped gently.

There was no answer.

She stood for a moment, thinking what to do. She ought to walk away, but her surroundings were so quiet, and the curiosity that had landed her in it on more than one occasion so great, that she found herself applying the slightest touch of pressure.

The door swung open to reveal a handsome office, wall to wall filled with books. A sliding ladder awarded access to a higher mezzanine, and a semicircular balcony jutted out above a large bust of Richmond Lomax. The smell was of leather, sandalwood and a recently burned fire. A bureau was opened to reveal scattered papers and hastily handwritten notes, and in the corner of the room a grandfather clock ticked mournfully. At the window was an impressive antique globe, polished by sunlight, and in the distance she could make out the dense green smudge of the forest.

She crossed the threshold. A mist of dust was suspended, dancing in the haze, and she felt if she walked straight through it she would leave an imprint, a mark of her trespass, like a hole punched in paper.

Without meaning to, Olivia came to his desk. Her fingers hovered over the clutch on the drawer, before slowly easing it open.

Inside was a jumble of ink-dry pens, loose drawing pins and a stapler snapped at its spine. She fed a hand in and caught the sharp corner of a piece of paper, which she slid into view. It was a black-and-white photograph of a young woman, worn at the edges as though it had been handled many times. She lifted it out.

At first Olivia thought she was looking at Beatrice Lomax, before deciding it was too contemporary. This looked as if it had been taken in the last five years.

The subject was reclining in the shade of a tree—here at Usherwood, Olivia guessed—and she wore a white vest with a pretty lace collar, beneath which the picture was severed. A loop of hair was wound around her finger and a playful smile danced on her lips. There was a glimmer in her eye, of secrets, of intimacy, that suggested she was sleeping with whomever was behind the camera.

Olivia brought the image closer. She flipped it round. On the back it read: *Now and always x*

Her phone beeped. It made her jump, the tinny chirrup at odds with this dusty, history-soaked space. She placed the photo on the desk and scooped the phone from her pocket. An unrecognised number flashed up and she clicked on the message.

Drink at the Anchor, Friday, seven p.m.? Addy x

Pleasure soaked through her. She stared at it.
Get a grip, Olivia.
She couldn't help it. Was it a date? It sounded like a date. A flurry of butterflies flew free in her tummy. There was a kiss on there. He never did that.

Quickly she replaced his number with the old one she had for him. Her fingers were shaking. She told herself off for being silly.

She was fumbling to compose her reply when a voice came from the doorway:

'What do you think you're doing?'

The phone slipped from Olivia's hand and she scrambled to retrieve it.

'Sorry,' she mumbled, 'I, er...'

'This is private.' Charlie's stare was fierce, his words violently quiet.

'Of course.' She moved towards the door. He grabbed her elbow. It hurt.

'What were you looking for?'

'Nothing, I—'

'Something you could sell to the papers?'

'No.' She was wounded he would think that of her.

'I'd never do that. The door was open and I… I don't know.' Her mouth went dry. Why did he have to look at her like that, stripping her naked, making her feel like a silly like child?

'Let me go.'

Their faces were inches apart. He was huge, his frame engulfing hers. His grip was painful. 'I told you when you started here that the house owes you nothing,' he said. 'This is a job, do you understand? Not a fucking museum.'

'I understand.'

He released her. 'Never let me find you here again.'

She rubbed her arm. It was the same he had tended to the night Cato had knocked her down. A confusion of feelings assailed her and she translated them as anger. How dare Charlie Lomax make her feel like this? How dare he bully her, intimidate her with his size, his presence, his aristocracy, the advantage of his sex?

'I won't,' she retorted. 'Don't worry.'

He frowned at her hard.

'You work for me,' he told her. 'Watch what you say.'

What *she* said? There was only one person in this room who needed to get their attitude checked. The words were free before she could swallow them.

'I've told you I'm sorry,' she answered furiously. 'What do you want me to do, beg? A working relationship goes both ways, you know. You can't demand respect if you've never shown any to me, and from where I'm sitting you haven't even bothered. You think that because of who you are and because of what you have we should all bow down and worship the ground you walk on—well, that's not me and it never will be, and if that disappoints you then I suggest you find someone else to sort out your precious estate. Perhaps if you weren't so aggressive all the time, I might have a better idea where I stand. Perhaps if you weren't so shut off I mightn't be afraid to say two words to you in the morning. Perhaps if you talked to me once in a while I might like you a bit more. Perhaps if you cared at all about other people or what they might be feeling then you'd have a shot at understanding what I'm on about. I'm only trying to do the right thing here; I'm only trying to do my job. I'm sorry if you feel I've overstepped the mark, but it's not my fault Cato drags me along to things just so he doesn't have to spend time alone with you.'

Charlie watched her, steady except for a lightning flinch. It was like glimpsing the solution to a profound mathematical equation, only to have it snatched away.

His eyes fell on the desk, as she had known they would.

He picked up the photo of the woman, examined it before replacing it in the drawer. The wood slid back into place with a grateful hush.

'Get out,' he said.

She didn't wait to be told again.

CHAPTER ELEVEN

LATER THAT DAY he took the dogs up Lustell Steep, the highest point of the cove. In winter, harsh winds thrashed in from the Atlantic, the chalky, salt-encrusted walls of the remote Candle Point lighthouse taking the worst of the poundings. Today, at the height of summer, the tower seemed a different world: a peaceful, patient thimble on a rocky outcrop, the ocean silent and still.

The contrast was one of the things Charlie liked most about being by the water. Knowing it from childhood, he could never consider a land-locked life. The sea was an eternally changing animal; black with fury one day and smiling blue the next.

For years he had taken refuge in the moods of the ocean. It was impossible to imagine not waking to it each morning, the slender ribbon of water a reminder that the earth held mysteries he would never be able to answer. As a child he had spent time at his Uncle Barnaby's cottage, further down the cove, overlooking the waves: he would sit at the window for hours, gazing at the sheet of iron and waiting, half hoping, for some disturbance to its surface. *We know more of outer space than we do of the ocean*, Barnaby had told him. *It's deeper than you can imagine, and full of wonderful secrets.* It was a half remembered house, and his uncle a half remembered man.

Barnaby had been his mother's brother. He had left the cove when Charlie was five: he had fallen out with Richmond, though about what it was never discovered. They had neither seen nor heard from him since; his name was never spoken. Where was he? Was he even still alive? Childhood acceptance of his uncle's dismissal had somehow seeped into maturity. It was just how things were. Charlie rarely thought of him, and pushed him away now. The past was a foreign land.

Comet was sniffing about in the gorse, his tail emerging from a wiry tangle before he heard his master's whistle and his head shot up, ears keen. Charlie launched a stick and both dogs darted after it across the heath, legs scrambling, and the tussle seemed to tip in Sigmund's favour before a third hound appeared over the brow and joined the frantic pursuit. Charlie recognised it as the Montgomerys' young sheepdog, and sure enough Fiona followed behind, shouting her puppy's name.

She managed to untangle him from the mêlée. 'Charlie, hi. Long time no see.'

Fiona owned the Quillets Vineyard with her husband Wilson. The winery was renowned for its grapes and was annual supplier to the prestigious Dukestone Flower Show, as well as, many moons ago, to Usherwood. Fiona had become friendly with the Lomaxes, she and Beatrice especially close. Since the tragedy they had fallen out of contact. It was Charlie's fault, partly—she reminded him too much of his mother. He recalled the women outside on the veranda on late summer evenings, sipping cordial and conversing in shadowy, private murmurs. He had wanted badly to know what they spoke about. After bedtime, pressing his ear to the stuck-fast window, he could see their heads dipped towards one another, exchanging thrills and surprises.

'Fiona.' He nodded. 'How are you?'

'Oh, fine, fine.' Her dark hair was escaping from her trapper's hat, and around her neck she wore a lanyard and whistle. She sounded it to zero effect and shot Charlie a wry grin. 'Being kept busy with this one.'

'Is the business going well?'

'We can't complain. It's been a super year for champagne. You must come by,' she urged warmly. 'Wilson and I would love to see you at the house.'

'Thanks. I might.' But they both knew he wouldn't.

'I hear Cato's back?'

'He is.'

'It's ages since I've seen you both. I catch him on TV sometimes—it's hard to believe it's the same person.'

'Oh, he's the same.'

'Send him my regards?'

'Of course.'

She smiled. 'What about you? Are you still taking photos?'

How lightweight that sounded against his brother's

achievements. A while ago Charlie had exhibited at the Round House gallery, to the cove's unanimous acclaim, but since then he'd become buried by the estate and it had seemed an indulgent pursuit. Someone had to dedicate himself full-time to the running of the house, and it wasn't going to be his brother in LA. It had occurred to Charlie that this might be a lame excuse, and the real reason he had turned his back was because it was painful; that it brought Penny too much back to life when he had to accept she was dead.

'Not really,' he admitted, 'not any more.'

'That's a shame. You always had such a love for it.'

The wind picked up, an eerie whistle as it blew across the grasses. Fiona said, 'I was so sorry about your girl-friend.'

'Oh.' He lifted his shoulders, looked to the ground. 'It was years ago.'

'I know. Even so.'

'Even so.'

'I kept meaning to come to the house, and there never seemed to be the right opportunity. Time passed and then... After Bea and Richmond, I don't know, it just seemed too unkind. If I'm totally honest, Charlie... Well, I didn't know what to say.'

'That's OK.'

The dogs rushed over, sniffing the ground. Charlie was relieved at the diversion. Fiona's pup was begging attention from the others, scampering after their tails, rangy with adolescent spirit.

Perhaps if you cared at all about other people...

Olivia's words came back to him. He held them down.

'Is it true Usherwood's throwing a party?' Fiona was watching him brightly, buoying the conversation with what she imagined to be a positive topic.

'Ah, just an idea.' He ran a hand across his chin. 'We haven't confirmed it.'

'I overheard the girls at the yacht club talking,' Fiona explained. 'There are certainly a lot of eager young ladies out there willing to make up the numbers!'

News travelled fast. And while it pained him, the facts couldn't be ignored. Charlie had consulted the budget for the coming year, and the party, with its grisly entourage of press attention and media deals, would help no end. He would have to swallow his misgivings and consider the wider picture. It would be one night, and after that only a week before Cato and Susanna returned to the States. Usherwood would become a singular detour in their whirlwind calendars, a diversion they would describe to friends in a fond, patronising way, and life on the estate would resume as before. Only this time, there would be cash at his fingertips. Charlie's share of the profits would lift the place back on its feet—he had to believe it.

'I should get home, Fiona. It was good seeing you.'

She paused, as if she wanted to say something more, something important, before changing her mind. Instead she said, 'We all miss them, you know.'

It looked for a second as if she might reach out to touch him. She didn't.

'I know how proud she'd be,' Fiona said. 'Of both of you.'

Bringing the dogs to heel, he started up the slopes and didn't look back.

Usherwood had just slipped into view, a castle on the sweeping horizon, when he spotted a couple of figures mounting a stile, and by the look of it making a meal of the descent. Cato was clad in Charlie's old Barbour and was jabbing the air with a stick.

'That's it, Mole; one leg over, now the other!'

The summons carried across the empty field. As Charlie got closer, he saw Susanna struggling over the gate, one leg dangling in trepidation over a slick of mud.

'You want me to put my feet in that?'

'You've Wellington boots on, what's the problem?'

'I'll slip!'

'You will not slip. A bit of muck never killed anyone.'

Daintily she managed to sidestep the bog, falling dramatically into Cato's arms and gripping his shoulders. Charlie would have preferred to return alone, but this was the direct path, and besides, he'd already been seen.

'Charles,' said his brother rigidly.

'Cato.'

'What a beautiful afternoon!' sang Susanna, carefully scraping her boot against a knot of grass in an attempt to get it clean. 'We're just out for a walk.'

'I can see.'

'I feel so much better now, baby… This really was the thing.'

'That'll teach you to drink so much,' admonished Cato, who had been nursing his own hangover for the majority of the morning.

'It was the oysters,' said Susanna testily.

Cato turned to him. 'Who were you talking to down there?'

'Fiona Montgomery.'

He scoffed. 'That old crow's still flapping her wings, is she?'

'She sends her best.'

'I'll bet. You've got to watch out for these gossipy bats; the way they see it, if they rub up against you long enough some of the shine might eventually come off.'

Susanna tittered at her boyfriend's analogy. 'Darling…' she feebly rebuked.

'Believe it or not,' said Charlie, 'not everyone requires you to buff them up. Fiona's got her own business—a very successful one at that.'

'And a damn sight more successful with my endorsement, no doubt. Don't think I didn't see her ogling me whenever I came home from school.'

'No!' Susanna gasped. 'Were you underage?'

'I'll say. The hag couldn't help it. I'll vouch if you'd left me alone with her for one minute she'd have grappled into my trousers like she hadn't eaten in a week.'

Charlie was disgusted. He was tempted to remind Cato that far from Fiona making a fictional pass at him, it had in fact been Caggie Shaw who had awarded him his sexual initiation. On Cato's sixteenth birthday he and the house cook had been discovered in a state of dishevelment, Caggie on her knees in the stables while Cato reclined *in flagrante* across a bale of hay. For a while it had looked as if Caggie might be fired, until Richmond intervened with a disinterested 'Boys will be boys' rationale and promises of 'a stern talking-to', though whether or not that materialised was anyone's guess. Cato had been a formidable young man, sly beyond his years, and it was impossible to say from which side the persuasion had come.

Judging by the state of him this morning, old habits died hard. Cato couldn't help himself. Each time he returned to Usherwood, no matter whom he was with, it was the same routine: he and Caggie were unable to keep their hands off each other. Charlie had his suspicions about why. Cato had never come to terms with the vanishing. After the news he had shot off to France, from France to Hollywood, from Hollywood to the stratosphere. As far as Charlie was aware his brother had never wept. He had never fought it. He had never stared himself down in the mirror and asked the eternal: what if? *Not that depressing nonsense again*, Cato would say, whenever the subject was raised. But the trauma had to escape somehow. Caggie harked back to his childhood. She was a fraction younger than their mother, the same blonde hair and the same green eyes. She signified the world before it ended. She was his gateway to another life. She was his carer, the only one left. She was denial.

'We're meeting about the party tonight,' Susanna trilled. 'Will you join us?'

Cato observed his brother for a reaction, and gave a

satisfied smirk when Charlie consented: 'I expect it's best if I sit in.'

'Knew you'd come around, old chap.'

'We have to make money, don't we?'

Cato's smile faltered. For all his superficial magnanimity, he knew deep down that he wasn't quite playing ball, and that his millions hoarded in the bank were little but a spiteful ransom. 'Indeed we do.'

'In that case, there's little time to waste!' Susanna seized her boyfriend's arm. 'I think I've had enough country air for one day. How about I fix us all a Tom Collins and we get down to business?'

Instead of negotiating the stile for a second time, Cato chivalrously lifted her over, eliciting a squeal of delight.

Charlie followed behind, keeping his distance.

CHAPTER TWELVE

OLIVIA SPENT ALL of Friday counting down the hours to her appointment with Addy. She managed to clock off early at Usherwood—she'd weeded the verges and deadheaded the Sweet Williams in good time, and Charlie had gone AWOL amid the party planning. That was fine by her. The less she had to see of him, the better. After their altercation she'd been fully prepared for an unceremonious dismissal, but as yet it hadn't come.

Back at the caravan, she rifled through her chest of drawers.

'You look lovely in what you're wearing,' Flo said from the bedroom door, nettle tea in hand. 'I shouldn't think he's making this much effort.'

'Come on.' Olivia gestured at her work clothes, scruffy dungarees hanging from her waist, white vest covered in soil and torn at the hem where it had snagged on a nail. 'I know the Anchor isn't quite The Ritz, but even so.'

'Why are you going?' asked Florence. 'He'll only hurt you again.'

'Addy and I have unfinished business.' She yanked out a grey silk top. 'And if you don't mind me saying, that business is none of yours.'

'All right, sweetheart, no need to be sensitive.'

'I'm not. I just wish you'd keep your opinions to your-self.'

'I'm only concerned for you.'

It was no secret that over the years Florence had taken against Addy. *He's terribly vain, isn't he? What does he think he is, God's gift to women?* By Flo's judgement Addy had once been a lovely boy; it was when he'd taken work at the Blue Paradise that things started to go wrong. Girls swarmed to him like bees to honey. Suddenly his plans to go travelling had evaporated, his ambitions for the future dismissed. Addy had become solely concerned with how many customers he could secure dates with in one day, and the honing of his immaculate reflection in the surf shop's full-length. *Goodness knows how many he's been with*, Flo would comment, twisting a knife in Olivia's heart. *He's not the same person he used to be.*

It was kind of understandable. After all, it had been Flo who had wiped the tears after every Addy knock-back throughout her teens; each time he'd swaggered on to the beach with the latest in a catalogue of beauties, all gamine girls with long legs, streamlined stomachs and chests so flat that if you arranged them into one of Flo's more ambitious yoga positions you could use them as an ironing board. Olivia couldn't blame her for being wary, but she wasn't in the mood for a reality check.

'If I'm going to be living here,' she said, 'I have to do things my way. You brought me up to think for myself, didn't you? So that's exactly what I'm doing.'

Florence held a hand up in surrender. 'OK. Just don't say I didn't warn you.'

The Anchor was a traditional seaside pub at the westernmost point of the cove. On the beachfront terrace an arrangement of picnic benches looked out on to the water, while inside it was buzzing with locals. She spotted Addy in a booth, nursing a pint and as usual scanning his phone. His forearms were tanned against the white of his T-shirt. He looked impossibly hot, his golden hair rumpled and sexy.

'Hi.' She slipped in next to him, wondering why out of all the men in the world he had to be the only one who turned her knees to jelly.

'Hey. Wow, you look nice. Want a drink? I didn't know what you wanted.'

'A glass of wine, please.'

'Red or white?'

'White. Thanks.'

Addy scanned the bar. 'I just spent bloody ages queueing for mine—do you mind going up? I'll give you a couple of quid.'

'Don't worry, I'll get it.'

'Sure? You're a legend. Oh,' he caught her as she departed the table, 'maybe get another of these?' He lifted his pint. 'Saves me going up again…'

When she came back ten minutes later he greeted her with a grin. Since the beginning of time she'd been addicted to it—would she ever grow out of Addy Gold?

'So,' she smoothed her top, 'this is nice.' It was such a banal thing to say but she couldn't come up with anything else. They had been friends for so long—why couldn't she talk to him normally, about normal things? They had tons of interests in common, didn't they? They must do. She just couldn't think of one right now.

'I'm quitting the Blue Paradise,' he blurted.

She nearly spat out her wine. 'Why? You can't quit!'

Addy lifted his shoulders. 'I've been at it for years, Oli. I'm bored. I need some… I don't know, some excitement in my life. Maybe it's time I actually *did* something instead of bumming round the cove chasing the next wave.'

She went to object but the summary was succinct.

'What will you do?'

'Not sure,' he mused. 'I've got a few ideas, stuff I meant to get round to but never did… You know how life catches up and then you wake up one day and look around and think: Shit, man, is this it? Well, wake-up call, Addy!' He did a flustered little jig as if an alarm clock had fired off nearby. 'Maybe it doesn't have to be.'

She swallowed her selfish reservations. It was great that he was finally taking charge of things. She should try to be supportive.

'Well,' she managed, 'it sounds like a brilliant decision.'

He took a frothy sip of his beer. Olivia watched the
foam on his top lip and wanted to kiss it off. 'Actually,'
he said, blue eyes twinkling, 'how'd you fancy helping
out a mate?'

She returned his smile. 'With what?'

'Life at Usherwood… It must be a kick being around
film stars all day, huh.'

'Yeah, they're OK. Charlie's doing my head in though.'

Addy smirked. 'He always was an arrogant twat.'

'You were never friends, even at school?'

'Are you kidding me? Lomax thought he was some
hot deal, made up his own rules and everyone else could
piss right off.'

'Sounds about right.'

Addy's eyes strayed to the bar, where a blonde was
digging into her purse for change. 'I remember this one
time,' he drawled, 'we had this cricket match against
Rudgeley Boys. Rudgeley was, like, the most interesting
thing that happened all year; their team was the best in
the county but we were totally on it to take the trophy.'

'I remember! You used to go to the Farley Ground
for playoffs.'

'Yeah, that's it. Anyhow Lomax had it in for the
Rudgeley captain, this brick-shit-house fat kid called
Sedgwick, because Sedgwick used to call him to his
face all the things we called him behind his back: toff
wanker, posh prick, that kind of thing.'

Addy laughed. Olivia considered that Addy's own

family wasn't that badly off, in fact none of the boys who attended Towerfield were exactly poverty-stricken.

'So Lomax bowled this totally vicious ball against him. It got Sedgwick in the nuts and Sedgwick freaked. The two of them started beating the crap out of each other. The master had to drag them off. There was blood everywhere. Lomax got smashed in the face and Sedgwick was staggering about like he'd been winded. Sedgwick was mashed up good; only he was so fat that when he fell over he kind of just rolled, like a massive squidgy meatball. It was pretty entertaining, but we were all majorly fucked off at the time. The match got cancelled, and since it was Lomax who started it, Rudgeley took the trophy and we got banned from ever playing in the tournament again.'

'Shit. You must've been gutted.'

'Sure was. I mean, not me personally, I wasn't playing anyway—I'd put my shoulder out that season, remember?'

'Oh. Yeah.'

There was a pause. She had something she wanted to ask him.

'Did Thomasina Feeny set you up to this?'

'To what?'

'This…' Olivia gestured to the table, as though the Feenys had taken to selling cut-price furniture. 'Tonight.'

'Why would she do that?'

There was a trace of humour in his voice. She could never quite tell if he was joking or not, like when he used to tease her about being a gypsy because she didn't live in a proper house, or because her clothes were from charity shops, or because they used an outside loo, but then before she could take it seriously Addy would grin and give her a playful nudge, his blue eyes sparkling, and promise her he was only being affectionate.

She'd clung to that word—*affectionate*.

'Never mind.' She smiled. 'Just a hangover from school, you know?'

Addy wouldn't know. His adolescent experience had been entirely different to hers. He'd always been cool, and popular, the one everybody wanted to be friends with. As teenagers Taverick Manor had endured socials with the Towerfield boys, insufferable episodes geared solely towards securing that first kiss and that longed-for first fumble. All the girls had flocked to Addy, while Olivia looked on, dejected when he had pretended not to know her. Afterwards she saw it made sense—she was a couple of years below, she'd purposefully distanced herself from the handbag crew and besides, Addy had a reputation to protect. Instead she had danced with a boy called Steven who had worn a tangerine sweater and had curtains, and had wedged his fourteen-year-old erection between her legs for the duration of a Radiohead song.

'Those Feenys are trouble,' Addy observed, and she didn't press him because she had no desire to find out just how naughty he knew one or both of them to be.

'Usherwood's work.' She returned to safer ground. 'I need the money, so in that respect it's a job like any other.'

He scooted a little closer to her on the bench.

'Jez and Simon said they saw you at Saffron the other night, like it was a family outing or something.'

'Believe me, it was anything but.'

'Bet Cato fancies you.'

She laughed openly at that. 'Right.'

'What? You're gorgeous. I've always thought so, ever since for ever.'

Her tongue wound itself in a knot.

'Fair to say you're getting close to them…' He started playing with a beer mat—how she loved his hands, the fingers long and strong and slender. 'Right?'

'When I first turned up, there was this thing that happened—just an accident. The Lomaxes taking me out was an apology, that's all.'

'What accident?'

'It doesn't matter.'

Addy looked unconvinced so she added: 'You're right about Charlie. I don't know if it's because Cato's here or if he's always like that. He hates everyone.' She gulped the wine. 'He definitely hates me.'

Addy watched her. 'You're sexy when you're angry.'

'I'm not angry.'

'You are, a bit.' He leaned in. She noticed he'd barely drunk half his pint, and his eyes moved slowly, very slowly, down her face and towards her lips.

'Hey, man.'

Addy's friend Dax interrupted them. Even at this hour he was still wet from the ocean. Dax spent so much time in the water he was practically amphibious.

'You surfing tomorrow?' He moved to sit down, then

paused, looked between them, and Olivia sensed but didn't see Addy's expression of: *I'm in the middle of something here, buddy.*

'Ah,' said Dax, 'right on. Catch you later, dude.'

'Where were we?' Addy pressed when he'd gone. Olivia could feel his thigh against hers, the heat of it, and drank more wine.

'Usherwood,' she mumbled.

'Yeah.' He put a hand on her leg. 'D'you think I could get an introduction?'

The question threw her. 'What?'

'To Cato.' Addy cocked his head and delivered that smile again. 'Or Susanna—either, really.' He stretched, and with the movement came that intoxicating aroma of salt and sweat. 'I've always seen myself as getting into Hollywood—hanging around movie sets, going to functions, looking sharp all the time, acting a bit... I used to get told I could model, y'know, and aren't actors kind of just models who learn lines? So I figured that's what I wanted to do, only I don't know how to get *into* it, like, where you even begin, and now Cato's turned up and it's like a sign. I'm thinking, if I get to speak to him then maybe he could get me mixing with the right people?'

'I don't know...'

'I've tried with Charlie, but he totally blanked me.'

Olivia frowned. Addy caught her expression and tacked on, wide-eyed: 'Hey, I wouldn't want to put you on the spot, if it was awkward.'

She recalled Charlie's words: *This house owes you nothing...*

'Well, they are having this party,' she began. 'You could come if you want.'

Addy jumped on it. 'For real?'

'I'm not sure who they're inviting, but if I say you're with me—'

'OK.'

'I mean, not like that—'

'Why not like that?'

'Because we're not… I mean, we're not… You know—'

And then, like magic, his mouth was on hers. His lips were soft, hot, insistent, fitting to hers as neat as a glove and she reached up to touch his face, making sure it was really there, really him, and felt his tongue wrap deliciously around hers.

'You'll let me know when it is?' He took a slug of his pint.

'Sure,' she breathed, stunned. 'Sure I will.'

They stayed until the pub closed, Addy treating her like a queen, hanging on to every word she said and gazing deep into her eyes. Every so often he would squeeze her hand, or claim another kiss, and the whole night felt like walking on air.

When it was time to leave, Addy pulled her close against the chill.

'Come down to the beach,' he urged. 'I'm horny.' He held her hand and they ran through the darkness towards the water. At the shore he kissed her again.

'Let's go in,' he murmured.

'It'll be freezing!'

He was already peeling off his T-shirt. His jeans followed, and then he was bounding into the sea, splashing through the white-capped baby waves as they broke and lapped around his ankles, knees, waist, the sky above bursting with stars. Through her drunken haze Olivia thought he looked just like a painting. *Boy, Sea and Sky*, he'd be called.

'Come on!' he yelled. 'What are you waiting for?' He dived into the swell, arms churning, and surfaced seconds later with a dog-like shake of the head.

Olivia shrugged off her dress. She had forgotten that the ocean was warmer at night, and the temperature had to be close to her own blood.

When she caught up, he held her, his touch running down her back, skillful and deft, unclipping her bra. Her breasts sprung free, light and buoyant in the water, a strange sensation. Addy grasped them as he kissed her. She felt him grow against her stomach and she moaned. So many times she had imagined what this would be like…what sex with Addy Gold would be like.

His fingers were fumbling a path into her knickers.

'Hang on—'

'What?' He grabbed her hand, dragged it beneath the surface. The surprise of his flesh on hers made her gasp.

'You like that, don't you…?' His mouth moved lower.

'Wait…' Her head was thrown back, the sky spinning sickeningly in her vision. This was happening too fast, way too fast. A wave heaved, washing them into shore. Olivia felt the bump of sand against her knees as they hit the shallows.

Addy grabbed her, lifting her on top. Her throat bloated. The wine churned.

'I want to go in,' she said, abruptly aware of her nakedness, and the twinkling high street in the distance. She wanted to be there, on the road, going home.

Addy attempted to drag down the elastic on her knickers. 'Me, too.'

She was horribly drunk and she was about to have sex with Addy. Addy. This was Addy. It wasn't meant to be like this.

'Don't,' she said. 'Stop.'

'I won't, baby, I won't…'

'No, I mean, we can't…' She was slurring.

'Relax; it doesn't matter. I'll pull out. I've done it loads…'

'I need water. I don't feel well.'

'You'll feel better after this.'

Somehow she found the strength to push against him. He swiped to catch her but she evaded his grasp, heading for the bundle of clothes and hauling her dress on.

'Can't you at least wank me off then?' He glowered. 'You've got me all hot now. What am I meant to do? I never had you down as a prick-tease, Ol.'

She clutched her head. 'I'm really drunk.' The beach was wheeling and tipping, as if all the sand was being poured back into the sea. Her stomach tensed and cramped and then in the most mortifying few seconds of her twenty-three years she vomited a splash of white wine on to the sand.

'What the fuck—?' Addy cried, disgusted. 'Gross-out or what! Are you a lightweight these days or something?'

'Sorry.' She wanted to burst into tears. Fragments of people, voices, swung through her addled mind. Charlie Lomax, glaring. *What do you think you're doing?* For a crazy second she wanted him here, safe and solid, sorting her out; and the wide, musk-scented bulk of his chest. Hot shame crashed through her. Her dress was on inside out but she didn't care.

'Let's get you a cab.' Addy tugged on his jeans and patted her awkwardly on the shoulder. 'You'll be all right. Pint of water and some Marmite on toast…'

They hailed a taxi on the high street and Olivia crawled inside. After assuring the driver she was purged, Addy leaned in. 'Call me about the party, yeah?'

The car sped off. His figure receded on the road until he was gone completely.

CHAPTER THIRTEEN

SUSANNA SWEPT INTO Usherwood's Grand Ballroom and raised her arms to the gilded ceiling. 'This,' she announced regally, 'is it!'

'It's filthy,' Cato stated, striding in after her and running his finger along a grubby windowsill. 'It's utterly inhabitable.'

'We don't have to *inhabit* it.' Susanna gestured around. 'It's one night, darling, and where else should we host the occasion but here?'

Cato could think of a few places. The oval ballroom hadn't been used since his parents were alive and it showed. Its arched windows were glazed with age, sunlight straining weakly through the glass. Weighty drapes were riddled with mothballs, releasing a musty, mildewed smell. Gauzy cobwebs were strung across the corniced ceiling, in the centre of which an enormous chandelier glinted sleepy-eyed. Most of the furniture had been moved, or sold, and what remained—the oak display cabinet, several ladder-back chairs, a Bechstein grand piano—were shrouded in dustsheets.

'I mean, what will the villagers think?' she went on. 'You said yourself they haven't seen Usherwood since back in the day: they need to be impressed!'

'They're not villagers; it's a town.'

'Oh,' she flapped her hands, 'what's the difference?'

Cato stood in front of a relative's portrait and mirrored his pose, hands on hips, eyebrow slightly raised. Susanna giggled.

'They'd be impressed by a tent in the garden, Mole. How could they not? They're plebs.' He yawned. 'Merely setting foot across the threshold will have them wetting their knick-knacks. They'll be living off this party's coat tails for a year.' His footsteps smacked cleanly across the floor. 'Are we getting coverage?'

'Four nationals have already confirmed,' Susanna rhapsodised, 'as well as *What's Up?* magazine. It's going to be just perfect!'

'I'm sure it will be, with you in charge.'

Susanna beamed in the spotlight of his praise. Cato wanted everything to be just right because she knew, she just *knew*, it was the night he planned to propose.

'Do you want a run-down of the itinerary?' she fished, checking his response for a flicker of his intentions—but of course Cato was far too composed for that. 'Guests arrive at seven for drinks and canapés in the main hall, after which we'll invite them through to the ballroom for dinner and dancing. I thought round tables, not long, and no less than eight to each or else conversation flags. I've booked the caterers. Oh, that reminds me, we're shipping them over from France. I couldn't find one I liked over here and *L'Atelier Noir* looks sublime…'

'Very well.'

'I spoke to Jennifer this morning.' Jennifer was her powerhouse agent. 'Word of the party's made it back home. There's a piece running in tomorrow's *USay*. It's entitled "From Hollywood Royalty to Usherwood Royalty".'

Cato whipped the dustsheet off the piano and sat on the stool, adjusting the height so he was comfortable. 'Hmm. I rather like that.'

'I thought you might. Getting the family name on the map.' She was about to add something about the family they might start together when he began a stumbling rendition of *Für Elise*. The instrument was pitifully out of tune.

'Any news on the *City Sirens* role?' he asked, wafting from side to side like a tormented maestro.

Susanna's good mood was momentarily pricked.

'It went to Carla Jessop,' she answered crisply. '*The bitch!*'

'She's ugly, Mole. Her teeth are too big for her mouth.'

'Clearly the director didn't think so.'

Cato stopped playing with an elaborate flourish. 'Probably because he had said mouth bobbing up and down in his lap on the casting couch.'

'I suppose the teeth ought to be good for something,' she agreed. But it still stung that she hadn't had a sniff of a decent script in months, and when finally she did it was snatched from her grasp by a younger model. Jennifer had told her not to fret, but Susanna couldn't help wondering if she ought to have perhaps said yes to that complimentary eyelift she had been offered in the spring.

'Right,' Cato boomed, rising. 'I'll leave these affairs with you, shall I?'

Susanna glanced around, thrilled more than daunted at the task. Carla Jessop didn't have all *this*, did she? The designers would be arriving any minute. Perhaps she could persuade them to take a look at the rest of the house while they were at it.

'Do you want to help?' she asked.

'Oh, no.' Cato crossed the room. 'I've other matters to attend to.'

'Charles?'

'To hell with Charles: he may not like my way of doing things but he'll soon get used to it. I plan to tell him my takeover intentions the night of the party.'

'Gosh.'

'Quite. But for now, I'm ravenous. I think I'll seek out the cook and have her,' he licked his lips, 'serve me up an old favourite. I wouldn't want to interfere with your artistic vision.'

'I won't let you down,' Susanna pledged, coming to kiss him.

'I know you won't, Mole.'

'By the way, Cato…?'

'Yes?'

'Do you think you might refrain from calling me that at the party?'

He turned to her quizzically. 'Mole?'

'Yes.'

'See?' He touched a finger to her nose. 'You can't help but respond to it.'

'That was a trick,' she protested coquettishly.

'As may be. But I'll call you what I like, understand?'

The door closed. Susanna breathed the silent grandeur of the space.

Cato liked to tease, but she felt certain that when he popped the question in front of everybody, he would do the right thing. He would call her by her name—Susanna Genevieve Alexandra Denver—and she would clamour her acceptance from the rooftops. It was going to be the most magical night of her life.

She clasped her hands together.

'Right,' she said jubilantly, 'now where do we start?'

CHAPTER FOURTEEN

MIDDAY. THE SUN was climbing. Charlie drove the axe into the butt of the decapitated oak. It caught on the wood and required a quick, sharp tug to bring it free. Raising the blade, he pounded into it once more. Chunks of kindling felled with every chop.

The heat was extreme, even in the spotted shade of the Thistle Wood canopy. He shed his T-shirt, a film of perspiration across his chest and shoulders, gleaming in the dappled light. He pitched another log on to the mounting pile.

A creature rustled in the undergrowth, a flap of agitated wings followed by a panicked ruffle, then silence. Charlie rested the axe and followed the sound. Comet darted to join him in the pursuit. He put a palm flat to the dog's nose.

'Wait, boy,' he said gently. 'Stay back.'

It was a swift. One wing was torn and beating hopelessly at the ground in an attempt to take flight. The bird's tiny body hopped dizzily beneath a dried, brittle leaf. Charlie scooped it up and held it in his hands. It was quivering, the heartbeat faint and frantic against his thumb. Carefully he lifted the wounded limb. The feathers twitched and cowered in his hands, damaged beyond repair: a flightless bird would die slowly and in pain, if it weren't claimed first by a cat or a fox. He knew what he had to do.

He tethered Comet to the tree and found a smooth, flat stone, on which he rested the injured creature. 'It's all right,' he murmured. 'It's all right now.'

The bird's chest was swelling and collapsing, swelling and collapsing, taut with fear. Charlie raised the rock and brought it down hard. After that, it was still.

He spent all morning heaving wood through the entrance. Susanna was relaxing on the terrace, sheltered beneath a wide-brimmed hat and punching arrangements into her iPad. Every so often Charlie would catch her glimpsing him over the top of her Prada sunglasses, before glancing away when she thought she'd been seen.

'Need any assistance?' Cato emerged from the house, as usual with precision timing: Charlie was bringing in the last armful.

'All done.'

'You'll do yourself an injury, boy,' his brother commented, splaying his expensively moisturised hands as if to prove that wealth should be a natural precursor to inactivity. 'Oughtn't you to hire some numbskull to do it?'

Charlie wiped his brow with his T-shirt. It rucked up

over his stomach and he saw Susanna's eyes flash over the exposed skin. 'How am I meant to pay for that?'

'I'd give you an allowance,' Cato said generously.

'Really? How much?'

As usual, his brother changed the subject.

'Speaking of roping in the cavalry, where's that English Rose of yours?'

Charlie streaked his hands on his jeans. 'Olivia's off sick.'

'Fat lot of good that is.'

Susanna muttered snippily: '"Fat" being the operative word.'

'She called on Monday; she's got flu.'

'I expect she'll come back in time for the party,' Cato offered cynically.

Charlie wondered if Cato had made a pass at Olivia and she had rejected him. Once his brother got bored with Susanna, bored with Caggie, she was undoubtedly next in line. The thought bothered him deeply.

'Excuse me.'

He entered the empty solace of the hall, leaving Susanna gushing over the menu for Saturday night. Charlie was dreading it, but had to set his concerns to one side. Despite himself he had been unable to stop imagining what the cash injection might achieve. He would be able to repair the roofs, to restore the chapel, to rectify the heating… All he had to do was swallow his pride. It was a bitter pill, but still.

He pushed the door to the hallowed ballroom. Susanna had done a fine job, even if it was a little outré for his taste. A stately array of tables and chairs had been imported—he'd witnessed a team of designers arriving on the estate earlier that morning—and were laid with elegant porcelain and elaborate floral displays. The surfaces had been cleaned and polished to perfection, the Corinthian pillars shining pearly-white, and the raised platform at one end played host to a beautifully buffed Bechstein grand. He looked up. The higher windows had been harder to reach and the diamond skylight hosted a lace of telltale gossamers that shivered in the draught.

The last occasion he had spent time in here, proper time, had been with Penny. In the depths of a freezing winter, the Usherwood grounds had been blanketed in snow, and every sound, every birdcall, muted in the frost. The east had been the last to receive a faltering heat so they had camped here, bringing a mattress, blankets, socks for Penny because her toes stung in the cold. Charlie had stoked the burner. The moon had risen bright-eyed in the night, visible at the very window he was looking through now, and they'd had blazing, breathless sex in the glow of the flames.

Distantly he could hear Cato's untroubled chatter, flirting carelessly with his girlfriend and eliciting her laugh. How could his brother have forgotten? *Had* he forgotten, or was it just another act?

All their lives Cato had possessed this ability to simply *flatten* events, to take traumas, accidents, *distasteful* occurrences, and press them into a thin even line that he could fold and then fold again until it was a tight nub that could be hidden in a drawer and locked away.

Anything that marred Cato's impeccable image was as good as extinguished. Perhaps Charlie should learn from it: he could benefit from letting go, he knew.

How different the brothers were. It was a leap sometimes to believe that they had come from the same parents. If they hadn't, if they had been mere acquaintances, it would have been so much easier. Charlie wouldn't have to be reminded every day that the person responsible was his flesh and blood. As if their parents dying—no, disappearing: for who knew if Lord and Lady Lomax weren't marooned on an island somewhere, or snatched by pirates, or floating on the water in the thirteen-year-old remains of their lost biplane?—hadn't been enough. Cato had stolen it all from him.

Five years ago. His brother's first film had just been released. Cato had returned for a flying visit, instantly captivating, hopelessly glamorous, fragrant with a promise beyond the Usherwood walls, both exotic and tantalising.

Charlie had found them together. The pale lines of Penny's ankles wrapped around his brother as the lovers writhed against the walls of the cellar stairs.

I'm sorry, Charlie, she'd said. *Cato and I are going to be together. We're helpless to resist it. We have to follow our hearts...*

In retrospect, he should have known. Perhaps he had been foolish to expect more of Penny; he had reckoned her to be unfazed by those pretensions. Yet Cato's fame had proved a temptation too hard to resist. He had vowed to whisk her off to LA; even, at one point, to announce their imminent marriage. The months she had spent with Charlie and the connection they had shared (or he had imagined?) evaporated in a single, horrifying evening: for her, it had been worth the sacrifice.

He would never forget the night of the storm. Their bags had been packed, set for the airport, and a swift, useless kiss had hit him like a slap in the face.

The Jaguar's tail lights disappearing down the drive, rain slashing the windows, a red torch bleeding into darkness…

The very last time he had seen her.

News had come in later that night. Barbara had delivered the only blow that could possibly contend with the one revealed eight years before. Cato had drunk too much. He had slammed the car into a tree.

Police and paramedics had been quick to arrive on the scene. Charlie had swerved through the night, crashing through country lanes in the driving rain, almost killing himself in the process and not much caring if he did. His brother had been taken to hospital, where he recovered over the course of a week, surrounded by sympathetic nurses and the respectful (though not discouraged) curiosity of the press. Penny died in Intensive Care at 11.29 on a Thursday morning.

As was Cato's way, his own denial about what happened somehow filtered into the world around him: if Cato didn't talk about it then there was nothing to talk about. The manslaughter charge had been short-lived. Charlie had his suspicions about the cheque Cato had written, a vast sum in exchange for his freedom. After a brief ripple of interest, followed by a couple of feeble eyewitness accounts that put bad weather at the wheel instead of Cato, the incident was all but forgotten.

It might be forgotten for them, but it wasn't for Charlie. Cato had never apologised, never got to his knees and begged his brother's forgiveness, never even *mentioned* it. Charlie wondered if he might have been able to mourn better (was grieving a skill, something you could improve at the more you had to do it?) if this conversation had happened. There were so many things he wanted to ask Cato, so many ways in which he needed to express his fury, but always there was this suspicion that the second he did, Cato would turn and sneer: *I don't know what you're on about, old bean...*

So much for Now and Always... And yet Charlie knew that he had lost Penny before she was gone. It was typical of Cato (how petty that sounded, *typical*, but there was no other word). Never had he been able to stand Charlie having something he didn't. Even though Cato had jetted halfway across the world to claim a life of fame and riches, his brother's happiness at Usherwood was something he could not abide.

All their lives there had been this jealousy, latent but potent, festering under the surface. Why? What could Cato possibly have to be envious of?

A voice snapped him out of his reverie. Barbara was at the door.

'Mr Lomax, there's a photographer outside. I'm afraid Cato's disappeared. Would you be able to deal with him?'

The housekeeper's expression was a practised kind of neutral. 'I've explained he's a day early, but…'

'Of course.' Charlie dragged himself from his thoughts. They clung on; it was like wading through a sucking marsh, sticky and cloying on the calves.

When he passed Barbara they exchanged a look of understanding, so fleeting it was barely there, which stemmed from a lifetime of knowing just what the other was thinking. Barbara didn't want this party to happen, and neither did he.

But, it was beginning.

CHAPTER FIFTEEN

'WOW,' BREATHED BETH, shaking her head in wonder, 'this place is incredible.'

On the night of the festivities, the girls arrived at Usherwood on foot. Flo had dropped them at the cemetery and they had elected to walk the rest of the way (the 2CV had now been resurrected, and while Olivia wasn't normally one to care too much about what other people thought, there were already enough reasons why she and Beth would stick out from the glossy crowd without adding one more). A queue of sleek dark cars was slipping greasily through the gate, their blacked-out windows a frustration to the clique of unauthorised photographers gathered there.

Cameras snapped half-heartedly as the girls passed in the hope they might be someone important. Beth was in a cocktail dress she'd picked up in the sales but had never had occasion to wear, while Olivia wore a duck-egg-blue creation she'd sewn herself, scalloped at the

knee with capped lace sleeves. A winding path of flickering candles lit their way—hundreds, dancing in cups
at the roadside and snaking off into the distance. The
evening was warm, the sunset thick, and from afar the
liveliness of the house drifted over. It was strange to
hear anything except the usual trickle of the Usherwood
brook and the gentle swish of the trees—life, civilisa-
tion, *people*, as if they had found a split in the fabric of
time and had slipped into another decade.

'Wasn't "rundown" the word you used?' Beth raised
a sceptical eyebrow when the building appeared, a fairytale illustration of shimmering windows, the sun settling above the spires as if it were a balloon about to
burst on a needlepoint. A swathe of red was laid at the
door, bright as a letterbox, where VIPs were posing for
paparazzi, emerging from cars in expensively tailored
suits and gowns that sparkled like starlight. 'You should
see the flat Mum and Dad have just moved into. I don't
know, somehow I get the feeling they'd be happy to
trade…'

Olivia felt bad. Beth's parents had recently been forced
to sell their home and relocate to rented accommodation.
It was a further blow after another tough year with the
bank. She wished there was something she could do—
she'd grown close to them over the years and it was horrible to see them struggle.

'It doesn't normally look like this,' she reasoned. In
fact she thought that Usherwood was far more beautiful
the less adornments it boasted—no doubt the house had
dressed impressively for the ball, but in the way of an

already attractive woman who had slapped on too much make-up and whose shoes didn't quite fit.

'Can we give you a lift?'

A gleaming Mercedes stopped and the window wound down. A guy with perfectly arranged hair and a face the colour of leather leaned out.

'No, thank you,' answered Olivia, just as Beth gave her a sharp dig in the ribs.

'Be a shame to get those dresses dirty,' the man pressed, with a glinting smile that flirted on the wrong side of lascivious. 'Are you sure I can't tempt you?'

'Quite sure.'

'I'm not practised in the art of persuasion, you know. Ladies tend to say yes.'

'That must be nice for you.'

The smile vanished. 'Suit yourself,' the man growled, as the car sped off.

'Ugh,' commented Olivia, 'what an absolute creep.'

'Do you realise who that was?' Beth exclaimed. 'Sam Levy!'

'Is he on TV?'

Beth rolled her eyes. 'That's what you get for having been brought up without a telly. Seriously? Sam Levy, of *Charterhouse Priory*? Dating Emily Windermere?'

'Who?'

'I despair.'

Olivia laughed. 'Look, Susanna's organised this whole red carpet thing. It'll be a jungle of egos and guaranteed to be all over the papers tomorrow. We're walking in like anyone ordinary, *which we are*, not climbing out of Sam Levy's A-class. He's a total perv. I can't believe you get reeled in by all that bullshit.'

'Spoilsport.'

'Star-fucker.'

Beth stuck out her tongue. 'Speaking of fuckers,' she said, 'where's Addy?'

Olivia tried not to flinch at his name. Each time she thought of their date she wanted to curl up in a ball and die. Fortunately the whole disastrous beach thing was a blur, but unfortunately not quite blurry enough to spare her the sporadic rearing up of an agonising detail: his touch, his kiss, his breath in her hair, the lap of water against her skin…and her buckled, bedraggled figure as she bent over the sand.

It was the most embarrassing thing ever. She never got sick through alcohol and could only put it down to the adrenaline of the night (but as Florence had pointed out the following morning as she had groaned and writhed in bed, the five large glasses of Pinot Grigio might have had something to do with it).

'Dunno,' she admitted.

'He hasn't called?'

'What do you think?'

'I think he's an arse,' diagnosed Beth loyally. 'Scrap that—I *know* he is. Big deal if you puked. I've done worse. My opinion? You're lucky it happened.'

'Lucky?'

'It spared you. Honestly, it's high time you got over Addy. He's a dick. Don't you remember how he used to ignore me when we were little? Just pretend like I wasn't there whenever you invited me along to things. He still does it now, like I'm not cool enough for him or something. It's tragic.'

'Come on; he was, like, eleven. Hanging out with one girl was bad enough.'

'That isn't you talking. It's him. Filling your brain with his shitty excuses. He picks you up and drops you whenever he feels like it; and, big surprise, he's gone and done it again. When are you going to wise up and move on?'

Olivia stopped. 'Beth, seriously, it isn't your concern.'

'Yes, it is. It's my concern because I care about you.'

'Well, don't—at least not tonight. Right now I don't want to see Addy, I don't want to hear about Addy, I just want to forget about him. OK?'

'Fine by me.'

'Good.'

At the entrance to the house, the girls linked arms, their almost-argument forgotten. They wandered through, Beth grabbing her every thirty seconds with another hissed name Olivia had only vaguely heard of. In the Usherwood hall, waiters weaved with trays piled high with canapés: figs wrapped in crispy prosciutto and tiny salmon blinis lumped with caviar. Gold flutes were raised amid the contented hum of conversation. A string quartet played Pachelbel's *Canon in D*—a predictable choice of Susanna's, Olivia thought, before telling herself off for being mean.

Susanna tilted her chin, pushed her chest out and admired her reflection in the mirror. She could hear her guests arriving downstairs and all but swooned with anticipation.

'I give you,' she murmured through crimson-painted lips, quietly lest Cato hear her from the bathroom, *'Lady Susanna Lomax!'*

'Jesus wept!' exclaimed Cato from the en suite, making her jump, as another blast of freezing cold water shot through the taps. 'Wretched pipes!'

Batting her eyelashes, Susanna composed herself, hand to chest, to practise her acceptance. *'You really mean it? Moi? Why, of course, Cato, I'll marry you!'* Her eyes widened prettily. *'In front of all these people, how irresistibly romantic...'*

'What in Christ's name are you doing?' boomed a voice as the door swung open, releasing an angry puff of apple-scented steam. 'Talking to yourself?'

Susanna smiled. 'Something like that.'

Cato strode to the bed and began tugging on his clothes. 'Everybody's here: enough dilly-dallying, woman. If I hadn't had to spend half the evening in the bloody shower trying to get a lather up we'd have been down there thirty minutes ago.'

'There's no rush, darling. We can be elegantly late.' She turned to award him an unobstructed view of her designer gown. It was deep red, velvet at the shoulders and sheer across the bust, and pinched her waist with just the right degree of pain.

'Goodness, are you wearing that?'

'Don't you like it?'

'It's bloody see-through.'

'No, it isn't.' Susanna smoothed her hands over the material. It was—a bit. You couldn't quite make out her nipples, nestling behind a velvet detail, but the outline of her tits were there, and who knew, at the right angle...

'You know me,' she purred, 'I like to make an impression.' And with any luck that impression would be all over the tabloids in the morning.

'Not always the right one,' he growled.

'Don't you dare ruin this for me, Cato!' she screamed, shrill as a bird, her hands balled at her sides as tantrum clouds gathered ominously.

'Keep your knickers on.' Cato was unfazed. 'If you're wearing any.'

It was hard to stay mad when her lover looked so obscenely handsome. Oh, but it had to be improper to wear a tuxedo this rakishly. The suit made him look every inch the British scoundrel, and Susanna half wished he had shaved himself an RAF moustache.

'Wouldn't you like to know?' she replied, pausing to catch her breath. It wouldn't do to appear highly-strung and flustered when they took their positions at the top of the stairs. Susanna had rehearsed many times her sweeping descent, flanked by family portraits, arriving at the party like Cinderella at the ball.

'Come on, then.' Cato knotted his tie. 'Let's get this show on the road.'

In the event it was even more magical than Susanna had anticipated. As she and Cato hovered regally above their minions, a reverential hush descended.

The compere she'd hired stepped forward and boomed: 'Ladies and gentlemen, allow me to present your esteemed hosts for this evening... Lord Cato Lomax and Susanna Denver!'

Cameras rushed to capture the moment. Susanna linked her arm in his and threw her best red-carpet smile, which she tinged with a whiff of refined detachment.

The sea of upturned faces was smacked with awe. Someone started an impromptu round of applause, and she sensed the beady eyes of every woman trained upon her: her dress, her man, her beauty. Never had she felt so coveted.

All too soon it was over and they were mingling with the hoi polloi. Susanna felt fizzy from the champagne she'd quaffed.

'Darling, you are a *vision*!' A British star she'd worked with years ago craned in for an air-kiss. 'We *are* pleased to be here, what a fantastic venue. Did you hire it?'

Did this person not read the papers?

'On the contrary, Annabel,' she replied, 'this is Cato's ancestral home.' She leaned in, unable to resist. 'Soon to be mine, darling, but let's keep that between us.'

She was satisfied at how the actress's Botoxed face cracked with the news. Annabel Lacey-Smythe was a West End dinosaur, devoted to the theatre, and during their acquaintance had always made Susanna feel like a half-baked aspirant because she had never taken to the boards herself. In Susanna's view it was far easier to dance about a stage at arm's-length from the audience than it was to have a lens shoved in your face and every flicker, ever waver, captured for criticism.

'Well, that is rather fortunate,' enthused Annabel sourly.

'Isn't it?' Susanna tossed back another flute of champagne. She clocked one of the bar staff and made her excuses, floating across to issue her instructions.

'Fix me a martini,' she told him. Cato was across the room, charming the Marquis of Sallington. She wondered whether if she fed a hand into Cato's suit pocket right now she would be able to feel the telltale box waiting to be opened...

'Dirty, two olives—I'm in the mood to celebrate.'

After the entrance of the Queen of Sheba (come to think of it, that piece of music might even have been playing), everyone began filtering into the ballroom.

Olivia spotted Barbara clearing glasses and headed over. 'You're working?' she asked incredulously. 'They didn't give you the night off?'

The housekeeper wiped her brow. 'Heaven forbid Ms Denver allows that.' Sensing she'd spoken against the family, she quickly added, 'Mr Lomax, Charlie, did insist, but all this...it isn't for me. I'm far more comfortable behind the scenes.' She swiped away Olivia's efforts to help with a ticking-off, 'Stop that, you're a guest!'

'Barbara, meet my best friend Beth.'

'Well,' Barbara smiled, 'it's nice to see two such normal-looking people—and I mean that in the best possible way.' She lowered her voice. 'Have you seen how much plastic surgery there is floating about? It's like a waxwork museum in here.'

Beth giggled.

'Speaking of looking under the weather,' she turned to Olivia, warm with concern, 'are you feeling better?'

Olivia nodded. She had been laid low at home with a cold, most likely brought on by her drunken night with Addy. 'Yes, much,' she said, ignoring Beth's sidelong glance. 'How've things been at the house?'

'Not a great deal to report except for what you can see. We've had more strangers in ahead of this party than I care to remember.' Barbara amassed a fist of discarded napkins, one of which bore a pout of red lipstick. 'Charlie's missed you.'

Olivia blinked. 'Well, I—'

'The sun's been relentless, he's worried the planting won't take.'

'Of course.' What had she thought Barbara meant? 'I'll be back tomorrow.'

'Go on, then.' Barbara shooed them on. 'Have fun!'

Beyond the vaulted entrance, the magnificent ballroom was festooned with lights. A chandelier twinkled up high and strings of tiny bulbs, delicate as bracelets, threaded to all four corners of the room like a giant, glittering spider's web. Olivia spotted a dazed gaggle of Taverick Manor sixth-formers, the boarders released on special privilege and chaperoned by a portly matron wearing a chintzy floor-length number and a pained expression. Close by were Serendipity Swain and Finn Avalon, exotically glamorous as they regaled a circle of admiring hangers-on, and after a bout of good-natured jostling Finn took to the piano and struck up a high-tempo jazz tune. Olivia listened for Susanna's squeal of delight and sure enough it rang out.

'Oh, God, look who it is.' Beth whipped round. 'Don't let him see me.'

'What? Who?'

'I've probably got stuff in my teeth from all those spinach blinis. Have I?'

'Your teeth are fine. What on earth are you talking about?'

'Sackville Grey—I should've known he'd be here.'

'So why don't you go and talk to him?'

'I can't! What am I meant to say?'

'How about, "Hi, it's Beth, good to see you again"…?'

Beth looked at her as if she'd suggested stripping naked and crawling up to him on all fours. 'Are you *insane*?'

Olivia smiled. Her friend had carried a torch for Sackville, owner of the Round House art gallery, since his car had broken down outside the stables one day and Beth had phoned for help. Sackville was achingly Hoxton, tonight donning a pair of drainpipe cords, suede lace-ups and a sharp blazer. His dark hair relinquished a flash of silver around the temples and he carried the air of someone who spent their evenings in a candlelit attic scribbling romantic poetry into a battered leather-bound notebook. Since moving from London Sackville had made a raging success of the gallery space and now it was one of *the* places to be exhibited in the West Country.

'Go on.' Olivia handed her a glass of champagne. 'Dutch courage.'

'No way.'

'Why not?'

Beth glimpsed him again. 'OMG. Look who he's talking to. That's our way in. Will you? Please?'

'I can't believe you said OMG. I'm considering never speaking to you again.'

'Fine, you don't have to, so long as you do this one last thing for me.'

Olivia sighed, and followed Beth's gaze. Sackville had been accosted by a fiercely nattering Imogen Randall, owner of the tennis club, a stout, matter-of-fact woman with close-cropped ginger hair and wide, muscular haunches not totally dissimilar in shape to one of her cherished racquets. He wore an expression of faintly concealed alarm. Alongside them, sure enough, was Imogen's son Theo.

'Nice try,' said Olivia. 'Forget it.'

'Come *on*!'

'No. Absolutely not.' Theo Randall was Olivia's first boyfriend, with whom she had spent an entire summer aged twelve practising how to French kiss (not easy because Theo had just had train-tracks fitted and they kept getting caught on her top lip). A year after the break-up (lots of sobbing, love notes, wild flowers on the doorstep—Theo was a romantic) she had bumped into him at a party, at which he'd sported an unsightly rash of chin-based acne boils that he'd tried to pass off as an injury after he'd been hit in the face by one of his mother's fast-flying balls.

He was shorter than she remembered, and almost as spotty. She was surprised he hadn't flown the nest in pursuit of a glittering tennis career—certainly Imogen had poured every determined ounce into making her son the next Andy Murray—but then whenever Olivia had seen Theo rally as a child he'd been arrestingly ill-coordinated, blundering about the court and earning for his efforts a hotly embarrassing lambasting in front of his friends. Imogen, in her day, had once played doubles with Sue Barker.

It was too late. Theo had seen her. Raising his hand, he made his way over.

Sackville, desperate to escape Imogen, moved with him. Beth presented herself in a great big rush—'HidoyourememberImBethIworkattheBarleyNook'—and Olivia just had time to inwardly groan when across the room she spied a flash of golden hair and the broad line of a familiar pair of shoulders.

Her heart flipped. What was Addy doing here?

Her eyes travelled down. Piece by piece it became clear.

He wasn't alone. His arm, the arm that just last week had been looped around her waist, had pulled her close in the swaying lull of the ocean, was now wedged proprietorially in the fly-trap grip of Thomasina Feeny.

A tinkling glass ahead of a speech was one of Susanna's favourite sounds in the world. It reminded her of warmly lit society functions and very good quality red wine, and of rich men in suits who kissed your hand on introduction.

After a sumptuous dinner of tuna and asparagus salad, golden baby chicken and lemon pudding brûlée, Cato stood from the head of the top table, glass in hand, and began to address the crowd.

Susanna closed her eyes, savouring the moment.

'Everyone, if I could steal your attention for just a couple of minutes…'

She stared up, waiting for her cue. Would Cato do it now, right now, and catch her off-guard by dropping to his knees?

'Some of you have been to Usherwood before; for others it's your first time.'

No, he would ease her into it, the gentleman that he was.

'For me, well,' he swirled the glass, 'it's damn emotional to see the place as it should be.' His voice splintered and a respectful silence fell. Susanna reached to touch his arm. 'When my parents were with us this house was no stranger to such lavish gatherings. I'm sure you'll agree that Usherwood thrives on light and laughter, of which I trust there will be plenty more to come this evening.'

'Hear, hear,' said an old fogey at the back. The guests raised their glasses.

Susanna's gaze flicked across the room. She spotted Charlie. Darkly suited, he had slipped into the room unnoticed. His hair was rumpled and he needed to shave. His shirt was unbuttoned at the neck and he wore no tie.

'To Richmond and Beatrice,' pronounced Cato gravely, and the room echoed his words. Susanna pressed a tissue to her eyes.

'Not that tonight would have been possible without the help of several very special people,' said Cato. 'First, Fiona and Wilson Montgomery of the Quillets Vineyard, whose generous donation I dare say we'll be enjoying long into the night.'

He lifted his glass and the salute came back: 'Fiona and Wilson.'

'Second, my housekeeper Mrs Bewlis-Teet, who has allowed us to turn the place upside-down and has been unflinchingly good-spirited at every stage. Mrs B-T.'

'Mrs B-T,' sang the repeat.

'And this woman.' He motioned to Susanna. Now—it would be now! She looked demurely to the floor. 'She really has put her all into organising this event and for that we must be thankful.' Gosh, it was like the Lord's Prayer! 'Dear old Mole.'

There was a pause, and seemed to be some confusion as to whether another toast should be raised. A few uncertain rumblings of 'Dear old Mole' staggered across the assembly. In the corner, Caggie Shaw stifled a laugh.

Bitch! Susanna thought. Once she was installed she would be firing that upstart cook so fast her head would spin.

'I'm thrilled so many could join us to help put Usherwood back on the map,' Cato concluded. Susanna wanted to grab him: *Haven't you forgotten something?* 'Hollywood might be my mistress, but England, glorious England, remains my wife.'

There was a long, deliberate quiet.

'Which is why, as of the New Year, I will be assuming my position as heir and successor to this estate… As the rightful Lord Lomax of Usherwood.'

A ripple of interest passed through the space.

'I will be relocating permanently to Cornwall and taking the reins from my long-suffering brother. Goodness knows Charles has struggled with the property, so doubtless this will be a relief to everybody concerned.'

Susanna's eyes swung to Charles. She watched the colour drain from his face, top to bottom, like a leaking fish tank.

'And that brings me to the most important point of all.'

She steeled herself.

'To thank you: this community. Heaven knows this family—such as it is—has been through the mill. I treasure this town, just as my parents did, and their parents before. That's the crux of the duty I pledge to undertake: never to forget what brought me here, my history, my chronicle, because whoever said, "With great power comes great responsibility" was bang on the money. It's all of *you*, Lustell Cove, who make this part of the world such a special place, and such a great pleasure to return to.'

The ballroom rang with applause and the band resumed playing. Cato stepped off the podium and gladly received his flock of supporters.

'You must be terribly pleased,' said a producer acquaintance, sidling up to Susanna with a smile. 'I take it you'll be relocating with him?'

'Of course I will,' she snapped. She caught him ogling her see-through attire and failed to mask her scowl. 'Now, if you'll excuse me, I must go and find a drink.'

CHAPTER SIXTEEN

'CAN YOU BELIEVE IT?' Addy raved, diving into Beth's seat the instant the speech was done. Beth had received a phone call partway through the oration and had taken it outside. 'Tony Jeffries, Elizabeth Caulder, Sam Levy... Oli, this place is like a who's who of everyone—it's mental!' He craned to see. 'Do you think you can introduce me to Cato now? I can't believe it's really him. He's shorter than I imagined. Susanna's a fox, though, isn't she? I've got this wicked idea for a thriller—well, it's kind of like *Die Hard* only a tropical version, like *Predator* with sex, sort of, and it's set on this island with all these super-fit women. They're castaways who were on this mad party boat but then it sank and they got washed into shore and then they have to wrestle this alien thing that comes after them and it's so hot they can't wear any clothes, like *any*. It's got Cato all over it, for the hero, and I've got my part pegged...'

Olivia tuned out. She absorbed how handsome he

looked in a too-small tux that clung in all the right places. With his corn-coloured hair and butterscotch skin, he was heart-stoppingly gorgeous. What was he doing with Thomasina?

Finally Addy wound to a pause. Clocking Olivia's nonplussed expression, he checked himself. 'Hey,' he reached out, 'I'm sorry I wasn't in touch after Friday. My phone died and then I had this batshit crazy night and after that I just bunned, like seriously, I slept for a week, and then Dax was bunking down with me and then I got held up at the Paradise and then suddenly it was tonight...' He shrugged with boyish innocence, the shrug of someone adept in charming his way out of tricky situations. 'Anyhow Thomasina's dad got invites, so I didn't need to tag with you, after all.'

Tag with you... Was that all it came to?

Of course Daddy Feeny had been on the list—he was an MP. Across the room a crab-faced Thomasina was eyeballing them, Lavender skulking behind. The twins were searingly orange in floor-length silk kimonos that probably cost near on a thousand pounds and made them look like giant Wotsits.

He touched her arm. 'No hard feelings, yeah?'

'Look, Addy, about that night—'

'Shit, he's coming over.' Addy straightened. 'Can you take a photo, Cato and me together? I want to tweet it.'

Olivia had checked out Addy's Twitter page. It described him as 'Model, Actor, Surfer,' and the shot he'd picked was like something out of a Davidoff ad.

'I'd rather not,' she said.

'Why? You work for him, don't you?'

'Exactly. It's unprofessional.'

He grinned that grin. 'For me?'

Cato disappeared through the terrace doors, cigar in hand, and his crowd of hangers-on followed. Olivia found it excruciating to be joining them, but Addy insisted, and anyway the coolness of the veranda turned out to be a welcome break. It was clammy inside the house, saturated with perfumes and wine breath.

'Can I talk to you for a second?' she asked.

'Hmm?' Addy's eyes skimmed over her. 'Oh. Right. Sure.'

They ducked round the side of the orangery. A wooden swing seat was bathed in moonlight. It was deserted. Olivia sat and he flopped down next to her.

'It's about…' she began. Typically she hated skirting round subjects, it was better to just get to the point, but somehow with Addy it was always so difficult. She never quite found the words she meant to say. Nervously she twirled the chain around her neck. 'It's about us—'

He cut her off with a kiss. Dazedly she returned it, as sweet as it had been on the beach, his fingers on her chin and the back of her neck, stroking her hair.

'Hey,' he told her, breaking away. 'What is there to talk about? I'm not with Thomasina, if that's what you're worried about. She's nothing to me. I came with her so I could see Cato. And you, obviously, I wanted to see you. I've said I'm sorry for not calling. What else is there?' He leaned in. 'You taste good…'

'But Addy, I have to know where—'

He put a finger to her lips. 'Shh… We've known each other our whole lives. Let's just go with it if it feels right.' His mouth was on hers again, passionately this time, and she melted into his warm chest, drowning in the light, citrusy notes of an expensive aftershave, and decided that Addy's kiss was the only answer she needed.

Olivia heard Beth before she saw her. Having deposited a blusteringly enthusiastic Addy with an acutely uninterested Cato, she took a shortcut round the back of the gardens and detected a muted snivelling blowing towards her through the portico.

'Beth…?' She stepped through. 'My God, what's happened?'

Her friend was slumped on the crumbling wall. She wiped her nose on the back of her hand and sniffed wetly. Her tear-streaked face glowed eerily in the dark.

'That's it, Oli,' she sobbed. 'We have to sell Archie.'

Olivia's good mood evaporated. *What?*

'That was Dad. He's received an offer. It's too good to refuse.'

Olivia sat down next to her and pulled her close. She'd feared this day would come—perhaps Beth had, too, only it was too painful to talk about so neither girl had mentioned it. The horse was way too costly to keep, an expense they could no longer afford, even if he had become part of the family. The fact that the Merrills had kept him this long, had preserved him even over the sale of their house, spoke volumes.

'I'm so sorry, Beth.' She hugged her. 'Really, I am. I'm so sorry.'

'It's stupid.' Beth dried her cheeks. 'He's just a horse, right?'

'No, he isn't,' comforted Olivia. 'I know how much he means to you.'

'I feel like I'm orphaning him,' she wept, 'like I'm deserting him. He doesn't understand what's going on!'

Olivia rooted around for something her friend could blow her nose on and surfaced with a broad-leaved dock. Beth snorted loudly into it.

'There must be something we can do.' Olivia couldn't bear seeing her so unhappy. This was Beth she had played knights and steeds with in the rainy moss, Beth she had dyed her hair pink with to avoid having their school photographs taken, Beth she had paddled on the ocean with until four a.m. on her sixteenth birthday, sad because her dad wasn't there. She knew Beth better than anyone.

'There isn't.' Beth shook her head. 'It would take thousands for us to match this offer. Since the business folded we just can't justify it. It's over.'

The chiming laughter of the Feeny twins blew over on the breeze and Olivia prayed they wouldn't materialise. Sure enough, seconds later, the sisters popped their matching heads round the wall, goblets of wine sloshing in their fat hands.

'Yoo-hoo!' trilled Thomasina. 'We thought we heard someone out here.'

Beth attempted to shield her face but it was too late.

'Or should we say *boo-hoo*?' Lavender crowed. 'What's the matter with *her*?'

'Nothing.' Olivia didn't want their grubby paws all over Beth's misery.

'It must be about having to pawn off that tatty old horse,' pondered Thomasina, arranging her porcine features into something she imagined to be sympathy. 'We heard about that… It's a crying shame, isn't it, Lav?'

Lav was what her mother called the loo, which normally pleased Olivia, but right now she felt too glum for it to register any satisfaction.

'At least he's going to a good home.' Thomasina examined her manicure.

Olivia glared. 'How would you know?'

'How would we *know*?' Lavender giggled. 'Isn't it *obvious*?'

'Daddy's the one who put in the offer!' declared Thomasina smugly. 'You ought to be grateful; otherwise I expect he'd have to get put down or something.'

'*You're* the one buying him?' Beth could barely get the words out. '*You?*'

The twins beamed.

'But you've already got seven horses!' she spluttered.

'So this one should fit right in. I suppose he's all *right*, don't you, Lav?'

Lavender screwed up her face. 'Hmm, yah, I guess he'll *do*.'

'We'll allow you to visit,' Thomasina offered sweetly. 'Daddy wants to purchase in the autumn, so we'll invite you round for Christmas.'

With a final burst of self-satisfied sniggering, they zigzagged back inside.

'Oh, God.' Beth turned, stricken. 'Oh, *God!*'

'It'll be OK,' Olivia managed. 'It will, you'll see...'

'How?'

'I don't know. It just will.'

'It can't be. It's fucked. The whole thing's fucked.'

'Don't say that...'

Beth got to her feet, frustration spilling to anger. 'What would you know? You don't understand what we've gone through; the sacrifices Mum and Dad have had to make. You've been in London the whole time. You weren't here when I needed you. And even now you're back all you care about is bloody Addy.'

'That's not true,' she protested. 'We emailed all the time while I was away. I'd do anything for you, Beth; you're my best friend. Don't say things like that.'

'Why not?' she choked, swiping her eyes. 'It's true. All you can think about is your precious relationship with Addy—Addy this, Addy that, ever since you came back you haven't stopped talking about him. Anyone would think working at Usherwood might have given you something else to think about, but no, as far as you're concerned the rest of the world can just disappear. I saw you just now, draped off him, hanging off his every word, all pathetic and moony-eyed. Can't you see he's come with someone else tonight? Can't you see him for what he really is? You're not yourself when you're with him, Oli. You're embarrassing.'

It was as if she'd been slapped.

Beth was upset. She didn't mean it. She didn't know what she was saying.

'I'm trying to help,' Olivia said thickly.

'Don't bother. Leave me alone.'

They had never fought before. It felt horrible. 'Beth, please…'

'No. Go away. I want to be by myself. Haven't you got your boyfriend to get back to? Until he latches on to some other girl, that is.'

Olivia's patience snapped.

'Exactly how are my feelings for Addy anything whatsoever to do with you?' she blasted. 'I thought friends were supposed to confide in each other. I wouldn't have bothered if I'd known it was such a chore for you to listen, and that I'd get it all thrown back in my face. You don't know him like I do—'

'You're right. I don't. No one does, because you're deluded.'

'Well if I am then so are you. How do you think Sackville's ever going to look twice at you if you're too much of a wimp to go and talk to him? It's just like at school. What do you want me to do, go and do it for you?'

'Don't you think maybe I've had other things to deal with?'

'According to you it never crossed my mind. I don't care, remember?'

'You said it.'

'I've had enough of this.'

'So have I.' Beth stormed across the patio. 'I'm leaving.'

'Good. I wish you'd never come in the first place.'

The patio door slammed.

Olivia kicked the wall with one of the stupid uncomfortable wedge heels she hadn't even wanted to wear. She stubbed her toe and bit back the pain. Yanking the shoe off she flung it into the night and limped miserably back inside.

At eleven p.m. Susanna decided to take matters into her own hands. Men! Sometimes they needed a firm shove in the right direction.

'Come for a walk,' she breathed, clutching Cato's elbow as he engaged in a charm offensive with RAMA Award-winning actress Meredith Castille.

'You're pissed,' he slid back through gritted teeth. 'Hoick that dress up.'

She glanced down. The shadow of a nipple was peeping out from behind the velvet detail and she yanked the material to correct it.

'Oof!' she exclaimed merrily. 'That's better.'

Meredith and her catalogue model husband appraised her, smiling stiffly.

Husband. The word had taken on magical powers, elusive and essential.

'Right-o,' said Cato jovially, 'I think some fresh air might be in order.' A smirk passed between the men and Susanna squeezed his hand gratefully.

'I'd like another martini,' she garbled.

'I don't think so,' came the gruff reply. Roughly Cato steered her though the hall, past the library and into a passage that smelled of rotten wine. The muddle of corridors was disorientating. She struggled to balance in her stilettoes.

'Where are you taking me?' She giggled, slipping off her heels. 'Ouch!'

'Somewhere discreet.'

'Are you going to lock me up in the cellar?'

'Maybe, if you don't start behaving.'

Abruptly he hauled her through the rear doors and across the lawn. In her peripheral she spotted a comet, a soaring shape launched out of the walled garden. It looked like...*a shoe*? She blinked away her drunkenness. The Usherwood maze crept towards them out of the night, a dense bank of labyrinth.

'I've a good mind to abandon you out here until you sober up,' said Cato.

She couldn't tell if he was kidding. The prospect of Cato leaving her, in any capacity, was all of a sudden abominable, and she grabbed him.

'Careful!' he objected. 'Do you know this suit cost me two thousand pounds?'

'I was hoping you might ask me something,' she drawled.

'I just did.'

'Not *that*...'

Susanna waited hopefully. It made sense, of course: there were too many people in the house and he would prefer to do it in private. She should have known—Cato had to play out so much of his life on the public stage, it was no wonder he had opted to save this just for them.

'I know where we can be alone.' She stepped through the entrance to the maze. 'But if you want me,' she murmured, turning at the last moment to catch the flame of lust ignite in his eyes, 'you'll have to catch me.'

In a flash she darted from sight, the maze swallowing her, red dress rippling then dissolving like paint in water. The hedges were higher than her head, dark green and lush and scented like moss. She felt panicked and excited, unable to see further than a foot in front. She held her arms out, palms flat, feeling her way.

'Cato!' she called. 'In here!'

At one moment his footsteps were incredibly close, the next a distant patter. The thrill was flirting on sexual, the promise of release when Susanna imagined rounding the next wall and slamming straight into that broad, brawny chest. Deeper in the hedges were thick and overgrown, a tangle of ivy reaching out to brush her shoulders or the back of her neck as she hurried on: which way she was going she had no idea, only certain that the next junction would be identical to the last, and the huntsman's cry as it dashed at her from every angle, tempting, tantalising…

'I'll root you out, Mole. Then you'll be in trouble!'

The sky, though black, seemed a lighter shade above the gloomy hulk of foliage, the endless grid as dense as bricks. She wondered if anyone had become lost in here, properly lost, and how far the path could take her in; if there might be a centre to the web in which a lone soul had perished, unable to break free, and Susanna would discover their long-forgotten skeleton, bones glowing like pearls beneath the moon.

The possibility hit her in a sobering punch.

The ghost!

Hadn't Susanna heard a weeping woman? Hadn't she sensed a troubled spirit? Who was to say the wailing had come from within the house…and *not outside it*?

Susanna's breath choked in her throat and she flung herself into the privet, hands across her chest like a vampire in an upright coffin. The hedge resisted her with a gentle bounce, like a testing finger on the surface of a bowl of jelly. A pair of arms locked around her from behind and she screamed.

A hot gust of breath assaulted her ear.

'Stop right there,' it commanded. 'Lift up your skirt.'

Susanna's stomach contracted with desire. Before she could respond Cato's bear paws were on the underside of her bottom, raising her, his knee wedged between her legs. Her toes left the ground, her face pressed into the bush, whose flat-leafed creepers were waxy and silk-smooth. She heard him unbuckle his suit pants, the shiver of material as it fell, and the rip of her own underwear as his fingers roughly tore them aside. The inescapability of his cock was exquisite.

Cato took her violently. 'You've been wanting this all night,' he snarled, slamming into her, his hand snaking round to claim one of her errant breasts.

'Oh, I have! I have!' Susanna cried out, close to pain as he delivered a sharp smack across her ass. 'Say you want me, Cato! Say you want me for ever!'

'I want you right now, you harlot. Showing me your

tits like that when everyone was watching. What do they think of you, hmm? What do they think?'

'I'm a naughty girl, Lord Cato. I need to be taught a lesson!'

Another slap. The impact stung. She was all but devoured by the shrubbery now, and Cato's rutting quickened with a series of guttural groans.

'You like being punished, don't you?'

'I do! I do!' She had a flash of their forthcoming nuptials, and how it might feel to say those words to him on the altar.

'Ask me, Cato!' she begged. 'I'm ready! Ask me!'

'Do you want me to make you come hard, little nympho?'

She pictured herself in her bridal gown. 'Yes!'

'So hard you pass out?'

The ring slipping on to her finger… 'Yes, yes, yes!'

Susanna was engulfed by a crashing wave of pleasure, ripples of ecstasy chasing up her spine as Cato climaxed in tandem with her, driving through her aftershocks and burying his dark mop of hair in her neck.

'I will marry you, Cato,' she whispered through the tingling haze. 'I will.'

Seconds later she heard him secure his trousers, the flick of the zip.

'Sober up,' he instructed her coolly. 'I'll meet you inside.'

'But…' Her knees were weak, the skirt of her dress up by her head. 'Cato, please! I'll get lost! I don't know how to get out!'

His reply was invisible, taunting her from a direction she couldn't decipher.

'Keep left, that's the trick.'

CHAPTER SEVENTEEN

CHARLIE WAS SMOKING a cigarette outside the library. His wild black hair and scruffily worn tux made him look like a moody date on prom night.

To the south lay the forest. A highwayman's moon was slung above the dark peaks of firs. Beyond, the pale grey line of the sea sparkled like a chain.

The dogs were with him, lying on their stomachs, their muzzles on the gravel. When their ears pricked he listened out for sound, deciphering the crunch of approaching footsteps. Olivia came into sight. She was wearing only one shoe.

'Hello,' he said.

She stopped and folded her arms. 'Hi,' she said tightly. She was still pissed off at him. They hadn't spoken since the argument last week.

Charlie blew out smoke. He had seen her earlier on the swing seat, kissing the pretty boy: the pastel of her dress and that distinctive swirl of burned-copper hair.

He'd turned away before he was seen. The pretty boy wouldn't know how to kiss. Olivia needed to be kissed properly, with intent. She needed to be kissed hard. She needed to be kissed ambitiously, every hour and every day of her life.

'Tonight's awful, isn't it?' he said. 'Bloody awful.'

'No kidding.' She didn't sound right, not her usual self. Her eyes met his. She asked, 'I'm guessing you caught Cato's speech?'

'Moving, wasn't it. I especially liked the quote from *Spiderman.*'

Her smile flickered in the dark. It was surprised. Genuine.

'What are you going to do?'

'I don't know.'

'Can he really take Usherwood from you?'

Charlie ground the cigarette out.

'Yes,' he said, 'if he wants. As the eldest he's entitled. He's Lord Lomax; the estate belongs to him. I'm not fussed about having the name or the status or any of that. I love Usherwood. That's all. Cato's never loved it. It might be different if his reasons were noble, but this is about ego. That's the way it is with my brother. He wants the house because of how it's going to look, not how it's going to be. He has no idea how it's going to be, he hasn't even thought about it, and that's why he'll get bored after six months. Cato always gets bored.'

He couldn't remember the last time he had shared this much with anyone.

'If you hadn't stayed,' ventured Olivia, 'he'd never be in a position to return.'

'Maybe.' He drew a hand across the back of his neck. 'But do you think he cares about that? My staying only makes him want it more.'

'You could have sold up. You could have moved away, like he did.'

'Doubtless I'd have had to if I'd wanted Cato's life. The reality is, it isn't possible to do both. You can't have Usherwood at the same time as being away from it. It's needy. It's demanding. It takes everything.'

Olivia watched his bowed head. Never had she seen anybody so tired.

Charlie looked at her feet. 'Where's your shoe?'

'I threw it away.'

'Why?'

'I had a fight with someone.'

'About your shoes?'

'No.'

'About what, then?'

'It doesn't matter.'

The leaves shivered on the trees. 'Are you all right?'

'Yes. I hate these shoes anyway.'

There was another silence.

'I should go in,' he said.

'I should go home,' she said.

Charlie fished a pair of boots from the porch. 'Here.'

'It's fine, really.'

'Don't be stupid. You'll cut yourself.'

Grudgingly she took them. 'Thanks.'

· * * *

In the end, the firework display dictated her path. Susanna reeled blindly through the maze, her dress torn and her hair a mess, at panicked, bewildered intervals weeping at the possibility that she would never emerge from this infinite nightmare. At midnight the explosions ripped through the sky, gold and purple and red, and she could hear her guests' admiring gasps floating into the air like Chinese lanterns. She thought of old ships navigating their way across oceans by virtue of the constellations, and mapped her way by the serpents and strobes that whistled overhead.

At last she surfaced, the relief dazzling, and was spat out on to the lawn like a dummy from a baby's mouth. Her own mouth was dry and she had an ache behind the eyes. Stumbling across to the house, Susanna detected the tail end of a procession disappearing through the doors. She wanted to scream: *What about me? Wait for me!*

Wasn't she hosting this damn party?

Fired by rage at Cato's desertion, she stormed through to the kitchens.

'Where is he?' she demanded.

Caggie Shaw was wiping her hands on a tea towel. Even in raggy old jeans and a blouse that strained over her too-big, heading-south tits, she still looked fresh and sexy—a bit like Helen Mirren, troublingly, in the right light.

'Crikey,' Caggie exclaimed, 'what happened to you?'

'Where is he?'

'Who?'

'Cato.'

'How should I know? Out there entertaining your guests, I assume.' Caggie's eyes travelled downwards. 'Your dress is undone.'

Susanna consulted her gown. Either Cato or the hedge had ripped her bodice and her left breast was now fully visible, caught in the netting like the catch of the day.

She dragged it up. The disappointment of the night rushed at her unchecked and she blubbed out a sob. She felt dirty and used and stupid.

Caggie held out a glass of water. 'Perhaps you ought to drink this.'

'Perhaps you ought to keep your opinions to your damn self!' Briskly Susanna located a fresh bottle of Bollinger Blanc and wrestled with the neck, angling it perilously like a madman brandishing a shotgun.

'Turn it to the wall,' Caggie shrieked, 'to the wall!'

With a satisfying pop the cork blew off, striking a hanging casserole and then the lip of a copper pot, before bouncing off the bread bin and rolling across the floor. Susanna seized a used flute, wiped the lipstick off the rim and filled it too quickly so that the bubbles surged over the top and spilled down her hand.

'I don't think you need any more,' observed Caggie.

'Who cares what *you* think?' Susanna lashed. 'You figure you're something special round here, don't you? Looking down your nose at me, acting like I'm not worthy.' She caught her reflection in a brass-bottom pan and laughed emptily. 'Well, newsflash, old lady: you're a fucking *cook*. Nothing more! And Cato and I will be making some changes once we move in so I would tread carefully if I were you.'

Caggie watched her evenly.

'I don't think Cato would get rid of me, if that's what you're insinuating.'

There it was again! That *tone*... Oh, she couldn't bear it!

'Give me that water,' Susanna directed, 'I've suddenly got a terrible thirst.'

She snatched the glass from Caggie's grip, and in a swift, utterly rewarding instant chucked its contents in the woman's face. The cook stood stunned for a moment, fingers splayed, hair dripping grimly like a creature from the swamp.

'I'm dreadfully sorry,' Susanna twittered. 'If you'll excuse me.'

She felt a damn sight better as she threaded her way back to the ballroom. Heads turned as she entered, a frisson of murmurs.

Landing on Cato, she sashayed sexily across the dance floor.

'Oops!' Her shoe got caught in the hem of her dress, the heel eliciting a scorching *riiiiiip* as she burst from the barely-clinging confines of the material. The ceiling cartwheeled and with a slam she was splayed face down on the deck.

Cato was on her, capturing her elbow, dragging her up. 'This takes the biscuit,' he hissed, struggling to conceal her naked breasts, which shone like white orbs in the candlelight. 'What on earth has got into you?'

Susanna buried her face in his neck, inhaling his spicy cologne, and sobbed. Cato steered her towards the exit. Just when the evening couldn't possibly get any worse, a new voice boomed from the hall.

It was horribly close, and horribly familiar.

'Well, well, well.'

A six-foot-plus giant was obscuring the doorway, blocking their path. It was jauntily dressed in checkered trousers and a flat cap, its nose purple with port.

'Susanna Denver,' the man said, holding out his arms. 'Remember me?'

CHAPTER EIGHTEEN

LUSTELL'S CLIFFS WERE sparkling chalk. The beach was deserted, white sunshine hazy on the water. Sigmund and Comet frolicked in the morning shallows, dashing for the ebbing tide and barking when it chased them back. Charlie threw a piece of driftwood and the setter bounded after it, pedalling anxiously through the waves, snout raised above the surface like a floral-capped aunt doing a nervous breaststroke.

He had been up since five. Evidence of last night's revelry had infiltrated far and wide: champagne flutes were found in fireplaces, on bookshelves, in the ancient east-wing loo that had a NOT IN USE sign pinned to the door; canapé scraps in the bird bath; extinguished cigars on carpets and in flower pots (and in Caggie's thyme rockery, which hadn't been a popular discovery); a sack of smashed china where one of the waitresses had tripped over with a tray of whipped cream. The caterers would arrive mid-morning to collect the hired pieces, and going

on the final twenty minutes of her evening it was un-
likely that Susanna would be in a fit state to greet them.

After the last of the guests had gone, Charlie had been
the one to help her to bed. Cato had been too busy entertaining their surprise arrival to bother.

'The old bird's pissed,' his brother had diagnosed,
before steering their visitor into the drawing room for
a brandy nightcap.

'Oh, no,' Susanna had whimpered as they had shakily
mounted the stairs, Charlie's arm securing her beneath
the waist. *'Not him... Please not him!'*

In the bedroom, he had eased off her shoes and laid
her back on the pillows.

'I should have known he'd come,' Susanna had
howled. *'It was only a matter of time!'* Panicking, she'd
gripped the sheet. *'Where's Cato? Where is he?'*

'Downstairs.'

'With...' She'd shuddered. 'With him?'

'Yes.'

She'd mewled. Charlie had pulled a blanket over her.
As he did so Susanna had reached for him, taken his
hand and brought it to her lips.

'Do you want to screw me?' she'd invited huskily.

'You're drunk.'

'I've seen you looking.'

He'd drawn back. 'Close your eyes.'

'I want you, Charles. I've wanted you since I got here.
Don't you feel it? The chemistry between us is lethal. I'm
one of the most famous women in the world. Aren't you

curious? Millions would kill to be in your position—and I could show you a hundred more positions besides…'

'Go to sleep.'

'It could be our secret.'

'Goodnight, Susanna.' He'd flicked off the lamp.

She had cried, then. Charlie hadn't known what to do and so he'd put his arms around her, wet sobs soaking into his shoulder, until eventually her breathing slowed and gave way to a gentle snoring. Quietly he had left the room.

He crouched now and took up a stick. A surfer was out on the ocean, a far-off shape beyond his dog's bobbing head. The figure was sitting upright, riding the tide. Every so often it would paddle, leaping to take a crest or at the last moment changing its mind. The majestic burst of that vertical position was awesome.

As Comet splashed up the beach, stopping to shake his fur, Charlie carved an arc in the sand. To be that free, he wondered…what must it be like? Weightless: without restraint or responsibility. All his life he had been bound to something—his parents' legacy, his brother's ultimatums, his home, always his home—anchored by a load that tied him to the deeps. Usherwood was at once his beloved possession and his cross to bear. It was time to let Cato claim his share.

Last night, his brother's news had horrified him. Today, it glinted with faint, tentative possibility. He and Cato might not get on, they might never get on, but their partnership could be the only thing that helped the estate.

Each man needed Usherwood for his own reasons.

The past was the past. Charlie could spend his whole life eaten up by it, but what kind of a life was that?

He would do it today. He would extend the olive branch. There was no reason why the men couldn't share their inheritance, and, in doing so, preserve it.

The surfer was drifting in. Nearer to he saw she was a woman, and as she came to land and ran up the shore, a hundred metres or more from where he sat, he recognised Olivia. It was the hair: that warm flame colour a smudge against the blue.

Susanna drifted into the dining room at midday. Breakfast had turned into brunch had turned into an all-morning graze, and after dismissing the caterers she took her seat and poured herself a very large, very sweet cup of coffee.

'How is everybody?' she sang gaily, flicking out her napkin.

Caggie, busy refilling a fruit bowl, scowled. Baps glanced to the floor. Cato's disapproving eyes appeared darkly over the top of his newspaper.

At the opposite end of the table, Jonathan 'Jonty' Baudelaire, London film and TV agent extraordinaire, grinned at her over his buttered croissant. A flake of pastry clung to his top lip, and when he took a gulp from his mug she noticed he hadn't got past the irritating habit of slurping his tea.

'Jonty,' Susanna got straight to it (it was always best to address the elephant in the room, and 'elephant' really was the word—he was so fat these days!), 'how long are you planning on staying?'

'I was just saying to the girls,' Jonty tossed a cavalier glance at Baps and Caggie, 'I hope you don't mind my dropping by unannounced. Only, when we heard you were over—and how could we avoid it, darling: you always knew how to court the press—the opportunity seemed too good to miss.' He guzzled more tea.

Susanna forced down a mouthful of grapefruit, and with it her conscience. Of course Jonty had been going to make contact: she'd hardly kept this visit under wraps, had she? The society pages were full of it. It was just that her life with Cato, her life *now*, was so far removed from the foolish misdemeanours of the past that it was easier to bury her head in the sand and pretend like they'd never happened.

Hopefully he'd be gone by tonight. The reconciliation had been inevitable, but that didn't mean it had to last any longer than was necessary.

'You weren't hiding from us,' Jonty raised a bushy eyebrow, 'were you?'

'Of course not,' she replied primly. She'd had every intention of making contact with them before returning to the States, of course she had. It wasn't her fault Jonty had beaten her to it! 'I suppose you brought Thorn?'

'Naturally.'

Caggie and Baps retreated. Cato raised his paper. Jonty continued beaming inanely, his crab-apple cheeks and gammon-pink jowls badges of a decade spent boozing over power lunches and living on a diet of steak tar-

tare and quails' eggs. She found him repellent. In his green-and-yellow country gent's get-up he looked absurd. It was hard to believe she had ever slept with him. He was like Toad of Toad Hall.

Yet Susanna had resolved that morning, surfacing through a migraine that felt as if someone were wringing her brain like a sponge, that it was better to face these things with dignity. She had made a rotten fool of herself last night, and while Jonty's reappearance was an unsavoury surprise, she would simply have to deal with it.

'A boy does need his mother,' put in Cato unhelpfully.

'Indeed,' resumed Jonty, done with the croissant and now slathering jam on to a hunk of toast, 'which is why we're here. I know how much you've wanted to see us, darling, and how difficult it must be with a schedule as…' he narrowed his eyes, no doubt kept abreast by his LA associates of her floundering career, '*demanding* as yours. So if the mountain won't come to Mohammed… Well, I thought Thorn could stay with you for a few days, get to know a little about his absent mum.'

Absent mum. Jonty always did know how to put the knife in.

'You put it so charmingly,' she responded archly, 'how can I resist?'

The clock ticked on the mantelpiece. Jonty bit into his toast.

'He's six, Susie.' She didn't know which was worse— Susie or Mole. 'Don't be alarmed if he needs a little reminding. I mean, when were you last in touch?'

'I sent him a card on his birthday,' she threw back,

fully aware of how weak that sounded. 'And I visited last summer. I took him to see *The Marriage of Figaro* at the Royal Opera House, remember?'

'Which was grossly inappropriate for a five-year-old.' Cato smirked.

'Where is he?'

'In the garden.'

Susanna peered out of the window in trepidation. Bless the child, for he had not been planned…a two-week love affair and a single mistake. She had been naïve at twenty-six, her dreams of becoming an actress only just flourishing, and during a publicity jaunt to the UK Jonty had taken her under his wing. In the end she had been persuaded to go through with the pregnancy, consoled by the idea that at least life with Jonty would be financially viable *and* a boost to her career, but after Thorn had been born (Thorn? *Thorn?* However had Jonty talked her into that one? It had been his grandpa's nickname or some such nonsense—she must have been off her head), the arguments had begun. Susanna had fled, her Hollywood debut at last within reach, and though she had tried to justify her abandonment in a number of ways over the years, it always came to the same thing: Jonty had fought harder than her, for Thorn to stay in England, to be raised the English way, to know his country. Put simply, he had *wanted* the boy more than she had. But, then, he always had.

'I'm not sure when we're heading back to LA,' she said lightly, pushing around the fruit in her bowl. 'I wouldn't want to mess Thorn about. Cato?'

'You can do what you like, Mole.'

How she wanted to wring his neck! It was his fault. If her boyfriend had done the honourable thing and proposed, she could have brandished her sparkler in Jonty's direction this very morning. That would have sent him on his merry way.

'Oh, do shut up,' she snipped. 'If you haven't anything useful to contribute then don't contribute at all.'

He didn't look up from his paper. 'Don't get in a strop because I didn't share a bed with you last night,' he said languidly. 'You were doing the most beastly snoring—I could scarcely hear myself think!'

She went hot with embarrassment. 'As a matter of fact *I* barely slept.'

'Could have fooled me…'

She bit her tongue. Cato would ridicule her if she told him her suspicions.

The ghost of Usherwood was back. Last night Susanna had seen her, actually *seen* the spectre with her own eyes, floating down the corridor in a gossamer gown. She had woken at two a.m., her rise to consciousness sudden and clean, breaking into darkness like a diver into water. Moonlight swam through the glass. She'd gasped for liquid, groping her way to the door, and stilled in her tracks as the first wail hit: that reedy, haunting yowl that spoke of such passion, such yearning. Her heart had lodged in her throat. She'd felt paralysed, waiting for the ever-increasing yelps to die down, before gently prising open the door. Silence. Head pounding, hoping the soundtrack might be a result of her drunken delirium, Susanna had crept into the hall.

That was when she had seen her. A flash of white, like a handkerchief waved by someone in distress, a slender figure glimpsed as it darted out of sight.

Susanna had retreated back inside like a fox down a hole. To think if she'd opened the door just a second earlier, she would have collided with the ghost head-on!

'Daddy, Daddy, Daddy!' The din of her child's voice pricked Susanna's reverie like a pin on a balloon. 'Look what I've got!'

Thorn came rushing him, grubby hands outstretched as he presented Jonty with a particularly ugly-looking snail.

'Me and Olivia found it,' he announced proudly.

Jonty ruffled the boy's wisp of blond hair and Susanna smiled back in a pained way. Trust that gardener to go encouraging him to forage about in the dirty undergrowth: the girl had no class.

'Do you know who this is, darling?' Jonty asked, patting the corners of his mouth with a napkin. 'Do you remember your mother?'

Thorn was shy, clinging to his father's wrist as Susanna lasered him with her most encouraging expression, and held her arms out because that was the sort of thing long-lost mothers did. Thorn regarded her warily. She replaced her hands in her lap.

'Why don't you show her what you've found?' Jonty prompted.

Uneasily Thorn approached, and even more uneasily

Susanna extended an upturned palm to receive the slimy offering. The snail soldered wetly to her skin.

'Is this a gift for Mommy?' she crooned.

'No,' he replied. 'I want it back.'

'Like mother, like son,' murmured Cato from behind the paper.

'See how he's missed her?' Jonty said affectionately, as Thorn clambered on to her lap. God, he was heavy. Wasn't he too old to be throwing his weight around? He didn't feel like her child; she might as well have been passed a wriggling piglet.

Susanna spied Olivia outside, digging the plots. Her hair was damp, her cheeks flushed with the bite of fresh air. She caught her own reflection in a silver teapot and the distorted throwback made her look like a beak-nosed witch.

'Would you like to go outside again?' She adjusted her position in the hope her son might just slide off, lifting slightly from the chair like someone trying to shift a cat. 'I've got the most terrible migraine, is anyone else suffering? I think it was that *fricassée de poussin.*'

'That'll teach you to rope in the French,' said Cato.

'I take it everybody's happy, then,' said Jonty, pleased, reaching for another mug of tea. 'Thorn stays with you for a week or two, Susie—he's going to love it.'

Susanna replaced her fork. The food looked as appetising as gravel.

'I'm sure he will.'

CHAPTER NINETEEN

WHEN CHARLIE ARRIVED home that afternoon, Cato was waiting for him in the library. He was sitting in Charlie's chair, at Charlie's desk, reclining against the leather Chesterfield that had once belonged to Richmond Lomax. He had his feet up, and was engaged in the important business of excavating his gums with a tooth-pick.

Surrounding him was a fortress of their father's tomes. Richmond had been a scientist, concerned with sums and specifics, points and particulars, and the steady reliable bulk of history. Buried among them were the stories their mother had loved—a du Maurier here, a Brontë there, a Christie gathering dust in a pile of papers—secret voices that no longer tried to be heard. Richmond hadn't wasted time with fiction.

'I'm sorry, old bean,' Cato said. 'There simply isn't room for the two of us.'

Charlie hung back, a visitor to his own space. The

words he'd rehearsed on the walk back dissolved. 'What?'

'You heard.'

'There's room enough for a dozen families.'

Cato turned the pick between his finger and thumb. 'I don't mean physically.'

'Then what do you mean?'

'Come now.' The feet came off the desk and Cato sat forward, elbows on knees like a benevolent boss at pains to make a dismissal. 'You and I might be cut from the same canvas but you know as well as I do that cohabitation is not an option. With regret,' he savoured it, 'you'll have to move on.'

'Like hell I will.'

'Before you overreact, think about it.' Cato touched the tips of his fingers together. 'I'd make it worth your while, Charles, you know I would; you'd receive a nice slug of money every month, a tidy allowance to keep things ticking over.'

'That would have been helpful when I needed it here. I came to you so many times. Do you know what it took for me to do that, after everything that's happened?'

'I feel for you,' Cato commiserated. 'Often I think how terrible it must be to be you. Which is why I'm offering to step in. Isn't this what you've always wanted?'

'Not like this. You know it isn't.'

'Have a break!' Cato spread his arms wide. 'Anywhere you want to go. Take a holiday. Lie on a beach. Soak up the rays. Have sex with a beautiful woman. Don't look a gift horse in the mouth, now, there's a sensible chap.'

It had to be a joke. His brother couldn't seriously imagine he was going to sit back and accept this preposterous consolation prize.

'This is just a game to you, isn't it?' he said. 'This whole thing, it's just a game. There I was thinking we could move things forward; try to put the past behind us. But you? You don't care. You led me to believe that last night's monstrosity was a shared venture; that if you weren't prepared to donate then at least this was a chance to bring in the cash together—'

'Together?' Cato snorted unkindly. 'Do you really think we'd have secured those tidy deals with the press if it weren't for Susanna and me?'

'And you treat her just beautifully, while we're on the subject.'

'A shame that we're not.'

'I take it she'll be moving with you.'

Cato made a face. 'I haven't decided yet.'

'You can't blackmail me into leaving: Usherwood's mine, too.'

'To a lesser degree,' his brother conceded. 'But if you insist on staying, well, let's just say I could make your life awfully uncomfortable.'

'More uncomfortable than you already have? I don't know, Cato, you'd need to stretch it pretty far to exceed your record.'

'Oh, you're bringing up *that* again, are you?'

'I've lost track of how many "that"s there are.'

'No wonder the finances are up shit creek if you can't count to two.'

'You're doing this out of spite. There's no other reason than because you can. If this is some warped reminder of your filial superiority—'

'You said it.'

'—then give up now. My hands are raised. Don't ask me to go.'

Cato sighed deeply. Eventually, as if he had been given no other choice than to break the news as gently as he could, he said, 'I'm going to present the facts for you as plainly as I can. As the eldest this house is my inheritance and therefore belongs to me. I'm afraid that is a pill you are just going to have to swallow. And since the property will be in my name, and will, to all intents and purposes, be in my possession, I have final say in who I share it with.'

'I suppose you'll be holding on to Caggie.'

'She rather likes being held on to.'

'And Barbara's for the chop—after years of faithful service, you'll be getting rid of her. You're brutal. You're absolutely fucking brutal.'

'Baps is a tough old turkey. She'll live.'

On cue there was a rap at the door. The housekeeper put her head round.

'Excuse me for interrupting, but this arrived by courier.' She held up an envelope. 'I thought you should see it right away.'

Charlie took the missive. The envelope was handwritten, addressed to both brothers, and one corner bore a large red stamp: URGENT!

Cato snatched it from him. He tore it open and un-folded a single sheet of A4.

His eyes scanned the document.

'Well,' he raised his eyebrows, 'this is a turn up for the books. Old Barnaby Cartwright, I thought he'd kicked the bucket.'

Charlie absorbed it. The letter was cryptic. Barnaby had been banished from the family when the boys were young. They had received nothing from him in over twenty years.

'Uncle Barney won't be coming to see us any more...' he remembered his mother saying, tucking him into bed one night, her face streaked with tears. *'Daddy's decided. But Uncle Barney loves you very, very much, never forget that...'*

'What must he be now, a hundred and seventeen?' Cato reclaimed the message and screwed it up. He strode to the fire. 'Clearly he's off his rocker.'

'Don't you dare.' Charlie grabbed him. 'This is the first address we've had for him since before Mother died. She'd want us to follow this up.'

'So he's dragging us to bloody Norfolk, of all places? Sounds deathly dull to me.' Cato turned on the house-keeper. 'Finished eavesdropping yet, Baps?'

'Forgive me, my lord.' She closed the door.

'Barbara knew our uncle better than we did,' said Charlie incredulously. 'God, you're hideous.'

'Not as hideous as a load of inbreds living in wind-mills.'

'We have to make the trip. It doesn't sound like there's much time.'

Cato grimaced. 'What the fuck is *"Hedge Betty"* anyway—surely he doesn't expect us to stay somewhere that sounds like a pensioner's muff? Can't he come here, for pity's sake? I'll send a chopper if he's at death's door.'

'That's a really wise idea. Haven't you read this?'

Cato unfurled the letter and perused it once more. 'Fine,' he barked, 'but it had better be worth it. If the old man croaks while we're there then on your head be it.'

His brother's voice caught him as he exited the library.

'Oh, and Charles?'

He stopped. He didn't turn round.

'Now I think about it, this jaunt could be a sensible move. It'll be good for you get away from the house for a while. You never know, you might get used to it.'

CHAPTER TWENTY

Barnaby G. Cartwright
Hedge Betty
Stickling
Norfolk
NF12 7TW

Cato & Charles Lomax
Usherwood House
Lustell Cove
Cornwall
LC20 3AU

August 1st 2013

My dear Cato, my dear Charles,
Please accept my apologies for writing to you out
of the blue, and after so many years have passed. I
pray this is not too much of a shock.

My health is failing and I have vital news to impart, the nature of which is of the utmost importance to you both. I should have done this a long time ago, had I possessed the courage—I'm sorry that I did not. If I depart this life without full disclosure of the facts, I fear it will only cause more suffering.

I request that you come to see me. I am unable to travel myself and trust this does not put you at too much of an inconvenience. My address is at the top of this letter. I await your arrival with anxious affection.

Yours, in anticipation...

Your loving uncle,

Barnaby Cartwright

PART TWO

PART TWO

CHAPTER TWENTY-ONE

THE HELICOPTER GENERATED a terrific wind. Olivia held Thorn's plump hand as the giant dragonfly came to land on Usherwood's lawn, its rotors a deafening blur. Susanna shot out of the house, Burberry luggage trailing after her, and rushed towards it.

'Are we going in that?' the boy asked excitedly.

'You are,' said Olivia, relieved that she didn't have to board. 'I'm not.'

'Then how are *you* getting there?'

'In the car.'

He pulled a face. 'Slooooooooow!'

Olivia was learning that Thorn had been raised to expect speedy results. He couldn't understand why plants took so long to grow, why morning took so many hours to come or why he had to wait to get the toy superbike he'd been promised because it wasn't his birthday until October. Jonty had left that morning, zooming off in an oxblood Porsche Carrera and spraying them all in a cloud of dust, impatient to get back to his full-throttle London life. It wasn't hard to see where Thorn got it.

The prospect of spending half a day holed up on the motorway with Charlie, however, was not one she relished. When she'd heard the party was heading off she had been relieved—a chance to press on with the Sundial Garden, peace and quiet in the house, time away from the brothers—until Susanna announced that if Cato were going then so must she, and if she were going then so must Thorn, and if Thorn were going, then… Well, there was no way she could look after her own son without at least a little bit of outside help. Naturally Olivia had rejected the offer, before Susanna had proposed an obscene lum-sum payment to secure the pleasure of her assistance.

It would take months to earn this kind of money. The trip to Norfolk, what would amount to a few days of her life, would be more than enough to fund her move back to London. Already she was dreaming of returning to the city. Since the blow-up with Beth all the magic had drained out of Lustell Cove, and now she could see it for the illusion it was: a childhood temptation, a sweet-scented nostalgia trip, an interval before real life resumed. She had to get away. Her head was a mess over Addy. Flo was in her space 24/7. Beth didn't want to see her. There was nothing to stay for.

Norfolk wasn't Cornwall, and right now Olivia wanted to be anywhere in the world but here. Besides, there were worse ways to spend one's time than playing sandcastles with a six-year-old in the sunshine. How hard was it going to be?

'Are we ready?' Susanna was yelling over the noise, as she attempted to harness her billowing headscarf. 'Do we have everything?'

Cato emerged with the last of the bags and marched across the lawn.

'Must we take *quite* so much, Mole?' he lambasted. 'For God's sake!'

'Oh!' Susanna squeaked, suddenly remembering. 'My son!'

At Cato's frantic beckoning Thorn hurried to join them.

'Wave at me from the sky!' Olivia called after him, watching his rucksack get smaller and smaller until it was tidied into the aircraft.

Minutes later the helicopter rose shakily from the ground. Olivia saw Thorn's excited face at the window, happily flapping his goodbye, before the chopper tipped its nose, hovered for a few seconds and then sailed off over the forest.

Without Cato and Susanna, Usherwood exhaled. The bricks seemed to relax, the cherub in the fountain seemed to sigh; even the swallow-song played a lighter tune.

She returned inside to gather her things.

Charlie's Land Rover had seen better days. The front was littered with spanners and screwdrivers, old cassette tapes, bottles of water and crumpled newspapers, and she'd seen less sand on some beaches. There was a pervading scent of salty dog, which wasn't altogether unpleasant, and with Sigmund and Comet's hot breath on the back of her neck for the duration of the cross-country journey, not altogether surprising.

The radio was bust, which meant the long silences she'd feared opened up uninterrupted. Neither Lomax seemed to know what the trip was about, or what would be waiting when they got there.

'Do you remember him?' she asked as they eased out of the estate gates and joined the main road. Usherwood diminished to a dot in her wing mirror.

'Vaguely.' He switched gear. He was a stoic driver, fast but safe. His knuckles on the stick were weather-cracked and wide, flecks of dark hair spilling from the wrist. They looked as if they could strangle something one-handed. 'I remember him not being there more than him being there. I remember him going away.'

'Was it something he did?'

'I don't know.'

Charlie's tone told her not to press further. She turned to look out of the window, at the receding cove, the houses steadily building to towns and the distant, charcoal sea: a fading strip that eventually vanished to nothing. This trip was a means to an end, and the family history had nothing to do with her.

After Bristol they stopped at a service station to give the dogs a run. Olivia went inside to browse for a book and was distracted by row upon row of glossy magazines, almost all bearing Cato and Susanna's blissful image. Most had been taken at the Usherwood party, Susanna's devilish dress stealing the limelight despite her lover's pristine good looks. Olivia resisted the onslaught of flashbacks. Each time Beth's stinging remarks came back they struck her harder than before.

She focused on the headlines: CATO RELOCATION! COUPLE TO RETURN TO CORNISH LOVE NEST! USHERWOOD WELCOMES HOME LORD! CATO AND SUSANNA TO WED!

It was strange seeing the place splashed across the press. This time a year ago she would have walked straight past such displays, untroubled by the serenely vacant smiles of the rich and famous. Now, she had peeled back their glossy veneer. They were still people, with dreams and hopes and fears just like anyone else. Every picture told a story. Every smile masked a truth. Every house hid its secrets.

Olivia lifted an article. Cato was ultra-photogenic, his debonair smirk lighting the page. Privately she thought he was more attractive in pictures than he was in real life. That kind of chiselled artifice worked on camera, a polished, airbrushed perfection, but was disconcerting close up. She squinted at it.

Weird, but Cato reminded her of someone, a face she knew from long ago. It had never struck her before. It was close, but she couldn't put her finger on whom.

When she arrived outside with two cups of coffee, Charlie took his without a word. He was on the ridge of the tailgate, securing the knot in a rope. His boots were coming apart, and she thought his feet must be cold.

'Are Cato and Susanna getting married?' she asked, blowing the hot liquid.

He slipped the loops over the animals' heads.

'Why,' he said at last. It wasn't phrased like a question.

She took a sip. 'Just something I heard.'

'I'd be surprised if they were.' He scuffed the dogs, rubbing them vigorously around the ears and muzzle. 'I don't see Cato getting married.'

'That's not what the papers say.'

'The papers are full of shit.' Charlie tugged them to heel.

She waited in the car for him to come back.

They came off the M11 after six. Olivia was tired and the drive seemed endless, pockets of time expanded and compressed by sporadic bursts of half-sleep. She dreamed of the man they were going to see, his mysterious summons, and would blink awake into a world she didn't recognise, halfway gone and halfway there.

Predictably, winding A-roads arrived with the weekender motorhome brigade, slowing to forty before Charlie overtook in an accelerating surge. Olivia glimpsed the caravans' signatures on the way past— SWIFT, VOYAGER, LIGHTNING.

The landscape was vast and flat, another England from the rolling dips of Cornwall. At home the sea always seemed to her the more abundant thing, the sky its painter's less preferred subject, but here it was the other way round. The dimming blue was a vast roof, closer to them than at Lustell Cove, and flush with brushstroke clouds that chased themselves to a distant point. The fields were wide and yawning.

Some time later it started to spit with rain. Charlie cursed the wipers when they froze, clearing their vision one minute and sticking the next, the windscreen pooling with water. In a layby he stopped and climbed out. The dogs were roused and craned to see what was going on, their heads appearing by Olivia's shoulder and their hesitant paws testing a path to the front. Sigmund yowled gruffly when he saw his master lean over the bonnet, and his tail thumped frantically.

Charlie's hair was wet. He frowned as he focused, leaning to examine the wipers. Dark water stained his coat. He didn't seem to notice or mind the rain. At this range there was a foot or less between them, the closest they'd been, and Olivia glanced away, rummaging in her bag for her phone.

Seconds later the door opened and he reached in, releasing a lever under the dash. The bonnet popped and he ducked back out to lift it, obscuring him from view. She was thankful for the curtain raised between them. The dogs were going crazy, desperate to be outside, and Olivia leaned into the back to reassure them.

The boot liner confessed yet more miscellanies. Dog stuff was everywhere, towels, rugs, more for them than he'd brought for himself, and a mattress covered in muddy prints, from which Comet gazed back at her with friendly inquisitiveness. At the rear a dust-covered box was partly open, its cardboard flaps fringed with age.

She reached into it for something to placate the agitation. To her surprise, it was filled with photographs. Intrigued, she pulled out a handful and flicked through them. Some were portrait, others landscape; some six-by-four, others bigger; some in colour, others black and white. All could be recognised as Lustell Cove. Olivia would know that ocean anywhere: the rugged moors and the ghostly, windswept bluff; the Candle Point lighthouse shot from below, its rusted gunmetal dog steps like stitches in a stone shaft, and the gleaming cage of its lantern; spray lashing against rocks, a whirlpool of living, liquid silver; heifers grazing in March, marmalade brawn against bountiful green; the forsaken engine house of a disused mine, its chimney castrated, the sea brimming through its arched windows; the beached sailboat *Atlantis* wedged in the sand, clumsily, like an old man leaning on an elbow; a washed-up jellyfish dried out in the sun…

There had to be hundreds. All were magnificent. The pictures made Olivia do more than see; they made her feel. They had been shot with an instinct for the living, vital moment, and stripped through with raw, violent passion. Stills of Usherwood featured heavily. She tore through them, each frame more powerful than the last: the lake, the chapel, the stonework…the pillars, the pond, the statuary. This wasn't about documenting the building's collapse; it wasn't about recording crumbling bricks or time-worn mortar for posterity, or to articulate the failings of the estate. It was simply an ode to the beauty of Charlie's home, a song he sung entirely by himself and for himself. The tenderness with which its scars had been captured made her want to cry.

Why should she be shocked?

It just wasn't how she'd pegged him. Charlie didn't see the world as she did. He worked with his hands, not with his head. He was a man who built, who made, who put things together; a man who was physical; a man who swore and sweated, who fixed car engines and eased thorns out of dogs' paws; a man who split his palm and wrung out the blood and called it a scratch. He was obtuse. He was rude and bad-tempered. He was tactless and blunt and boorish. He was proud and conceited and up his own arse. He didn't know how to express beauty or fragility or angles or shade or any of that, because that required intuition, and he had never intuited anything with her because if he had then he wouldn't have been so hostile from the moment she'd shown up. He would have known they weren't so different, after all; that despite his wealth, despite his upbringing, despite his home and his lands and everything that set them apart, they had a shade of a soul in common.

He wasn't these photographs, or anything like them. He was Charlie Lomax.

A light crept under the door she had locked him behind. A changing Lustell morning when she would lean from her bedroom window, praying for sun, the dense bank of grey blinking for an instant and flooding the fields with gold.

The door to the cab opened. Hastily Olivia replaced

the stills, shoving the box away and returning to her seat as Charlie climbed in and told her: 'We're fixed.'

Sigmund was soothed by his master's voice and settled as the engine roared to life. Rain was dashing hard at them now, the wipers working briskly.

Charlie pulled out on to the road. It was deserted. Though she wanted to turn to look at him, to see him in the glow of her discovery, she resisted.

CHAPTER TWENTY-TWO

'THERE—THAT'S IT.'

Olivia pointed to one of the houseboats, on the stern of which HEDGE BETTY gleamed in the headlamps' glare. The boat was third in a chain of vessels moored to the mossy bank, obscured by dripping foliage and tethered by a wooden gangplank. In keeping with its neighbours, the aft deck of his uncle's barge revealed a makeshift yard boasting an array of stone ornaments and flower troughs.

He parked and they climbed out. Olivia stretched in the drizzle. The dogs bounded from the back, rooting into the ferny undergrowth. Charlie whistled for them, roping them to a sheltered post and scratching their soggy heads.

'Stay, pups,' he told them. 'I'll be back for you.'

They crossed the walkway, Charlie shouldering their bags. Rain pattered on the leaf canopy, plopping thickly into buckets and empty pots. A tin mailbox had been erected at the gate, partway up a pole, and much higher, clearly out of reach of anyone of reasonable height, another was facetiously marked BILLS.

A promising blaze was coming from inside. As Charlie was thinking about changing out of his damp clothes and feeding the dogs their supper, the door opened and a woman stepped out. She was sixtyish, pretty, her silver-blonde hair tied in a loose, wispy bun and a jangle of bracelets adorning her wrists. She wore swathes of richly coloured fabrics, chiffon and silk, and a generous smile.

'You must be Charles.' She hugged him, a proper tight squeeze that caught him off guard. 'It's a brilliant relief you came. I'm Decca.'

'Call me Charlie. And this is Olivia.'

Olivia returned the embrace without question. He liked how easy she was in company, how natural, and wished he could be more like that.

'I hope I'm not imposing,' she said.

'Not a bit,' Decca assured them, 'there's plenty of room. Cato and Susanna dropped in earlier—heavens, she's glamorous, isn't she? They've opted for a hotel in town, so as it happens we've more than enough space. Look at me, forcing you to stand out here in the rain. Come inside, let's get you warm and fed.'

Olivia almost tripped over the heap of shoes at the entrance. Decca kicked off her sandals, adding to the pile, and stopped to light a roll-up from a scented candle.

The interior of the barge was a treasure trove of curios, its surfaces packed with souvenirs of a colourful, travelled life. Shelves teemed with artifacts, paraffin lamps and pewter jugs, hatboxes, candles and books. A printer's tray was fixed to the wall and filled with keys, pocket watches and miniature glass vials, shiny pennies and spiky watch cogs. In the corner a traditional queenie stove glowed orange. A picture of a younger Decca, draped round a man Charlie recognised as his uncle, hung above a sofa that had burst at its seams, a single velvet glove thrown across one arm. On the table was a handsome record player, a library of vinyl wedged beneath, and a glass diamond-shaped ashtray in which half a joint had been ground out.

Steps led them down into a galley kitchen. Whatever was cooking smelled delicious, smoky and robust. Vases of wild flowers were scattered on the window ledge and a heap of plates piled up happily on the draining board.

'You must be ravenous,' called Decca, lifting the spoon from a simmering pot and touching it to her lips. 'I'm making Barney's favourite—Sennet stew. It's a family recipe,' she tapped her nose, 'if I told you I'd have to kill you.'

Olivia examined a picture tagged to the fridge. 'Is this Barnaby?'

'In better days.' Decca tried for a lightness of tone but the context was wrong. 'He's asleep,' she explained to Charlie, apologetically. 'He sleeps a lot these days. It can take him a while to get off so I like to leave him when I can… You'll be anxious to see him, I understand that.'

He nodded, though part of him was relieved at the delayed encounter. Barnaby Cartwright was the closest thing to Beatrice they had left. How would it feel to be reunited after all this time, after so much had happened?

They were shown to their rooms, identical cabins made up with dozens of cushions and ripe with the smell of incense. Across the passage Olivia knelt on her bunk and wiped condensation from the porthole. The back of her hair was a nest from where she'd slept in the car. She yawned. The yawn turned into a sigh and she stared out of the window. Charlie watched her for a second before returning to the kitchen.

Their host was adamant he brought in the dogs. Decca's own, an Irish wolfhound called Bess, 'almost as ancient as he is', was snoozing on Barnaby's bed.

Olivia offered to fetch them, and headed into the night before he could object.

'Bess refuses to leave Barney's side,' Decca admitted wistfully, 'especially now. I worry myself silly thinking she's got a sixth sense about these things, that she's making the most of him while he's still here.' She shook her head. 'But that won't help anyone. Having your two indoors will be a welcome distraction.'

'Decca,' he began, 'do you know what this is about?'

She went to set the table. 'I know part of it,' she replied carefully.

'And…?'

'And when I ask for the full account Barney tells me that's for your and Cato's ears only—no one else's. I must respect that.'

'Can you tell me?'

'No.' She was definite. 'He will.'

'It sounds critical.'

Decca regarded him squarely. 'I know his getting in touch so suddenly must have put you both at sixes and sevens, but rest assured you'll be abreast of everything soon enough. Barney wants to speak to you and Cato together.'

'Which won't be tonight,' Charlie granted, 'because Cato's in town.' It was a typical manoeuvre of his brother, changing plans to suit his own ends.

'I don't think our standards are quite up to Susanna's.' Decca was diplomatic. She said it without a trace of affront. 'She wanted a hot bath, you see, and I'm afraid our little shower's temperamental at the best of times...'

As Decca chatted on about what a novelty it was to have film stars in their midst, he caught sight of a closed door beyond her shoulder. Anticipation prickled. Questions assailed him.

What did Barnaby have to tell them?

Was it about his parents? Was it the mystery of the Lomax disappearance?

Why hadn't he contacted them before?

Why hadn't Barnaby come to say his goodbyes on that horrible day of the memorial, when they had stood like ravens in a dark September field and the ground swallowed up his invisible mother and father...nothing to bury and nothing to kiss?

Decca interrupted his thoughts.

'I've put you and Olivia in separate rooms,' she said, 'I wasn't sure if you...?'

'No,' he said quickly. 'It's not like that.'

'I'm sorry. I didn't mean to embarrass you.'

'You haven't.'

Retrieving a loaf from the oven, Decca tore into it. Steaming, floury hunks fell apart and she winced at the heat on her fingers. She smiled. 'Good.'

He changed the subject.

'How long have you and my uncle been together?'

'Fifteen years.' Her tone grew serious. 'Long enough to be sure that he's thought of you boys every single day. Barney was heartbroken—he still is—that things ended the way they did. There wasn't any choice. Beatrice was everything to him. He wept for months when she died. I didn't think he'd ever get over it.'

'Did they make peace?'

'The animosity was between him and Richmond—it had nothing to do with your mother. They were always close, even when separated.'

Charlie thought of his mother on her desert island, plane-wrecked in the clothes she had vanished in, her hair matted and tangled with sand, her lips cracked with thirst, slowly perishing in the shade of a brittle palm tree.

'We never knew why.' His eyes flicked to meet her. 'What did he do wrong? Why did my father send him away?'

'This is a conversation you should be having with your uncle, not with me.'

An explosive coughing fit erupted from behind the closed door. 'Please excuse me.' Decca vanished into the depths of the boat, calling back, 'Open the wine, would you?'

Charlie busied himself with the extraction of a tricky cork. At last, the hacking subsided. He could hear the lilt of Decca's voice and the occasional burst of a deeper note, which he strained to identify, to grab hold of its counterpart in his memory. He could picture his uncle at Usherwood so clearly, the feel of his wiry jumpers when he lifted Charlie on to his shoulders; the smell of cut grass when they played hide-and-seek on the lawn; visiting the cottage by the sea, the path that led down to the beach…

A fiction, possibly, stemmed from wishful thinking. But there *had* been a man at the house when the boys were small, besides their father. There had.

Barnaby's letter had oiled a jammed cog free. Glimmers surfaced from depths he had never plumbed, flashes of recollection, cloudy and discoloured, glimpses fickle as rain. One thing remained: he had loved his uncle, and his uncle had loved him.

'How is he?' he asked when Decca returned.

'Not good.' She bit her lip. 'I'm sorry, Charlie, but he isn't up to visitors tonight. It's difficult. He doesn't want you witnessing him like this. Today's bad—the bad ones come and go, you take them when they're due.'

'I understand.'

Olivia returned with the dogs. All three were drenched. She knelt to run a towel over their coats and Comet took it for a game, chasing the rag round in circles.

'I hope you don't mind muddy paws.' Olivia worked the dirt from between their pads. There was a groove by her mouth when she smiled. He liked it.

'Not a bit.' Decca encouraged them to sit. 'I'm used to it by now.'

The stew was as tasty as promised, hearty and rich. As they ate, Decca regaled them with stories of her and Barnaby's life together, from meeting on a commune in the nineties to their nomadic adventures across South America and Asia, from living on ranches and Patagonian grasslands to a stint in a Mongolian yurt. Sigmund and Comet roamed, restless for supper, appetites staved by Decca slipping them scraps of potato and the diligent courtesies of Bess the wolfhound, who, after an introductory frenzy of sniffing noses, gently prodded their hindquarters for attention. Olivia shared her own unorthodox upbringing living in her mother's caravan. Charlie knew just where it was, even though he had never been. Up the green lane past the bend in the road, where every day she would turn off and vanish into that shadowy jungle.

At Towerfield he had been collected in the big, bragging Bentley that turned up like clockwork at the gates—three-thirty p.m. sharp, on Richmond's instruction. Teasing laughter would chase him into its soft interior. He would sooner have walked. If he had walked he might have caught up with her. She wouldn't have thought he was anybody out of the ordinary, just a regular boy, and he could have started the conversation he'd rehearsed so often in his head. Instead the car would pass her on her bike, silently aching, day after day after day, rain or sun, frost or wind, and Charlie would watch from the window as she weaved up the track, swallowed by foliage.

He thought of her caravan home as bright and original, just like she was.

After supper, they went to bed. By the time Charlie got in, he was so tired he couldn't sleep. The moon leached in, leaking across his chest.

He rolled over. Each time he closed his eyes he saw the rain-soaked road, glistening tarmac vanishing beneath him, the swishing wipers and Olivia's head as it rested against the window, her hands in her lap, breathing gently.

CHAPTER TWENTY-THREE

RISING FROM THE claw-footed bathtub, Susanna whacked her head on the ceiling and cried out in pain. She crouched to let the shock of impact pass, hunched naked like Gollum in the draining water and clutching her skull.

'Hmm?' was the extent of Cato's enquiry. He was sitting on the edge of the bed intently examining his Cartier watch, whose second hand had stopped.

'This is meant to be their "luxury suite", is it?' Susanna glared at the low beams, the quaintly sloped rafters and the tiny square window through which fishing boats bobbed in the dark. She never had been one for miniature dwellings that made you feel as if you were about to sit down to tea with a hedgehog. 'All that hypnosis I had against claustrophobia and here we are, stuck in a rabbit warren.'

'It was this or the pub. We're not in fucking Belgravia.'

'Clearly not!' She reached for a towel. 'I mean, come

on: bath in the bedroom? What a novelty. It couldn't be more dated if it tried.'

'Beggars can't be choosers.'

'We're beggars now, are we?' Certainly they were according to the girl at the hotel reception, who had failed to recognise either of them. Not a trace! She had even dared smirk when Susanna requested their most expensive lodgings. What kind of a place was this? Stickling was about as clued-up as the moon.

'What *is* the matter with you, Mole? Stop behaving like a spoiled brat.'

Susanna pouted. Understandably she was feeling tender. It had been a horrible day—in fact ever since Jonty turned up at that disastrous party things had gone from bad to worse. She had volunteered to come to Norfolk in the hope that the father of her child might deem it a step too far, but on the contrary it had been tagged as the perfect mother/son bonding opportunity. Having a kid she never saw was one thing when Susanna was in LA—after all, what was she meant to do from all the way over there? But in England it was a pick-sharp reminder of everything she had turned her back on. Every time Thorn falteringly called her 'Mummy', every time he gazed beseechingly up at her as if she had the answer to some profound philosophical conundrum, every time he asked why she didn't visit more often, guilt twisted like a barb in her stomach. Wrong as it might be, at least in California she could forget.

What on earth was she going to do with the child? Susanna didn't know how to be a mother; she'd never had to do it before. On the way over Thorn had been sick, splattering the inside of the helicopter with the goop of pulverised gummy bears Cato had fed him as bribery to keep quiet. Cato had gone ballistic, disgustedly pressing a silk handkerchief to his nose while Susanna cleaned Thorn up and told him not to worry. What else was she meant to do? The situation was impossible.

Come the morning she would offload him on to Olivia—heaven knows she had paid the girl enough for the assurance of her company. Finally Susanna would be able to exhale. She would root out a health spa for the day, enjoy a spot of pampering and indulge in a well-earned massage while Cato saw to business.

Buoyed by thoughts of her imminent wind down, she decided to try and make the best of the trip. Perhaps it was a chance for her and Cato to reconnect. He'd been appallingly shirty with her the past few days.

'Oh, darling?' She patted herself dry, taking time to do it sexily. In the mirror she caught her tanned, lithe twin, and was pleased with her reflection, sporting not an ounce of fat, the arms lean, the ass pert, her breasts high and round on her chest. How could he resist? She let the towel drop, tantalisingly slow.

Cato brought the watch closer to his face. 'Come on, you dicky bugger...'

'I'm cold now I'm out of the water...'

Still he didn't tear his eyes from that blasted timepiece. 'And?'

'I was hoping you might warm me up.'

'Go and stand by the radiator.'

Crossly Susanna collected the material and knotted it across her bust.

'What's eating you?' she demanded.

'You are,' he strapped the mended watch to his wrist, finally engaged, 'in about five seconds. Put your back into it this time, won't you; that last blowjob you subjected me to was terribly lacklustre.'

Susanna's mouth fell open. *Lacklustre?* She had always given a hundred per cent with Cato, even when she was tired and would really rather have nodded off, even when he took so long to come that her jaw seized up, even when bobbing up and down in his lap began to feel about as erotic as fellating a sausage roll.

Cato began unbuckling his trousers.

'Unbelievable!' Susanna threw on her dressing gown, knotting the cord fiercely across her waist, definite as a padlock.

'What?'

'Don't you think you've got some making up to do?' she snapped. 'After today, that freak show of a boat, bringing me here—'

'I didn't ask you to come.'

'I did it for you!' she lied. Thinking of his uncle's barge was enough to make her shudder. 'Excuse *me* if I thought you might appreciate some support when it came to greeting your long-lost family. Isn't that the sort of thing girlfriends do?'

Girlfriend. It sounded so flimsy, so incidental…so dangerous.

'For Christ's sake, Mole, keep it down; that tyke of yours is next door.'

'He's fast asleep. I checked.'

'Thank God for that. All that yabbering on the way over nearly split my head in two. Not to mention spraying the interior of my aircraft with that *Exorcist* gunk.'

'Try to be reasonable. He's a child.'

He snorted. 'And who made you Mother of the Year?'

'Jonty says I could be a great mom if I put my mind to it.'

Cato hooted a laugh. Susanna didn't understand what was funny and in that cruel guffaw heard confirmation of her fears. No longer did Cato see her as the sexy, successful siren he had met, clapping eyes on her across the crowded pool patio of a friend's Bel Air villa and deciding her beauty was *criminal*, and that anyone in possession of those kind of looks *needed taking down a peg or two*. How she had giggled at those arch British expressions, captivating him with her girlish charm, and they had fallen into bed later that evening, where Cato had proceeded to de-peg her for the duration of the night. Gone were those halcyon first forays. These days he was quick to ridicule, to dismiss her with a lash of the tongue or a snort of derision.

Was that why he hadn't proposed? Because he had simply fallen out of…

She couldn't bear to think it.

'To hell with Jonty,' he growled. Not normally one to admit defeat, he peevishly zipped his fly. 'The man's a joke.'

Was that it? Was Cato green about Jonty?

'You're jealous!' she crowed triumphantly.

'Of what? That beach ball you had sex with?'

'You're threatened.'

'I'm never threatened.'

'You can't stand sharing me.'

'I wouldn't mind sharing you,' he reached for room service and browsed for Eggs Florentine, 'with a big-titted brunette. But we've talked about that, haven't we?'

She balled her fists. 'Can't you take *anything* I say seriously?'

'Not when you get hysterical.'

'I am not hysterical!'

Cato snapped the menu shut so sharply she jumped.

'I am not in the mood, Susanna,' he warned. 'All I want is supper, a shit and at least twenty minutes of seri-ously filthy sex. If you must know I don't care a bit about whom you might or might not have dropped your knick-ers for before we became acquainted. All I'm concerned about right now is getting out of this dump as quickly as is humanly possible. The sooner the senile old goat gets whatever gibberish this is off his catarrhous chest, the sooner I can go home. I'm ordering for both of us.'

Sulkily Susanna plumped the pillows and rested against them, listening with her arms folded as Cato barked directions into the phone. His spinach was to be underdone and thoroughly drained, his yokes the colour of pumpkin, not apricot, and his muffin to be toasted golden but not brown, with both halves cut the same width.

'What's the betting Charles is staying with the gypos,' Cato mused once he'd hung up. 'He always was the pliable one.'

'Pity him if he is.' Susanna had a sneaking recollection of her post-party come-on and withered inside. Much of the night was a pickled blur but inconveniently Charles' rejection remained, an itch beneath the skin.

He'd said *no*? Why? Whatever was wrong with her?

And more to the point, when had she become so damn insecure? It wasn't just the absent engagement; it was her lover's flash acceleration into the fast lane. Cato's career was soaring from strength to strength—he had been tipped to star in titan Stanley Gooch's new venture— while her own had slowed to an almost stop. In the early days it had been the other way round. *She* had been in the coveted position: directors lunched her, producers craved her; gossip columns were rife with rumours of a new relationship, a sensational diet or a sought-after wardrobe.

Was she too old? Was the chick-flick dead? Was she dead with it?

She blinked her way into Cato's monologue.

'"Why can't you be more like Charles?"' His lips twisted into mimicry, his face distorted. '"Why can't you be more sensitive, more thoughtful, more perceptive, *more like bloody Charles*?"' Well, look how far sensitivity's got him. To get ahead in this world you've got to be brutal! If Father could see me now he'd take it all back, he'd be eating his words. He'd tell us this trip was a waste of bloody time. He'd say Charles was a fool for chasing it. He'd be on *my* side.'

Susanna watched him. 'Are you thinking about the letter?'

'Absolutely not,' he barked. 'Why would I be?'

'I don't know.'

In truth *she* was thinking about the letter—she had hardly stopped thinking about it since they had set off from Usherwood. Was it another inheritance for Cato, another property, perhaps—this one a castle, or a mansion abroad?

He sighed deeply, pinched the bridge of his nose and lay down next to her.

'Let's not argue, Mole, hmm?' Slowly he began to stroke the inside of her leg.

She saw he was hard through his jeans. Was it the promise of sex, or the anticipation of the Eggs Florentine? Cato really did like Eggs Florentine.

'Do you love me, Cato?'

'Don't be ridiculous.'

'Do you?'

'I adore you.'

'That's not the same thing.'

I don't care a bit about whom you might have dropped your knickers for...

Why *didn't* he care? *She* certainly would if he had knocked up someone six years ago and one day presented her with a child to whom he was eternally indebted. The thought sent her frigid with envy. If another woman so much as *looked* at Cato in a way she didn't like, Susanna would have no hesitation in wringing her neck.

'Yes, then,' he conceded.

'Say it.'

'What?'

'Say you love me.'

He sighed. 'I love you. There. Satisfied?'

She thawed, slightly. His hand slipped into her gown, tracing the outline of her breast, and then gave her nipple a sharp, unexpected pinch. She gasped.

'You do know I'm going to be forced to tell you off,' he breathed, 'don't you?' A chain of kisses was planted very, very delicately across her neck. She was fully melted now, spilling to meet his touch. 'Making me listen to every shade of nonsense when all we ought to be doing is fucking each other senseless.'

The cord on her gown was released with a sharp tug. Cato's fingers trailed down her chest, her stomach, across her carefully tended strip of honey-coloured bush, and plunged into the wetness between her legs.

'Oh, Cato…' she moaned.

'Open up, little piggy,' he growled, 'there's a wolf at your door.'

CHAPTER TWENTY-FOUR

OLIVIA WOKE TO the sound of church bells. At first the faraway peal was part of a strange and troubling dream. In it she was at sea, floating on her back, the sun bathing her face, when a distant alarm rang out from the beach. *You have to go back in now*, a voice insisted. *Go back in or it'll be too late.* She tried to swim, only to find her legs were useless, dead as driftwood, and with every thrash she sank deeper. Air was running out, salt filling her lungs. Churning waves tossed her on their surface. Panic devoured her. She became aware of somebody else in the water with her, an arm locked around her waist, and she fought to go alone but he held her back. Words against her hair were both threatening and kind. She couldn't work out who was speaking; they came from everybody all at once: Addy, Charlie, Cato, her father...

Don't struggle, I've got you, I've got you...

She drifted into consciousness and blearily checked the time. Eight o'clock. Her cabin was bright and the

sheets were hot. A dog-shaped imprint was at the foot
of the bed, the dent of a body that had kept her company
for most of the night. Olivia stretched and yawned, dangling her legs out of bed, her feet not quite touching the
floor as she wound her ankles and twitched her toes.
She peeled back the porthole curtain to reveal a gently
tipping line of green.

Breakfast aromas soaked through the door, left ajar
by her bedfellow when he had been summoned for his
walk. She could hear Decca in the kitchen, the pop of
the toaster and the scrape of a knife, and the muffled
hum of a radio programme.

In the bathroom she took a short, sharp, freezing cold
shower, and brushed her teeth. She dressed in jeans and
padded through to the galley.

'How did you sleep?' Decca asked, stirring sugar into
coffee and holding it out. She was in a sweeping robe
with gold stitching, her hair in a Mrs Pepperpot bun.

Olivia took the mug, inhaling the nutty aroma.
'Deeply.' She smiled sleepily. 'The journey took it out
of me; I was out like a light.'

'That's good. Barney didn't wake you? The cough
gets so much worse at night; the hours just go on and
on… Toast?'

'Please. How is he?'

'Better. I've made him go outside for breakfast.'

'Is Charlie with him?'

'No, he was up before either of us. He'll have taken
the dogs out, there are some brilliant routes round here.
Bess'll be having a field day.'

Olivia unscrewed the jam. 'When's Cato coming over?'

'Tonight.' Decca nodded firmly. 'Barney will spend the day getting his strength up, and he'll speak to them tonight.'

'Charlie's been through a lot. I know it isn't any of my business, but—'

'Oh, I'd say it was. Or that Charlie would like it to be.'

Olivia's toast all of a sudden became terribly interesting.

'You don't get to my age without developing an instinct for these things.' Decca gestured outside. 'Go on, then, aren't you going to join him?'

'He's back?'

Decca raised an elegant eyebrow. 'Not Charlie.' She smiled. 'His uncle.'

Outside, the sun was warming up nicely. Yesterday's rain had infused the air with a ripe, lush scent that reminded Olivia of wet woody walks back at Lustell Cove; those bright green ferns that burst by the path, fronds pricked with quivering beads and the reassuring squelch of mud beneath her boots. In the daylight she saw that *Hedge Betty* was part of a floating street, houseboats lined up on the water, merrily enjoying each other's companionship; some detached like Barnaby and Decca's, others connected by ropes and walkways. The river was spinach-dark, lapping against the flanks and slopping in the spaces between, its verges overgrown and wild.

Thick vegetation offered privacy from the road and a trail threaded up to the town.

It was with apprehension that Olivia made her way to the front of the boat. Barnaby was seated, a gentleman in his sixties with his back to her, his head tipped to catch the rays. She didn't know what to expect, how far the illness had ravaged him.

'Who's there?' he asked, without turning round. There was a blanket over his knees. He had a gentle, unpolished voice, mellow with East Anglian burr.

She touched his shoulder. 'Barnaby? I'm Olivia. Charlie's friend.'

He reached to clasp her hand, his grip warm, and she stepped round so he could see her properly. 'Come,' he urged, 'sit down. Sit with me.'

As it happened, the signs of Barnaby's illness—the hollows at his brow and cheekbones, the bluish bruises beneath his eyes—were easily ignored when on the receiving end of such a peculiarly penetrating gaze. Like his nephews, Barnaby's regard was soot-black, severe, as if compelled to disclose a matter of the gravest urgency, which, in this case, she supposed he was.

'You're kind to come with him.' Where Barnaby's stare differed from Charlie's was in its inclusiveness, its willingness to connect.

'Susanna invited me,' she clarified. 'For her son. You met her yesterday?'

Barnaby coughed savagely. 'I knew Cato would sooner or later attract the limelight.' He caught his breath. 'And that sort of woman with it. Charles is different. He's his mother's son. Has he talked about me? Have either of them?'

She searched for something to give him.

'He remembers you. Charlie remembers you coming to the house.'

'It was another lifetime.'

'And he remembers when you went away.'

He faced her. His eyes were alight. 'What I wouldn't give to go back and change things… But then there's the question: *what* would you change? What would you do differently? I've turned this over for more than twenty years and I still don't know the answer. I was who I was back then; so was Beatrice, so was Richmond. Denying what happened is the same as denying ourselves.'

She watched his fingers dance on the fringe of the blanket.

'I'm sorry about your sister,' Olivia said at last. He took a long time answering and she wasn't sure he'd heard, before: 'The words don't exist. I've tried to find them and I can't, even now. Some things defy language. We hadn't been in touch since '92. To know she died without our ever having spoken again…' Gruffly he cleared his throat. 'There's nothing to say, nothing to make it better. I was angry when I left. We fought. I told Bea to stand up for herself and to stand up to him. She told me I didn't understand; I wasn't the one…*dealing* with it.' A beat. 'So stupid to argue, when all I should have told her was that I loved her. That was all that mattered, all that ever mattered; the rest was a waste of breath. When it's over, is there anything else?'

A dragonfly landed on the table between them, gauzy wings trembling.

'It's silly,' Barnaby meditated, 'but I look for her everywhere—in fellows like him, in whinchats singing at the window, in the sighing sea, on days when the wind whistles through the boat and I think I can hear her, clear as a bell, right there next to me.' The dragonfly sailed off. 'There's a great trauma to never having a body to bury. It's a gap between what everyone tells you must have happened—what *has* happened—and what you accept to be true. Gone, just like that, and never coming back. How can I believe it? How can I, when the last time I saw her was on the lawn at Usherwood, holding her boys, protecting them and loving them? She isn't at the bottom of the ocean, cold and lonely...she's there. She's at home.'

'Did you go to the funeral?'

'I thought about it. Decca told me I should. Richmond's clan was out in force, and admittedly I was a coward. I couldn't face it. They knew how he felt about me and I couldn't stand Beatrice's memory being tarnished by a hurtful and avoidable squabble. I held my own farewell; I said my own things. That's the only good to come of being lost—no one had ownership of her, in the end— not then and never again. Really, it's what she always wanted. She's nowhere. She's everywhere.'

They sat in silence.

'My dad died,' Olivia offered. 'I was six, so I didn't really get it. Just that he was there one day and then he wasn't. There are things I wish I could have asked him.

I wish I knew the sound of his voice. I wish I had known him as an adult. I wish my mum hadn't had to do it by herself. He's at sea—he was a sailor, so it was right. We took a boat and poured him back in, that was how Mum described it, as if we'd only been borrowing him and he had really belonged there all along.' She brought to mind that glittering spring day. 'The powder felt so loose between my fingers, so light. It didn't make sense that that was *him*. My dad. The hand I'd held. The cheek I'd kissed. The shoulders I'd climbed on when he was try- ing to read his book, and I knew if I kept on he'd tickle me till I cried laughing.' She frowned. 'I don't remember anything else. But that was enough. That was life right there: hard to hold on to, running down till it's gone. It isn't silly to look out for her. When the sun shines on the ocean, whichever ocean, wherever, I smile back. It's as if we're smiling at each other.'

It was Barnaby's turn to smile. 'Charles is lucky to have a friend like you.'

'He needs friends. People he can trust.'

'That he will.' Barnaby was grave. 'That he will.'

CHAPTER TWENTY-FIVE

THEY ARRIVED IN Blakeney mid-morning, having arranged to rendezvous with Cato and Susanna on the sea front in order to, in Cato's words, 'deposit the cargo'. Barnaby and Decca had elected to stay behind.

In spite of Susanna's attempts to remain incognito—or perhaps because of them—she was instantly recognisable as she emerged from Cato's four-by-four, a scarf wrapped round her head and a pair of enormous dark glasses obscuring her face. Thorn clambered out of the back. When he spotted Olivia he came dashing over.

'We went pony trapping!'

She crouched to his level. 'You did?'

'The *Pony Trap Inn*,' corrected Susanna, bringing up the rear, as ever sapping joy from proceedings with vampiric precision. 'It was hideous.'

'Can I see ponies today?'

'You might,' said Olivia. 'Shall we look for crabs first?' All along the harbour children were crouched with buckets, weed-entangled nets dragging through the water and dripping brine when they were brought up and emptied. Shells scraped in plastic tubs as the crustaceans slipped and skated over each other. The sun beat down.

'I'm relieved *you* can think of something to do with him.' Susanna removed her shades and scoped her surroundings for prying eyes (a touch hopefully, Olivia thought). 'I'm shattered. Who knew looking after children could be so tiring?'

Cato joined them. He wore a coral neckerchief tied above a Breton T-shirt. On anyone else it would have looked ludicrous, but Cato managed to carry it off. Several people glanced their way, passers-by slowing to confirm their suspicions, a procession of nervous smiles and star-struck teenagers, all of which he seemed oblivious to.

'Greetings from the arsehole of England!' he announced.

Charlie put the dogs in the shade. 'Morning to you, too.'

Cato scowled.

'Miraculously I've located a hotel with adequate spa facilities, if their website is anything to go by,' Susanna chirruped. 'I'll be staying overnight. Cato, darling, you're sure you won't come? There can't be a great deal to do around here.'

He leered at Olivia. 'I'm sure I'll think of something.'

Gingerly Susanna patted Thorn's head. Thorn flung his arms round her neck and kissed her, and before she could stop it a short, delighted laugh flew out of her throat. Briskly she composed herself. 'Be a good boy now.'

'There's a first time for everything,' Cato murmured devilishly.

Susanna tottered off across the car park.

'He's still alive, then,' Cato tossed in his brother's direction, 'the runaway OAP? Didn't choke on his big reveal in the night?'

'Don't joke.'

'You can't imagine this is about anything remotely important?' Cato scoffed. In his voice Olivia detected the slightest ripple of genuine query. 'He just wants to clear his conscience before he carks it.'

'About what?'

Cato curled his lip. 'Pissing off Daddy Lomax? Wrecking Mummy's final years? Never sending Christmas cards? How should I know? I don't care.'

'You never do.'

'Come on.' Olivia took Thorn's hand. She had spotted a shack selling nets and steered him away: the poor child had enough sniping adults to deal with without two more. They perused the shelves and paid for what they needed, including a stick of rock for Thorn's friend Tudor (seriously, where did these people come from?) and a knobbly beaded periwinkle for him, which he had become taken with after Olivia showed him how to put his ear to the lip of the shell and listen for the ocean.

By the time they came back, Cato had gone.

'Look what we found!' Thorn held the shell up. 'Can you hear it?'

Charlie listened. 'Is it really in there?' he asked, shaking it as if he expected the water to come rushing out one end. Olivia smiled.

Thorn bounced up and down excitedly. 'It is! It is!'

They arranged to meet in an hour. Olivia and Thorn found a space on the harbour and began setting up their tackle, and she spotted Charlie's figure out on the salt marshes, the low, foraging shapes of Sigmund and Comet trotting behind. The Blakeney wetlands were golden and green beneath a vast, bright blue sky, across which an armada of gossamer clouds sailed to a vanishing point. Bursts of purple sea lavender flecked the wild grasses and a colourfully painted rowboat was lodged in the mud. Silver tributaries threaded through the fens. A tern screeched overhead.

Thorn was hanging off her arm.

'Are we ready?' He scuffed the brink of the wall with his shoe.

Olivia crouched, showing him how to tie his ropes and attach the bait, and filling up their bucket so the crabs didn't dry out. Gradually they lowered the line into the water. She had demonstrated this to Addy, one long-ago summer when they had been out on the water. It was a miracle she had been able to explain so much of it, given she'd spent the entire time staring at his mouth and wondering how to kiss it.

'Be patient,' she told Thorn when he begged to draw it out and peek, his fat legs knocking impatiently against the sea wall. 'Perseverance is half the battle.'

Her phone beeped. She dug it out of her pocket.

'Who is it?' Thorn waggled the line.

She subdued his hand in her palm. 'Keep still.'

Thought I'd come rescue you. Where you staying? A x

She read the message, and read it again. A knot of anxiety tightened in her belly. Addy was here? The mobile cheeped a second time.

Text me your address xxx

Olivia folded it back into her jeans. She pretended to focus on the task but could only replay Beth's accusation: *All you care about is Addy...*

Until just now, she hadn't been thinking about Addy at all. It was the first time in years she could honestly say that. Now, instead of filling her with pleasure, his promised arrival nagged at her as insistently as Thorn's grip on the crabbing net.

She didn't understand where she stood with him.

Was Beth right, or did he return her feelings? She'd done what he'd asked; she'd introduced him to Cato. She owed him nothing more. Surely, then, if he were getting in touch, it was for the right reasons?

She elected not to reply. Coming to Norfolk was about getting away and clearing her head for a few days. Seeing Addy would put her right back at square one.

'It's boring waiting,' complained Thorn.

Olivia looked out on the marshes, searched for Charlie's figure but couldn't find it. Next to her, a toddler with no pants on dropped a cornet of ice cream and burst into tears. 'Sure is,' she agreed, 'but sometimes the longer you wait, the sweeter it is.'

'Do the crabs taste sweet?'

'They taste like the sea, and lemons.'

'Is that because they eat lemons?'

'No, silly, that's what they get cooked in. If you like.'

'Are we cooking them?'

'We can, if we catch any.'

'Is it ready?' He jiggled the line. 'Can we bring it up?'

'OK, but lift it out very, very slowly.' Olivia helped him guide the net to the surface. Three deep-pink shields groped in the mesh, claws tweezering.

'See!' She put her arm round him. 'I knew you'd be a natural.'

After lunch they headed into Cley. It was a sweltering walk, the road shivering with heat, and Olivia distracted him by picking out flowers from the hedgerows and telling him their names. She piggybacked him part of the way, the bucket of crabs dangling from his tightly clenched fist and having to be consulted every few seconds as if its contents might have leapt free and side-shimmied back to the water.

Thorn wrapped his arms tight around her shoulders. The contact stung. When they stopped she checked her back and saw it was sunburned.

Olivia found a deli and picked out parsley, white wine, lemon and flour-caked bloomers with crusts thick as handbag straps. She bought Thorn an ice-lolly and they

had just emerged when a familiar mud-splashed Land
Rover screeched to a halt on the opposite side of the
road, mounting the kerb in the process.

A messy dark head appeared through the window.

'Where have you been? Bloody hell, I thought something had happened!'

She held Thorn's arm to cross. When they got to the
car he volunteered the lolly and crabs to Charlie as if
this answered the question.

'We waited past the hour,' she said affably, 'and we
have to get home or our spoils might escape.' Her grin
withered in the heat of his glare. 'Sorry.'

'I thought I'd lost you.'

'You didn't.'

His gaze was blazing. 'You're burned.'

'I know. It's fine.'

Charlie crunched the gears and reversed into a parking
space. When he emerged it was with two damp dogs and
a bottle of cream. Olivia applied it to her shoulders but
couldn't reach the back, and Charlie turned her round
so he could do it. He felt massive behind her. His fingers were coarse on her skin, not slender like an artist's,
or long like a pianist's, or adept in rolling reefers like
Addy's, but rough and solid and dexterous, fingers for
doing things. She was acutely aware of his proximity, her
senses heightened. She could detect that musky, earthy,
Usherwood scent, and feel his breath on her neck. The
lotion was cool, smelling of coconut and holidays on
Greek islands. His hands were firm on her skin; thumb
to thumb they covered her back, the tips snaking down

to her waist and she couldn't tell if he was doing this on purpose, making her feel like this, taking his time and knowing she was imagining what it would be like to stand stripped in front of Charlie Lomax, what would happen if his grip were to move round her body, beneath her arms and down her stomach...

Sigmund was sniffing for the final piece of Thorn's cherry ice. The boy lifted it from reach, giggling, and eager at the game Sigmund filched it from his hand, hunkering down to guzzle it, remnants of pink dripping on to the boiling tarmac. Thorn stared after it, bewildered, the naked stick in his hand.

The moment was broken. Olivia straightened, embarrassed.

On the high street they passed a cluster of tearooms, charming stone cottages with welcome boards outside advertising scones and raspberries and clotted cream. Tourists milled in floppy hats and shorts, pints of amber warming in the sun or the cool crack of ice in a glass of cola. A handsome windmill reminded Olivia of one she had stayed in at Hindringham, a thimble-neat tower with a boat-style cap, a fissured white petticoat and fantail sails that faced into the wind. She and her friends had spent the week sunbathing and drinking cheap wine, lying outside with their books and listening to old tunes on the woolly radio Beth had remembered to bring.

'What are they looking at?'

Thorn pointed to a bunch of sixteen-year-olds loitering excitedly at the entrance to a pottery shop. They were holding their phones to the window and kept rushing off to giggle with each other at the results.

'I bet I can guess,' said Charlie wryly.

Sure enough, as they approached, Cato's unmistake-able silhouette came into view. He was leaning against the shop counter, deep in conversation with a pretty blonde with Bambi eyes. With the tinkle of the shop bell he turned.

'Here comes the cavalry.' Cato winked at the girl. 'The kid's not mine.'

'No,' agreed Charlie, 'he's his girlfriend's.'

The assistant looked disappointed at the interruption, but naïve enough not to mind if Cato was attached or not. 'Can I help you?' she squeaked.

Olivia browsed the shelves. The ceramics were pleas-ingly sturdy to hold, a stout and squat assortment of mugs and egg cups, jugs and vases, with roughened clay bottoms engraved by their artist's initials.

'I've come to collect my brother.'

'You're brothers?' the girl enthused.

'Wouldn't know it, would you?' Cato removed his Marc Jacobs sunglasses and began polishing them. 'Someone had to draw the short straw, I dare say.'

Her eyes fell on a large grey-green plate, paint swirled and churning, flecked with white, like the surface of a roiling sea. Olivia lifted it, held tight to the edges and peered in, as if she were looking through a window. All at once it was as if she had dived straight in. She thought of the conversation she'd had with Barnaby that morning, how she had told him about her dad and the day they had

given him back to the ocean. Nothing could have captured so accurately the glitter on the water, the lifting,
invigorating spray, the warmth of sunshine, as this did.

She missed Lustell Cove. She missed her mum. She
missed Beth.

'Why are you sad?' Thorn asked, his hand sticky on
her T-shirt.

'I'm not.' She put it back. 'It makes me think of something, that's all.'

'What?'

She nudged him. 'You ask too many questions.'

The shop girl spoke. 'Sorry,' she wheedled, 'but do
you mind not touching?'

All three of them were staring at her. Charlie was
frowning.

'I do,' said Cato shamelessly, returning his attentions
to the assistant's sheer white shirt, whose top two but-
tons were undone. 'Especially if I take you to dinner, I
shall want to touch you so much I shan't be able to enjoy
my food.' He indulged in a long, syrupy pause. 'And I
like to eat *whatever* is put in front of me.'

The girl blushed. She couldn't have been more than
seventeen.

'I meant the ceramics…' she demurred feebly.

'Let's go,' said Charlie. 'Barnaby and Decca are waiting.'

Cato groaned. He lifted the girl's hand and kissed it,
like a prince in a fairy tale. 'I'm sorry, Miss Muffet, but
duty compels me to pass up your tuffet.'

'What's a tuffet?' asked Thorn.

'Ask your mother,' said Olivia.

Outside, Cato spent at least twenty minutes signing autographs. She sat on a shallow wall, looking out to the broads. She felt a blaze at her back, as if someone's eyes were trained there. It could have been the sunburn.

CHAPTER TWENTY-SIX

SEVERAL THINGS ABOUT Barnaby made sense. His uncle's frame as he sat in the armchair; the set of his mouth, straight teeth and a full lower lip; his keen, inquisitive gaze past which nothing went unnoticed. Memory was a cheat. Charlie didn't know if these were traits he recognised, or simply parts of his mother that he longed to see again.

Cato flopped down on the sofa. He rested an ankle on his knee and folded his arms behind his head. He looked like a tripper on the deck of a cruise ship.

Charlie was grateful for his brother's nonchalance. Despite the lost years, the brawls and the trickery, on some younger-sibling level he still believed Cato to know best. If Cato wasn't worried, why should he be?

Barnaby motioned for him to sit.

'There's no easy way for me to do this,' he opened.

'Just get on with it, then,' snapped Cato impatiently.

'Spit it out, for heaven's sake, man; before we all die of old age.'

'There's a reason why I haven't. I've prepared this story a thousand times and there's no avoiding it: the end is a blow and it's going to strike hard.'

Cato glanced exasperatedly to the ceiling. A muscle twitched in his temple.

'All I ask if that you listen very carefully.'

Their uncle closed his eyes. He was totally still.

'What I'm about to say,' he began, 'will change your lives for ever.'

'I was ten years old when your mother came along. All that time of being an only child, you'd think I might have been jealous. I wasn't. Our parents were absent for long spells of time: Father had a factory in Ridgeway, just round the corner from where we are now, and worked all hours God sent, while Ma kept busy spending what little he took home on fancy coats and shoes. Rarely would she stay to look after me, help me with my homework or cook my tea. Mothering was dull. She was a spiteful, selfish woman—it's taken me years to admit that, but there it is.

'My childhood was passed largely with my grandparents. The adult world was everywhere. Everybody was older and everybody was wiser. I was bottom of the pecking order, always needing to behave, to mind my Ps and Qs, before finally a new person came along who I could look after. Your mother wasn't planned and my own ma took it hard. Finances were tight and the last thing they needed was another mouth to feed. I remember thinking that if Ma didn't have a wardrobe full of furs then perhaps the baby wouldn't matter so much, but, as was habit, I kept my mouth shut.

'From the get-go I was protective of your mother, though the word doesn't do it justice. I'd have run to the ends of the earth for Beatrice. I'd have done anything for her. Our ma's disinterest meant I was responsible, in many ways, for bringing her up—she was a bright and lively child, full of laughter. I took care of her and I loved her.

'By the time she was eight, the family situation changed. Father's factory had boomed and we were one of the wealthiest households in the area. Ma was rarely with us, lunching with friends or perusing shop windows, and, as for me, I was eighteen and being groomed to take over the business. Everything seemed settled.

'Whenever you feel that way in life, it's prudent to brace yourself. One day Father came home and told us that he planned to send Beatrice away to boarding school. He had worked long and hard to come into his fortune, and now he wanted the best education money could buy. She didn't want to go, of course; she cried and cried and locked herself in her room, and Father and I fought viciously over it. We both believed we knew what was best for her and that the other was wrong. He told me it was no concern of mine; I told him he had made it my concern when he and Ma had washed their hands of us. He hit me and I hit him back. It wasn't my place to behave like that, but I was passionate and I wanted to fight for what I believed to be right.

'After that, there was no place for me at the house. Father demanded I leave and in the same blow hired my replacement at the factory. I moved out, sleeping at friends', sometimes on the streets. It was a difficult time.

'In a sense it was a relief when Beatrice went away to school, because then at last I could visit her—I hadn't been allowed back to the house in months. She seemed happy in her new life. She told me who her friends were, and which teachers she liked and which ones were beyond the pale. She was clever and now she was meeting her potential. I saw I'd been selfish to demand what I had of my father.

'As we grew older, the importance of our age gap diminished. Our lives, however, matured in different directions—if you can attribute the word "direction" to mine. Beatrice left school and won a place at Cambridge. I was travelling, through Europe, Asia, America, meeting women and finding work in fits and starts, and never home for more than a couple of months at a time, but I sent postcards and we wrote to each other when we could. If I ever had a problem, my first call was always to your mother—the same for her. We had wound up so unalike, and yet so much the same.

'On one occasion I returned, Ma made contact for the first time in years. *There's someone Beatrice wants us to meet.* She told me an hour and a place. *Have a shave*, she instructed. *Wear something reasonable.*

'When I arrived at the restaurant I could tell this was

no ordinary lunch. Ma was done up in her finery and fidgeting with a napkin, her eyes darting to the door. Father was stiff: we shook hands as if we were strangers. Only Bea greeted me warmly, squeezing my hand to let me know she was glad I had come.

'As soon as Richmond Lomax walked into The Coachman's Arms, I could smell the money. He was there before I turned. Perhaps it was that scent of fortune, perhaps it was Ma stumbling up from the table, flattering him and garbling her introductions, perhaps it was Beatrice who stood to receive his chaste kiss, perhaps it was my father who was dwarfed in the mighty eclipse of this prosperous gentleman.

'As for Richmond and me, we encountered one another as you might expect: he was my age, my height; we could have stepped into each other's shoes. He was as dark as your mother but with a cruelty about his mouth, the canines sharp, and a heavy brow that brought his looks just short of being polished. He wore a suit of the sort I had only seen in museums. He was tall, muscular around the shoulders and his eyes were black, like a Transylvanian prince who lives in a castle in the forest.

'The impression, it turned out, wasn't far from the truth. Richmond Lomax was a viscount, heir to a great property in the West Country and, he informed us starkly, seeking a wife to share it with. I'll never forget Beatrice's deference, so unlike the Bea I knew. She'd looked straight down into her soup. The Beatrice I had grown up with could look anyone in the eye. This man, this strange, exotic man with his jewellery and the oil in his hair, stifled her.

'From the start I was never Richmond's favourite person. *What do you do, old bean? I hear you're something of a drifter.* Ma had laughed at that. When I explained where I'd travelled, he chewed his pheasant placidly, boring me down, daring me to utter something that would snag just a corner of his interest. He dismissed me because I posed no threat. Nor was I enamoured with him, and less for those reasons as for in some strange paternal way it felt as if I had finally met the person who would take her away from me. Richmond Lomax had the air of a man seldom denied, and I knew then that if he had set his sights on my sister then it was my sister he would have.

'When news of the engagement arrived I was far from ecstatic, but by that time I had a marriage of my own to focus on: to a sweet girl called Daphne. Beatrice wed and moved down to Cornwall—we visited often but Daphne found the house intimidating. We disliked how Richmond holed himself up in the library for the duration of our stay, absent but all the same there, a hulk of latent disapproval. *I feel as if I'm on an island in the middle of the sea*, your mother would joke of Usherwood, making a point of ingratiating herself with the community at Lustell Cove. *I have to have friends or I'll go mad!* Richmond didn't agree. His fortress was enough.

'After two years, Daphne and I parted ways. We had tried for a baby, we had miscarried, and our fondness for each other couldn't stand the distance. She returned to Ipswich and I decided to move closer to your mother. By that time our parents were gone, there was little to stay for, and my skills as a labourer were easily transferrable. I found a cottage close to the cove and set about rebuilding my life.

'As it happened, the timing turned out to be perfect. Your mother had fallen pregnant, and, some months later, Cato arrived. Richmond named you after an uncle of his, who had fought in the Great War. Naturally, he was delighted you were a boy. We all fell in love with you, Beatrice especially. You were the apple of her eye.

'The seasons passed and on every occasion I visited, you had grown into more of a man. As soon as you could stand, you could ride; as soon as you could run, you could race; as soon as you could talk, you could argue. Richmond raised you in his own mould. You were his prized son, his *raison d'être*, his moon and his stars.

'The years rolled forward. Your mother confided they were hoping for a second child, but none came. As time went on I noticed her growing distant. She would drift in and out of conversations. I would catch her staring out of windows, gazing at the same page of her book for minutes on end, stopping mid-sentence as if a new, entirely unrelated thought had just occurred to her. I was worried. Richmond's temper was fierce. But she assured me that everything was well and I had to trust her.

'A little after Cato turned five, the longed-for sibling arrived. Bea's pregnancy had taken us by surprise. She hadn't suspected until late in her term and informed Richmond only a handful of months before the child was due. The boy was named Charles, but this time, Bea struggled. She hadn't been happy and the birth exacerbated things, leaving her ravaged by depression. She was tired all the time, sad and short-tempered. Believe she loved you, Charlie; she just didn't know how to show it.

'I took you off her hands. We put together jigsaws in my cottage, we paddled in the sea, we played with my dogs and I showed you how to stroke them and to keep your fingers away from their ears and eyes, and never to pull their tails. You were so different to your brother: careful and thoughtful, a quiet evaluator. Where Cato was rough and tumble, and would leap head first over a cliff, you would slide a toe over the edge, assess the drop and ponder the descent. You were happier by yourself.

'Richmond struggled to engage with you. He didn't know how to be with a son with whom he had nothing in common, and so left you to your own devices, hoping you would grow into it.

'The marriage strained. Beatrice was deteriorating. Richmond had always snapped at her over the slightest thing—now it was worse than ever. My sister began ignoring my telephone calls; hardly saw the friends she had taken such care to make. Some days I would drop Charlie home and she wouldn't be dressed, the curtains closed, her breakfast untouched on the dresser.

'I begged to know what was making her unhappy—whatever she told me couldn't possibly make a difference. It was Barney and Bea, for ever and always.

'And then, one day, I was granted my wish. We were

outside on the lawn. In faltering bursts, and with a great many tears, she revealed her secret.

'Bea had met a man. When she said his name her body caved, as if it was tension alone that had been holding it up. He was a farmer, and she was in love—madly, deeply, irrevocably in love. She told me she had never loved anybody else in the way she loved him, had never believed that kind of love was in her to possess.

'She confided that as a husband Richmond could be cruel. He would belittle her in front of acquaintances, he would laugh off her opinions and he would strangle her dreams; the years of their union a slow, simmering schedule of oppression. In the bedroom he was cold, they had never connected properly in a physical way, their desire for one another beginning and ending in the manufacture of their children. With this man it was different. He adored her. He respected her. He set her alight. He spoke to her fibre, of all the things she loved that were in her soul. The passion she had uncovered with him was without comparison. It was worth every second.

Worth risking everything? I asked. *Yes,* she replied, *worth risking it all.*

'I had to pledge that I would never tell a soul. She vowed to leave Richmond but she was afraid. If he found out, he would kill her and her lover. Did her farmer love her equally? Yes, and he was a single man. They had made their promises.

'Now I knew about the affair I was looking for it in every private smile, every letter delivered, every outing made, and I protected you boys from it with all my strength. I couldn't bear that you should be wounded by a bitter separation.

'Time marched on and Charles turned five. I'll never forget the night of your birthday. It was November 1992…the night that everything came to a head.

'There had been a party. I found Bea at midnight, locked in the bathroom. She wept that she could not go on. One more day with Richmond would surely kill her.

'She would do the right thing. She would confess all to her husband—tonight.

'And this, my poor Cato, my poor Charles, is where you enter the story, for it was in her confession about the two of you—the one of you, if I am brutal about it—that the truth at last comes free. Such a pitiful creature she was, slumped on the floor with her head in her hands, explaining that the affair had been happening for longer than I knew, longer than she'd told me…and how the farmer she loved had given her more than his adoration… There was more to her tale than what she had confessed.

'Richmond crept up unseen, the sting in the tail. Who knows what might have unfolded if he hadn't overheard, where we would have gone from that point. I shall never know. But there he was, a shadow at the door, and in all my days before or since I have never seen such hollow fury in a man's eyes. His wrath went past the confines of the word—it was debilitating, devastating, obliterating all around it, and yet it was totally, eloquently quiet. The three of us in that room, mute in the sharing of that unalterable knowledge, each of us disbelieving it had come to this.

'I was commanded to leave that very night. Richmond could have gone one of two ways. He could have retreated, maimed beyond healing, and licked his wounds in a faraway hole until life dragged him out by the scruff of the neck—but deep down Beatrice and I knew he was not that kind of man. Instead he took the other road: the road of vengeance. He held his wife and her two sons as ransom. If I ever spoke of this to another person, he promised they would die. If he ever heard a whisper on the wind, a ripple through the trees, he would know that I had leaked it and they would die. If I returned to Usherwood, if I so much as *looked* at Usherwood, they would die. If Beatrice ever saw her lover again, her boys would die. If she ever tried running away, or embarked on a noble gesture of self-sacrifice, her boys would die.

'She was the last person I should have fought but still I fought. I told her she had to act, she couldn't accept it, she couldn't agree to these demands, and it took me twenty years to realise that she had no choice. She did love you, both of you, till the day she died. I know this as clearly as I know my own name.

'How much of Richmond's threat was bluff I cannot say, but it was enough to keep Beatrice in her place for the next eight years. Every word she spoke, he heard. Every breath she took, he monitored. Every tear she cried, he drank. Richmond hired a man to visit her farmer, but word had already reached him and by now he was miles away. Every note that arrived was checked and vetted. Your mother was no longer permitted to answer the phone. Richmond never let her out of his sight. He watched her grow pale and thin, a ghost of her former self. Every attempt I made to see her was denied, every plea to speak to you both rejected.

'She didn't try to get in touch; she saw no point. A couple of letters and then that was it. She lived like this, a prisoner of the house, for almost a decade.

'When the plane went down, I couldn't help but wonder. At first I thought that Richmond might have done it, his final act against a trespass he could never forgive, but then I remembered Bea as a girl, laughing as she flew her kite, and I saw her at the controls, in a reckless instant deciding to put a stop to both their anguish.

'Whether or not she thought of you, that's up to your two hearts to decide. It would have been painful, perhaps it was easier to forget: a sacrifice to set you free.

'What I'm saying, dear boys, is this:

'Richmond only had one son to think of when he hit the waves…

'Because one was a Lomax child, and the other was not.'

CHAPTER TWENTY-SEVEN

CATO WAS FIRST to react. As if through a fog, Charlie watched him leap up. He watched him stagger across the room. He watched his brother's hands as they locked around the old man's neck and he lunged to spit the single word: *'Liar!'*

Shock slowed the world to a treacly roll. Barnaby's eyes bugged, his mouth slashed open. Charlie fought to contain the attack. 'Wait,' he roared. 'Cato, *wait*!'

Cato's chest heaved, saliva pooling at the corners of his mouth.

'Why do you lie?'

'I don't,' their uncle spluttered, 'it's—it's not a lie.'

'Let him go.'

'Which is it, then, old man?' Cato rasped. 'Which one of us is it?'

'Let him go!'

Barnaby's white-knuckled grip loosened on the arms

of chair. His body rattled. 'The affair...' he wheezed, hauling in air like a rock through a window.

'You've said that.' Cato was rabid. 'So which one of us is the mongrel? Which one of us is a useless farmer's son, you evil fucking bastard?'

The crash in Charlie's ears grew louder. His vision was spinning.

It couldn't be true.

And yet he knew that it could. He knew that Barnaby hadn't invented it. He knew their mother had never been an open book, no matter how he'd rearranged it in his mind. Whispers in hushed passages, the click of a key in a lock, silenced conversations, day trips where she would come home late...

History exploded. Everything true turned inside out. He wanted to unpick Barnaby's words, needle by needle until the tree they had come from was bare, but the tree had already been planted and its roots were in the ground.

'Which one?' Cato clutched his uncle's shoulders, shaking him like a rag doll.

Barnaby's face was swollen puce. 'I...can't...I can't breathe...'

'Tell us or I swear to God I'll fucking kill you and I'll do it now.'

'Let him speak.' Charlie's voice spilled out of him automatically, unthinking, as he dragged his brother off. 'You have to let him speak.'

Barnaby's chest lifted and fell, lifted and fell, brittle as a birdcage.

The men stood before him, fervour in Charlie's regard that was strong enough to sink a ship; anger in Cato's that knew no bounds…and terror, terror in both.

He didn't take his eyes off the floor when he said, 'It's you.' He lifted his head. 'It's you…'

Even much later, Charlie couldn't be sure which happened first. Was it the jolt that seemed to overtake his uncle, quick as an electric shock? Was it the hand that flew to Barnaby's chest? Was it the body jerking backwards, arched in its chair as the throes of the seizure took hold? Was it the twisted expression as his eyes came to rest at last, at last, on Charlie; apology and confession in the still, cool chamber of that dimming light? Was it the door slamming open and Decca rushing through, Olivia behind, and a young boy hovering on the threshold with a book in his hands, as if the scene were a mirror to Charlie's own childhood, the onlooker shut out in a mist of misunderstanding—bewildered, frightened, expelled?

Decca flew to Barnaby's side.

'Call an ambulance,' she commanded, 'he's having a heart attack.'

CHAPTER TWENTY-EIGHT

SIRENS SCREAMED THROUGH the night. Olivia clasped
Thorn on her lap as Charlie's Land Rover screeched
in the wake of the vehicle's flashing lights, close to its
rear where moments before his uncle had been fed in
on a stretcher. The knots of his hands were moon-white
on the wheel. His profile was bleached and unmoving.

She tried Susanna once more. It rang and rang.

*'You've reached the voicemail of you-know-who... I'm
busy right now...'*

Tension spilled off him like a force field. His body
was rigid, strung to breaking, as if she could touch him
with a fingertip and he would fall apart like chalk.

'Charlie—'

'Don't.'

She wanted to know what was hurting him.

Something bad. It had to be bad.

Cato had stayed on the boat, reeling about just des-
serts as he crashed across the decking. His hair had

broken from its usual arrangement, giving him a ma-
niacal, psychotic flavour; his usually pale skin was
blotched, and sweat patches gathered at his armpits. In
contrast, Charlie had been stoic. He'd carried his uncle,
he'd helped Decca with the paramedics and he'd climbed
into his car and started the engine.

There had been no question that she would accompany
him. He had opened the passenger door and told her to
get inside and there had been no argument.

Few things in life were bleaker than a hospital corridor. Surgical light bounced off bleach-polished floors
and the plastic seats of chairs. The smell of antisep-
tic was sour. Rubber shoes squeaked as nurses hurried
through swing doors that flapped tiredly in their wake.
Telephones bleated down distant corridors.

Olivia fetched coffee in Styrofoam cups. It was the
colour of a mud puddle, and just as thin. Decca left hers
to go cold. Her eyes were shut, her head cradled in the
heel of one hand. Olivia held the other and it felt freezing and small.

When Susanna arrived to collect Thorn it provided a
welcome excuse to escape. The film star had been interrupted from her spa break and was none too happy about
it, despite having been put abreast of the circumstances.

'What on earth happened?' she had barked over the
phone, when Olivia had finally got through. 'Is Thorn
all right?'

'He's fine.'

'And Cato?'

'Back on the boat.'

'I shall go there first.'

Olivia had gritted her teeth. 'This is no situation for a six-year-old. Thorn doesn't understand what's going on; he must be terrified. You'll make this your priority. We'll see you shortly.' She'd hung up, fired up by the daring of her reproach.

It was a relief nonetheless when she emerged into the car park and spotted the four-by-four wedged diagonally across three spaces, its engine guzzling. Susanna's hair was secured in a white towel emblazoned with the spa's gold crest, as if the call had wrenched her directly from the masseuse's slab. Olivia saw flecks of green kale-mask splashed beneath her eyes and at the corners of her nostrils.

'We drove fast behind an ambulance!' Thorn enthused, clambering up next to her, excited to relay the adventures of the evening.

'Did you really, darling.'

'It was like this!' He imitated the siren screech and Susanna brought her fingers delicately to her temples, as if she were in the throes of an exquisite migraine.

'That's lovely, Thorn.' Her eyes swung to Olivia. 'What's the news?'

'Barnaby's in Intensive Care. It's not looking good. We're waiting to hear. I'll call as soon as there's a development.'

'And Cato?'

'He was in a state when we left.'

'What kind of state? What do you mean? What's the matter with him?'

Olivia searched for the words and found no combination adequate.

'Honestly,' she admitted, 'I don't know. But whatever Barnaby had to reveal, it wasn't pretty.'

Susanna puffed air through her nose like a dragon in a picture book.

'Buckle up, Thorn!' She patted his knee. 'This is a rescue operation.'

The monster car departed with a shriek of tyres, squealing on to the main road and taking the turn back to Stickling. Olivia watched it disappear. On the deserted tarmac, the slow, lonely drum of her heartbeat served as a reminder that this wasn't really her life, playing au pair to a Hollywood A-lister and preventing a couple of aristocrats from strangling each other. She had stumbled across this strange detour by mistake, and in a few weeks the summer would end and it would be over.

She returned inside to where Decca and Charlie were waiting.

'Anything?'

Decca shook her head.

A doctor emerged and strode purposefully towards them. Anxiously the trio stood. Olivia attempted to hazard by the woman's expression some clue as to Barnaby's recovery, but she was inscrutable.

'No change, I'm afraid,' the doctor said kindly. She had a young, clear face. 'We're doing everything we can.'

Charlie asked, 'Is he awake?'

'He's still sleeping. He isn't in pain. I know it's tough, but try not to worry. He's in the best possible hands, I promise.'

'Can I see him?' Decca's voice was thick.

The doctor's pager bleeped. Briskly, she checked it. 'I'll take one of you through. Only for a few minutes, though.'

Decca turned to the others.

'There's no point you staying. Go back to the boat, get some rest.'

'Absolutely not,' said Charlie.

'Please. I wouldn't ask unless I meant it. I'd rather it was just me and Barney.'

'You're sure?'

'Absolutely.'

Olivia watched him pull Decca to him. The embrace wasn't tentative, or uncertain, like it had been when he'd arrived; it was a strong, definite, wholehearted hug, his arms around her, his hand on Decca's neck, his head dipped to her shoulder. She clung to the wool of his jumper.

'We'll be back after midnight,' he promised.

Evidence of Cato's rampage was rife. Books had been ripped off shelves, paintings flung from walls, artifacts trampled as if a tide had washed in, butchering everything in sight. The idea that he had abandoned the boat in this state was inhuman.

With the dogs fed, Olivia and Charlie set about clearing up. The activity enabled them to sidestep the shadows in the corners, busying themselves with the wreckage so they wouldn't have to address its cause.

Afterwards, Sigmund settled at her feet. When there was nothing else to say, she said, 'Do you want to tell me?'

Next to her, Charlie blinked. His eyes were dark as smoke.

Without warning he put his face in his hands. It happened very suddenly and for an embarrassed moment Olivia thought he might be crying. But there was no sound, no movement, just this dark giant of a man with his face in his hands.

He said it so softly at first that she had to ask him to repeat it.

'I don't think I'm my father's son.'

The boat should have tipped, the sky should have opened; the sea should have swallowed them whole. Nothing happened. The words hung between them.

His voice was flat, devoid of emotion. 'My mother had an affair.'

The hands parted and she saw the ragged turmoil he had been keeping in check all night. Brow knitted, irises gleaming. Instinctively she touched his sleeve. Once, when Olivia was ten, a fox had come to her mother's caravan. The season had been harsh and they had put food on the porch. She had crouched, absorbed on the fox as he ate, his shoulders hunched and his eyes brave, and she had longed to stroke him, to bring him inside, to feel his muscle under her fingertips and hold his trembling fur. Her mother had forbidden it: *Once a wild thing, always a wild thing.*

'My uncle knew and that's why he was sent away. My father...' Charlie's voice caught. 'Richmond forbid him to ever visit again.'

Piece by piece, he laid out the jigsaw, recounting it as he had been told. There it was, entire but fractured. Open to interpretation. A mystery to be solved, and Olivia thought of Barnaby, miles away and a world away, the keeper of the secret.

'It could be Cato,' she whispered. 'It doesn't have to be you.'

Charlie released a burst of eerie, humourless laughter.

'Wouldn't it be easier if it was? Cato was staking claim to Usherwood anyway, at least this way the fight's out of my hands.'

She battled through the repercussions, too many, too much, too serious.

'Cato was upset,' she managed. 'Surely he wouldn't have been if he were convinced this was about you. Barnaby didn't confirm it. It could go either way.'

Charlie stood. He went to the window, raking a hand through his hair. His profile was straight, as if it had been cut with a pair of scissors.

'Cato's a Lomax through and through. I'll tell you how I know.'

CHAPTER TWENTY-NINE

'I'M TO PLAY *the mother*?' Susanna belted into her cell phone. Despite the thousands of miles between them, she saw her agent shrink like a weed in the heat. She could picture Jennifer in her polished LA downtown office, coffee steaming, leather squishy, surrounded by works of art that Susanna herself had paid for. 'Are you *kidding* me?'

'This is a great role,' Jennifer encouraged. 'You know we've been trying to find a way in with Howard Brice for years. This is it. They want *you*, darling.'

'And I wanted the part of Janey. Who's that going to, then—an embryo?'

Jennifer named an upcoming actress whose flawless sixteen-year-old dolly face Susanna had seen plastered across the weekend glossies. Her cheeks flared.

'And just how old am I supposed to be?'

'We'd need to age you…slightly.'

'Oh, well that does sound appealing! For God's sake, Jennifer.'

'This is an opportunity to showcase your consider-able talents,' her agent put forward, with just the right marriage of clout and caution. A decade of working with Hollywood's biggest diva had taught her that persuasion was an art above all others. 'Those frothy parts never did you justice, Susanna—now let's show the world what you're really capable of. The role of Linda is a complex, colourful one.'

Susanna couldn't imagine how playing the insipid cookie-baking parent with a total of seventeen lines could possibly be either of those things.

'The name alone makes me think of an eighties perm.'

'If perms are eighties then chick-flicks are nineties.' Jennifer paused to let that one sink in. 'What have I al-ways said? Play *up* the age slide, not down. Young plays old gets an Award; old plays young gets laughed out of the building. You and I both know the industry has a challenging view of you right now, and this way we're preempting criticism. Isn't it time you sunk your teeth into something meatier?'

Cato thundered in from the bathroom. His zipper was undone and his face was like fury. Talk about sinking her teeth into a prime cut. No sooner had they arrived back at the hotel and she had put Thorn to bed, reading him his night-time story and waiting until he drifted to sleep, than Cato had ordered her back to the suite and ravaged her like a madman, flipping her wordlessly over the mattress and pounding the life out of her. He had demanded the Lord Cato routine more brutally than ever, insisting with a hectic desperation that she repeat his title again and again, so many times that the words lost all meaning. Susanna had glimpsed him over her shoulder, rutting grimly, shaped like a trident with his arms flexed and raised, biceps swollen like apples beneath a picnic blanket. He had resembled a Viking, naked and sweat-bathed.

On any other occasion she would have been pleased at this renewal of interest, but not today. He was behaving like a nutter. He'd barely spoken since she collected him from the barge.

Jennifer's question all of a sudden made her feel bloated.

'Fine,' she forced out. 'I'll meet them.'

'Good girl—you won't regret it.'

'That's for me to decide.'

She clicked off the call. Was this what her career had come to, wearing a wrinkle mask and having a head full of talcum powder? Next they would be wedging her into a fat suit, or giving her prosthetic warts. Perhaps she could be famed for it, the chameleon that suffered for her art, pursuing without vanity those characters lesser actresses shied away from, afraid to encounter the raw bones of their craft…

'I have news.'

That was meant to be Susanna's line, yet it came from Cato.

'So do I,' she responded, omitting the finer points of the conversation as she enjoyed instead the simple pleasure of the director's name coming out of her mouth. 'Howard Brice wants me for his new movie. Jennifer and I are meeting in LA two weeks from now. This is my renaissance. I'm heading straight back to the top!'

She inspected her reflection in the mirror for crows' feet.

'Well?' she insisted. 'Aren't you going to say anything?'

He didn't respond. Susanna straightened, peevish as a meerkat.

'Cato?'

'I've more pressing matters on my mind,' he said ominously.

Dutifully she remembered the ravaged patient in his hospital bed and arranged her features into an expression of concern. The skin on her face was terribly taut: if she hadn't been hauled from the peat pulp at the operative moment she might not have been left with the complexion of an overstretched balloon.

'Of course you have, darling.'

'You don't understand.'

'But you said yourself Barnaby was on his last legs…'

'You're not listening.'

She went to him, spreading her fingers across his shoulders. He was tense as scaffolding. It surprised her that he should care so much for an uncle whom just this morning he had been ridiculing, but that was the way with Cato—so much of it was for show. With her he let his guard fall, let her see what he was truly feeling. Susanna loved to uncover these new depths; she savoured opening them and fingering what was inside, like a delicately wrapped box of jewellery.

'I'm listening now,' she told him, resting her chin in the nook of his collar. They would celebrate Howard Brice once the deal was in the bag, and until then she would concentrate on being the perfect fiancée-to-be: supportive, sensitive, altogether wifely. She wondered what Lord Cato would say if she asked him to return the gesture; if she asked him to address her as Lady Susanna during the explosions of her orgasm? If he were to embrace the idea in role-play then he might start getting used to it in real life, like some kind of subliminal sex messaging.

'I need to find out,' he stated darkly.

'Of course—we'll call the hospital.'

She went for the phone but he stopped her.

His face was ashen. 'Not about that.'

'About what, then?'

There was a horribly loaded pause.

'Brace yourself, Mole.'

'It was the first thing he took.' Charlie had his hands in his pockets. The moon peered in at them enquiringly. 'I was four and he was nine. This would have pre-dated Barnaby's leaving, and back then my father and Cato were inseparable.

'On that day—it was a Friday in winter—Richmond took him hunting. Cato was shown how to fire a gun. We kept an arsenal of the things in the old barn, you've seen the racks, row upon row of sleek black barrels; I doubt they were legal. I heard the shots from across the estate, booming claps that ricocheted off trees and hurtled the birds to the sky. My mother was shut in her bedroom. Nobody else was around.

'They came back to Usherwood and blazed through the hall in their tweeds, Cato a copy of our father in his riding cap and sturdy boots. I was at the top of the stairs, peering through the banisters. Even the way Cato talked was the same, and the really weird thing would be when he spoke out against our father, those rare times when he would side with me over some lightweight dispute, and the intonation would be self-scolding, my father telling my father off, so that between them they had me caught in a whirlpool of concentric circles, a Lomax within a Lomax within a Lomax.

'I had my dog with me, a spaniel with a brown and white coat, and a whiskery nose. The week before he'd slipped in a ditch and broken his leg. We'd called out the vet and Peter had been fitted with a splint. He had a limp but he was getting better.

'My father disappeared into his study. Cato was searching for something to do. Over the years he'd been known to break things, hide things, kick things, all on purpose and all for sport. He craved provocation. He craved reaction. He yearned to bait, and, if necessary, to hurt. Now he looked up at me, wearing the expression I've come to know: a thirst for entertainment, a blood-lust borne of boredom.

'Before I could stop him—and in those days I couldn't have with all the warning in the world, because he was twice the size of me—Cato grabbed Peter by the scruff and dragged him down the stairs. *Want me to show you something?* The dog's bad leg went thumping behind him like an afterthought. *Want me to show you what I learned today? You can learn it, too, old bean. I'll teach you.*

'When I started yelling, Cato clamped his hand over my mouth and told me to stop, or he'd fetch the cane from the cellar and beat me with it till I was black and blue. He never did this, though he threatened it a lot.

'Those were the only times I loathed Usherwood. It was too big to be found. Things went unnoticed. There were too many hiding places. Nobody heard and nobody saw.

'Outside, the sky was frozen with drizzle. The lawns were grey, the air like lead. I raced after him but my legs couldn't keep up. I wasn't dressed for the weather and it was bitterly cold. Cato was making for the barn; Peter tugged roughly after him. What got me was the way the animal squeaked in pain each time his bad leg caught, but in between would go to wag his tail—it was pathetic, really, that innate trust that there was nothing to fear from these boys who were his playmates. Only there was.

'When I saw the barn approaching I felt convinced that Cato would back out. He had to. He was a bully, but he wasn't a killer.

'But the more I protested, the more he pushed. If I had walked away, he might have got bored. No audience, no point. But Cato enjoyed my cries. He mocked my pleas. He had embarked on a path unsure of its destination:

my reaction would dictate the outcome. I didn't know this then. All I knew was fear, and utter, utter helplessness. I was unable to reason with him because he could not be reasoned with. None of this could be articulated. I didn't have the words; I just kept saying, *please*, over and over again. Useless. Because the more I begged, the better the game became. Some days I wonder if my life with my brother hasn't been one big wind-up—that everything that's happened to us isn't simply a childish prank that somehow got out of control, and one day a curtain will get lifted and there it all is, how it should be, nothing lost and nothing sacrificed.

'The gunshot chilled me. I'll never forget it. Cato must have misfired because there was a thin, burbling moan before a second was released. Even then it couldn't have been true: I had to see for myself. When I peered round the door, Peter's fur was soaking red. The gun hung from Cato's arm. I screamed.

'Mother came across the lawn in her nightdress and knelt to comfort me—*What's happened*, she kept asking; *tell me what's happened*?

'*I didn't want to see him suffer*, Cato pledged when he came out of the barn, forlorn, traumatised, making like his sacrifice of Peter was humane: he'd been putting the animal out of its misery. Our uncle had shown us to do this, with a baby gull he had found on the beach one day, knotted in seaweed. *You should never leave a creature in pain if you can help it*, he'd said—all Cato was doing was following instruction. Mother dashed to comfort him, kissed him and told him not to worry.

'I remember Cato saying: *I thought it was the right thing*.

'To this day I don't know if my brother has ever done the right thing.'

He stopped. Olivia realised she'd been holding her breath.

'Don't you see?' Charlie finished. 'I'm not like them. I never have been and I never will be. I'm not a Lomax. I'm not.'

She stood, closing the gap between them. His dark eyes met hers. She reached to touch his face. It was hot, and coarse with stubble.

'What am I going to do?'

The glare of his scrutiny burned. Her whole body came alive, electric, and she was submerged by a feeling so massive and new that all she could say was: 'This.'

Slowly she raised her mouth to his. She felt his forehead brush against hers, the spill of his hair, soft and scented like pinecones, before the phone rang.

It was Decca. His uncle's struggle was over.

Susanna clutched the dresser. The floor sprang and bloated like a dish of blancmange.

'This can't be true,' she rasped, chilled with horror. 'It can't!'

'It is,' Cato confirmed grimly.

'But it has to be Charles,' she cried, her voice sliding up several octaves, 'it has to be! He's the younger one, this affair didn't begin until—'

'We don't know when it began.'

'But you were the first-born.' It was as if someone had just been sick all down her. 'Beatrice and Richmond conceived you—they were delighted when you arrived, Barnaby said as much! They struggled for a second baby after that, meanwhile she got in deeper with this farmhand of hers—it's obvious Charles is the love child!'

'Is it?'

'Yes! Cato, you can't possibly imagine…?' It was heinous, monstrous, a joke.

'We have to be sure.'

'We are sure!' Any alternative was criminal. Susanna simply could not entertain it. Cato was Lord of the Manor, with his impeccable British manners and thousand-acre bastion and ancestry solid as a mahogany closet. What was he without the Lomax pedigree—the son of a farmer and a factory worker's daughter?

It was unthinkable!

'I'm not surprised,' she warbled, clutching at possibilities, her words spilling out without thought or consideration, 'not surprised at all. The minute I met Charles I knew he wasn't half the man you are. He's not cut out for our way of life; it's plain to see he hasn't got a shred of refinement in him. If Barnaby had been given five more seconds, he'd have confirmed it clear as day.' She laughed wildly. '*Obviously* Charles is the impostor—oh, it makes such sense now, doesn't it, darling, him sloshing through puddles and getting filthy with those horrible dogs. He's not *like* you!'

Cato was pacing back and forth. 'Slow down, Mole, we must think about this.'

'What is there to think about? *You're* the successor to Usherwood, of course you are! There's nothing else for it.'

'I need answers. I need evidence.'

Oh, how she could throttle that bedridden crone! With the same wicked shock as a bucket of ice being tossed over her head, Susanna thought of her pursed-lipped long-limbed girlfriends back in Beverly Hills, who had always been so envious of her allegiance with a real-life aristocrat… Imagine having to confess Cato's illegitimacy! It couldn't happen. It couldn't and it wouldn't, because all this was nonsense.

He was heir to the Lomax legacy, not Charles.

'We're going back,' said Cato, spurred to action. 'That geriatric started this—and if he can't finish it,' Cato pounded his chest, 'then by God I will.'

CHAPTER THIRTY

THE ROADS WERE EMPTY. Cato bombed along deserted lanes, weaving between black walls of shrubbery as the headlamps swept ghostly beams across the countryside.

When they arrived at *Hedge Betty* the place was shrouded in darkness. Susanna had quietly woken Thorn and left him with the Pony Trap's landlady, explaining that there was something important she had to do but that she'd be back very soon. She couldn't risk bringing him here. Who knew what they were about to uncover? Charles could be storming through the place like a maniac. Decca could have flung herself into the water. Olivia might decide to release the dogs on them. Even under dire circumstances, Thorn's safety occurred to her as a significant thing.

Despite her premonitions, Charlie's Land Rover was nowhere to be seen.

'What the hell are you doing, woman?' Cato hissed as Susanna picked her way over the gangplank. His summons prompted her to slip on a squelch of mulch and flail urgently at the handrail, swinging from it like a monkey on a tree branch.

'What do you think?' she rasped back, righting herself with all the dignity she could muster. 'We're not going to stand out here all night, are we?'

'Shut up and follow me.'

Cato led the way round the side of the boat, where a narrow ridge just wide enough for a single shoe was tacked with knotted ropes. Big white floats shone like molars against the twinkling water. Susanna removed her footwear and tiptoed after him. Passing the galley window she saw that Cato's carnage had been cleared, everything packed and tidied away as it had been when they'd arrived.

'Quiet!' she entreated loudly. 'They're back!'

Cato whirled, exasperated, waving his arms to bat her down. Frantically she pointed into the window, yearning to flee but at the same trapped on an impossible precipice. He rounded the bow, disappeared from sight and seconds later there was a deep, single thud, followed by a disembodied hand waggling at her to approach. Tentatively she skirted round, just in time to see Cato's back-end vanishing through an open hatch. She was alarmed when his voice came back at her full volume: 'All clear, Mole!'

Susanna was attempting to fold herself through the aperture when a series of ferocious growls stopped her in her tracks. Wolves!

'It's me, you stupid mutts.' Cato's scold came drifting

through. There followed a thin whicker, as if the creature making it had been kicked.

As she flopped through she spied the dogs cowering on a blanket in the corner. There was another one with them, a great big ugly thing with fur like wire wool. It released a low rumble in its throat. Its eyes were yellow, like a witch's.

'Is it a hyena?' Susanna fretted, flattening herself against the stove.

'Don't be absurd. It's an idiot dog.'

Cato pushed open one of the cabins. Across the threshold was a boudoir swimming in fabrics and cushions, a tepee-style arrangement hanging from the ceiling and books scattered all over the floor. A joss stick rested in a bed of powdery ash, filling the space with a foreign, unpleasant aroma. He flicked the light.

'Can we find what we're looking for and get out of here?'

'Patience, Mole…'

Cato worked methodically. He opened all the drawers in sequence, top to bottom, left to right, rifling through before closing them, empty-handed but calm. He fumbled for a box on top of the closet, wobbling on a moth-eaten stool to reach it, and when he lifted it down he skimmed logically through papers, bills, statements, boring bureaucracy that, judging by the standard of living, Susanna was surprised existed at all. He crouched to inspect under the bed, dragging out a chest brimming with old photographs, mostly of the couple, hand in hand by the Egyptian pyramids, arms round each other at Machu

Picchu, grinning against a backdrop of the glinting Taj Mahal. Many of them were taken here, on the boat. In one, Decca was reclining in the open air with a glass of wine. In another, Barnaby grinned as he operated a lock.

They were in love, their smiles flaunting happiness. Susanna experienced a stab of bitterness and ground it out before she asked why.

'Do hurry, Cato!'

'What does it look like I'm doing?' He shoved the case back where it came from and scanned the room through narrowed eyes. Finally he tore back the bed covers, lifted the pillows and ripped off their cases, and chucked the whole lot on the floor. 'Damn it!' He stamped on the sheets. 'Damn it to hell!'

Susanna's eyes fell on a hardback novel tucked behind the headboard. A white sheaf of paper was escaping its pages.

Cato snatched it before she could.

'Let me see!' She clambered over the mattress. 'Let me see!'

Cato lifted it high above her head.

'Bingo.' He extracted a crisp envelope and held it up to the light.

It read, in elaborate script: *My darling brother…*

'I can't look,' Susanna choked, squeezing her eyes shut.

Cato sat down. Inside the envelope was a letter. Despite herself Susanna craned to see over his shoulder, her heart thundering against her ribs.

The date was August 1993, a year after his uncle's dismissal.

Beloved Barney,

There is no one else to turn to. God help me but I am trapped in this house. Every day is an eternity and I am so tired; I am tired of pretending for the sake of my boys and I am tired of the heartache. Have you heard word? Has there been news? I should give up asking—I know that he is gone and never coming back. Sometimes I scribble him letters, as I am to you now, and fold them up and keep them with me. Isn't that silly? They are never sent.

Forgive me for not writing in a long time. Richmond watches me as a hawk might a worm and I swear he reads my mind. He knows when I am thinking about the man who gave me my child; he senses when I turn from him at night… He has given up trying to touch me, which is some small mercy.

Never do I stop remembering that evening. If only I hadn't confessed my secret, if only Richmond hadn't been there, if only, if only… The façade would still be mine, and so would Ben. That makes me selfish, I know, but I cannot help it. Nor can I help the fact of Charles' birth; it should never have happened. I was stupid. I should have taken care because now look where we are—trapped in a web of our own making, spinning lies faster than we can tear through them, and Charles can never know where he came from.

A terrible admission, but one that Richmond would concede: Charles will always be the lesser loved.

How can it be different?

Yours affectionately,

Bea x

A slow smile spread across Cato's face. Susanna fell against him.

'That's it, darling!' she rejoiced. 'There it is!'

Cato scanned the note again, starched with age.

'Strange,' he mused, 'that it used to feel like me.'

She was beside herself with relief. 'What did?'

'The lesser loved. Daddy used to compare me with Charles, especially as we got older. And all that time…' He shook his head. 'I must have invented it.'

'You must have. A new brother arriving—'

'A half-blood.'

'I stand corrected. You were five when he came along, it was a wrench to share your parents.' She touched his arm. 'And they *are* your parents, Cato. They *are*. You're a true Lomax, there was never a doubt in my mind!'

Cato tucked the note into his pocket and replaced the hardback.

'The question now,' he exited the room, 'is how to break it to Charles…'

Susanna chased after him. 'What are you going to do?'

In the corridor he scanned the cabins, settling on one whose door was ajar. His half-brother's belongings were at the foot of the bunk.

Half-brother. Well that was a turn up for the books.

'It'd be terrible for the old boy to find this, wouldn't it?' Cato mused, running his nail along the edge of the letter. 'If he were to have it spelled out, just like that, in our mother's own hand,' he imagined it, a wicked gleam in his eye, 'no warning and no time to prepare. Such a brutal discovery that would be…'

'Certainly. Perhaps we ought to ease him into it gently?'

Cato put his head on one side. He considered it.

'Then again,' he laid the paper flat, their mother's writing naked for all to see, 'I wouldn't want to keep it from him longer than was necessary.'

He kissed Susanna hard on the mouth.

'That wouldn't be very brotherly, now, would it?'

CHAPTER THIRTY-ONE

AFTER BARNABY'S DEATH, arrangements were swiftly made. The funeral was scheduled for a week's time and Olivia stayed with Decca on the barge until her family arrived.

It wasn't easy. She could help in the practical ways—cleaning, cooking, accepting the sympathy bouquets that arrived at the door—but beyond that struggled to comfort the woman she had known just a few days. Decca would sit in the window for hours, bundled up in her cardigan and gazing blankly out, the occasional sad smile dimming her features. The discovery of a favourite mug, a song on the radio, a mournful glance from Bess the dog, was enough to trigger a cloudburst of grief. She wouldn't eat. She wouldn't sleep. She wouldn't talk. Olivia tried to be what she needed, but the only person Decca needed was Barnaby, and Barnaby wasn't there.

Neither, for that matter, was Charlie.

Since the night his uncle died he had retreated from

her completely. He was barely around. She'd thought she had reached him, the almost-moment they'd shared enough to compress the distance. Now it was as if it had never happened. He had reverted to the old Charlie, avoiding conversation, never meeting her eye; leaving a room as soon as she stepped in. He took long walks by himself with no indication as to where he was going or when he'd be back. He wouldn't speak of Barnaby, or his mother, or of Usherwood, and he categorically refused to see Cato. He removed himself utterly, reassembling the wall he had in a reckless instant allowed her to glimpse behind. Whatever confidence they had reached, it was gone.

Olivia reminded herself that he was dealing with the biggest uncertainty of his life. She could scarcely imagine how it must feel. The one person who could solve the riddle had taken it to his grave, leaving only a giant question mark where the answer should have been. Charlie's withdrawal wasn't about her, or anything to do with her.

Even so, it hurt.

Cato and Susanna were quick to organise their return trip to Cornwall. The Lomax helicopter arrived in a whirlwind of sound, tearing up the surrounding fields and attracting a flurry of attention from the locals.

Olivia went to see them off. When she arrived Cato was sharing a joke with the pilot, laughing jovially, his hands on his hips, his crisp peach shirt fluid in the breeze and the sleeves pushed up to reveal the wolfish black hair drenching his forearms. She thought such high spirits were inappropriate given the circumstances, not to mention inexplicable. Wasn't he going through the same turmoil as Charlie, wracked with doubt, the story of his life upended on a single shattering evening? She supposed each man must have his private way of dealing with it. Charlie certainly did.

Thorn was going with them, due to be returned to Jonty later that day. Olivia kissed him goodbye and promised to visit once she moved back to London.

Susanna helped him climb aboard. 'Now,' she said, carefully strapping him in, 'if you feel sick this time, you will tell me, won't you?'

The boy was absorbed in the plastic pterodactyl Susanna had bought him during that morning's trip to a local dinosaur museum. 'OK.' He beamed.

'That's my darling.'

'What about Roger?'

She stroked his hair. 'Who's Roger?'

Thorn held up the pterodactyl.

Susanna sighed. 'He'll have to tell me, too.'

Slipping on her shades, she turned to Olivia. Somewhere in that 180-degree movement, Mommy Susanna became Movie Star Susanna and she was back to the super-diva the world knew and didn't really love.

'It seems I didn't need you quite as much as I'd thought,' she said brusquely, easing on a pair of sleek leather gloves. 'Don't worry, you'll still get paid—I just think he's better off with his mother at a time like this, don't you?'

'Absolutely.'

Susanna checked that Cato was still occupied with the pilot.

'It's odd,' she mused, 'but I could get used to this. I never thought I'd say it, but, well…I've become rather attached to the boy.'

Olivia shrugged, and stated the obvious. 'He is your son.'

It came out a bit flippant, not how she'd intended, and she was sure Susanna would pick up on it. She didn't. Instead she considered it for a moment, her head on one side, as if this were an entirely new concept.

'Yes,' she agreed, with a smile. 'I suppose he is.'

On Thursday night the Sennets descended, and she and Charlie moved with the dogs to a nearby B&B. There was a misunderstanding at check-in, and when they arrived they saw it was one room, not two. Charlie returned to sort it out.

He came back moments later. 'They've only got this available,' he said, and put the key in the lock. It jammed. He gave it a hard shove with his shoulder.

Olivia followed him in. The double bed stared back at them accusingly.

'Isn't there anywhere else?' she asked.

'Not prepared to take the dogs.' There was an adjoining porch for Comet and Sigmund, who wagged their tails in approval. 'Besides, it's getting late.'

Charlie began tugging blankets out of a cupboard and casting them down. Immediately the dogs settled. He nudged their tummies with his foot.

'What are you doing?' Olivia sat on the mattress. It was hard, and lumpy.

'Taking the floor.'

'You'll be cold.'

'I'll be fine.'

She wished he would look at her. Why wouldn't he look at her?

'Please talk to me,' she said.

He crouched, straightening the sheet.

'If there's anything...'

'There isn't.'

'But—'

'Please, Olivia, don't. There isn't any point.'

'But you can't just bottle things up.'

'I can do what I want.'

'Everything isn't lost,' she tried. 'We don't have the facts yet, remember?'

'I'm not a Lomax.' He was cold. Empty. Resigned to his fate. 'I'm not and I'll never be. I'm sorry if that's a disappointment to you.'

'Why would it be?'

No reply.

'You can't be sure,' she pressed.

'Yes, I can.'

'But Barnaby said—'

'Barnaby didn't need to say.' He took a pillow from the bed and punched it violently into place. The impact of his fist left a deep penetration. 'Forget it.'

'I can't forget it. You let me into this and I'm not going

to abandon you to sort through it on your own. You might not like that, but tough, there it is.'

'I appreciate your concern but I don't need it. I don't need rescuing. I don't need your help, or anyone's.'

'I don't believe you.'

'That's your problem. Leave it.'

'Why?'

'Because I've asked you to.'

She waited a moment before coming to sit next to him.

His back was to her. Hesitantly she touched his shoulder. He flinched as if he'd been burned, and still he didn't look at her.

'I know it might feel like it,' she said, 'but you're not alone in this.'

Charlie bowed his dark head, turned it slightly. His chin was a shiver from her touch. She could feel the coarse stubble on his jaw and the heat of his skin. There was that profile again, arresting and exciting. As if it had been painted in broad, bold brushstrokes by someone who knew what they were doing.

'Trust me,' she said.

Finally he met her eye. His stare was hot. 'I'm not sure I can.'

She returned it. 'I am.'

There was a knock at the door. Neither of them moved.

'That'll be another room come free,' said Charlie.

'Yes.'

'Which is good.'

'Yes.'

The knock came again. One of the dogs barked.

'I should get it.'

Seconds passed. Her cheeks were blazing and her throat was in her mouth.

But when she opened the door, she saw it wasn't another room come free.

Addy Gold was standing on the porch, his grin wide and his blond hair rippling in the wind. In his arms was an enormous bunch of yellow roses.

'Surprise!' Addy beamed.

Words escaped her. She stumbled to find a response. 'Oh. Hi.'

He was holding out the flowers like the hero in one of Susanna's rom-coms.

'These are for you.' He laughed when she numbly took them. 'Hello? Earth to Olivia? Aren't you pleased to see me?'

Hastily she stepped outside and pulled the door shut. She shoved her brain into gear. 'Yes, yes, I am. It's a shock, that's all.'

'A nice one, though, right?'

'Sure. Of course it is. I just didn't expect you.'

'You didn't get my texts?'

'Well, yes, but…' She'd had so much on her mind that she'd ignored them all. He'd sent one on the night Barnaby died saying he'd arrived, but there had been so many other things going on that she hadn't thought twice about it…

'How did you know where to find me?'

'It's taken long enough,' he joked. With one hand on the door frame and the swathe of honey across his forehead, Addy could just as easily be propping up the counter at the Blue Paradise. Seeing him in this new context was weird. It felt wrong. It wasn't just in Norfolk that he didn't belong—it was here, generally, with her.

'I've been crashing with a mate for a bit,' he mused, 'he's got this party pad down the road. Everyone's wired about Cato being in town and then we heard the old guy bit the dust. A reporter gave me a tip-off about the boat, and the boat gave me here, so…'

'So.'

'So,' he held his arms out, 'here I am!'

'Here you are,' she echoed.

'Aren't you going to invite me in?'

Olivia glanced over her shoulder. Thought of Charlie and made a decision.

'D'you know what?' she said. 'I'm hungry. I think I'd rather go out.'

'Sure.' He seemed pleased. 'Whatever you say.'

The harbour at Stickling was twinkling with restaurants. It was a popular tourist spot, moonlight shimmering on the water from a clear canopy of stars. Couples roamed waterside and the aroma of seafood drifted through the night.

After supper, they strolled to the jetty. Addy took her hand. It didn't feel like the same hand that had held hers all those times before. It didn't feel like the same hand that had touched her at the beach that night, or the same hand she had gazed longingly at since she was eight, wishing and hoping and praying for this day.

'I've missed you,' he murmured, guiding her to a stop under the pagoda.

She had put those words into his mouth so many times. How it would feel to say them back: *I've missed you, too*. But now she was here, now it was happening, they didn't come. She hadn't missed him. For once, she really hadn't.

'I have to tell you something,' Addy said, against a tantalising soundtrack of rippling wavelets and nodding sailboats. 'It's taken me a while to realise, but I can't deny it any longer. Oli, I feel so strongly about you.' He claimed her hands. 'We've been friends all our lives, and I guess I never saw it before, but now it's become so much more. You're different, since you came back from London.'

His blue eyes sparkled in the night. The studio lights were glowing. The script was word-perfect. Her fourteen-year-old self couldn't have written it better.

'You mean since I started working with the Lomaxes?'

He was offended. 'What's that got to do with any-thing?'

She knew. Over the meal, Addy had filled her in. Since the party he'd taken pains to strike up a liaison with Sam Levy's agent, and had wasted no time inform-ing the woman he was 'a close personal friend' of the Lomaxes ('which is only half a white lie because you and me are so tight, Oli'). The connection seemed to have played in his favour, with the woman promising to get in touch with Cato's people to arrange a Kensington lunch. Given that Addy's isolated dialogue with the man himself could hardly be construed as a meaningful relationship, Olivia felt confident he would soon be putting his feelers out for a reunion. He had a matter of days to be upgraded from Sycophantic Wannabe to All-Time Best Buddy, and as far as he was concerned, she was his hot ticket. She had come on holiday with the family. She could open those doors for him. She could put in a good word. It didn't much matter who she was, or what she was about, so long as she could do that.

'When I took the job at Usherwood you were all of a sudden into me.'

'I was into you way before then!'

'Crap. When I first came back to the cove you weren't.'

'I was working up to it!' His expression was injured. 'Thought you weren't interested, didn't I? Moving hundreds of miles away kinda drops a hint…'

She searched his face—for truth, for honesty, for clarity, for what?—and realised then that she was never going to discover it, because this wasn't the face she wanted to be searching, after all. She could spend the rest of her life searching Addy Gold's face and never unearth anything new, anything that enthralled her, anything that had been for such a long time so deeply and determinedly buried that she was the first person to root it out and dust it off and hold it up to the light.

She had been searching Addy Gold's face for fifteen years and she still hadn't found what she was looking for.

It had taken most of her life, but finally she had it figured: Addy was habit. He was what she'd learned to accept. He was all the stuff she used to think she wanted to be, but now realised she didn't. She had known him before she knew herself.

Can't you see him for what he really is?

If anyone had treated Beth the way Addy had treated her, she wouldn't have stood for it for a second. The length of their friendship had always excused his bad behaviour, when in fact it should have been reason enough for the behaviour to stop. Beth had known it, her mum had known it—the two people Olivia cared about most in the world—and she had shut her ears to their counsel because she hadn't wanted to hear it. Infatuation was not the same thing as love. She understood that now.

'Look,' Addy soothed, mistaking her silence for shocked elation, 'the way I see it is: it's fate! I believe in all that stuff, you know? The cosmos and asteroids and shit.' He gazed up at the dome of constellations. 'See up there? That's Oreo's Belt.'

'Orion's Belt.'

'Whatever. I'm spiritual.' He held her shoulders. 'I see beneath the surface of things. It just so happens that our getting together coincides with my deciding what direction my life should go in, right? And why shouldn't it? It's all connected, don't you see? You're part of that, Oli; you're *part* of the direction.'

'Things have changed, Addy. I've changed.'

'If you'd rather I never mentioned the Lomaxes again, I won't. Happy?' He pouted. 'I mean as a girlfriend it *would* be kind of cool if you shared it, and it couldn't exactly do my prospects any *harm*, but none of that matters really because it's you I want. It's you. It's you I want by my side as I take this journey.'

'Not Thomasina?'

'Nah,' he rubbed his nose, 'been there, done that.'

The words that weeks ago would have ripped her to shreds now met her with barely a ripple. She couldn't help the bubble of laughter that escaped her throat.

'What?' He frowned.

'Nothing.'

Addy puffed air out, imploring the sky as if he had mislaid his vocabulary up there. 'The fact is, Oli, I'm putting myself on the line here. All signs point to you.'

'That makes me sound like a cul-de-sac.'

'You're not a cul-de-sac.'

'That's the most romantic thing you've ever said to me.'

She'd meant it as a joke, but probably it was true.

'Be serious for second, would you? Why are you giving me such a hard time?'

'I'm sorry, Addy, I don't mean to. I just don't think you're listening to me.'

'No,' he objected, 'you're not listening to me. I *want* us to be together. Do you hear? I *want* it to be us. I *want* you by my side. You and me, Addy and Oli…'

His features came closer, his lips millimetres from hers.

'I'm crazy about you…'

Abruptly she pulled back, and rested her hands on his chest.

'OK, Addy,' she conceded, and his face brightened,

not surprised because he had known she would come round. She had always been sweet on him, good old reliable Oli who worshipped the ground he walked on.

Stepping from his hold, she said, 'For the first time, shall I tell you what I want?'

CHAPTER THIRTY-TWO

THE FUNERAL TOOK place on a muggy afternoon, in a churchyard overlooking the bluff. Clouds brooded, darkening menacingly over the sea. The sky growled with the onset of a storm. Branches tangled and ivy crept, and a pre-Raphaelite angel rose in prayer, one wing crumbled to dust. A crow came to rest on a crooked headstone, yellow eyes flicking across the mourners as it picked its way along the slab.

Olivia hadn't deemed the couple to be advocates of turgid ceremonies, but the church had been Barnaby's wish. Outside seemed a more apposite goodbye, the fresh air bracing and cold, and as the wooden box was lowered into the ground she heard Decca's sob, a soft, sad song of a sob, her family huddling close. Olivia dipped her head in respect and caught a flash of blue hovering over the grass, its wings like lace.

I look for her everywhere...

She hoped that, wherever Barnaby was, he had found his sister at last.

Charlie was on the fringe of the congregation. Against the creepers he stood still as a tomb, as pallid as if he belonged in one. He was unshaven, his hair wild and unkempt. There was an absence about him, an uncanniness, as if he had been superimposed on to their backdrop and wasn't really there at all.

They retired to the wake for hushed conversation and an unappetising spread of sandwiches and quiche. Olivia looked for Charlie but couldn't find him, and after offering her condolences she headed down to the beach. The path from the road was a crooked arrangement of wooden planks meandering between profuse dark woodlands, arid shrubs and a fence of rickety posts, eventually disappearing into powdery sand. The tide was out, the sea a football pitch away, and Olivia spilled on to a vast stroke of pale beach. Grey sky whipped overhead. The air was raw in her lungs.

Rivulets threaded through the bay, slicing its canvas into waterlogged squares, knotted with lugworm trails and grit-filled shells. The path she had come in on had disappeared, swallowed by murky firs.

She put her hands in her pockets and looked out to sea. A figure stood at the shore, lonely and dwarfed, a fleck of paint on a sprawling landscape.

It took minutes to reach him. When she did he made no acknowledgement, just carried on watching the water as it rolled in on its endless, shapeless tide.

'So I found out,' he said, feeding a hand into his coat

and retrieving a scrap of paper. 'I've known all week. It's me.'

She read it.

'Cato got hold of it,' he continued hollowly. 'He left it on the boat. I picked it up the night Barnaby died… We came back from the hospital and there it was.'

'Bloody hell, Charlie.' She gripped the letter. 'Why didn't you say anything?'

Olivia pictured the question as an epitaph, inscribed on his headstone, fitting for a man who spoke only when there was something worth saying—and even then with the sense that words were futile, pebbles being thrown into a wide bottomless lake, a disturbance on the surface before nothing. Punctuation marks on silence.

'Pretending for a few days more?' he answered. 'I don't know. Now I let it go, it's really happening. I can't believe it's happening.'

Her arms dropped by her sides. 'Neither can I.'

'It doesn't matter. I saw it coming.' His voice skidded before righting itself. 'I'll go away for a while. I can't be there when Cato comes back to live.'

'You can't leave.' She couldn't think of Usherwood without him, of the cove without him. He belonged to Lustell as much as the sea.

'Can't I?' The wind picked up. Finally he gave her his face. 'It's been a fake, hasn't it? All of it. That house was never mine, my father was never mine, and now what do I do? Who do I talk to? Who gives me answers? No one. There's nobody there. Years of devotion, and what it amounts to is a fucking illusion—a waste, a complete and utter fucking waste.'

'You can't think like that—'

'How am I supposed to think? What would you think? Come on, since it's so easy looking in from the outside, since you haven't a clue what I'm going through or what I'm dealing with, why not tell me what you think?'

She ignored it. He was angry.

'Cato can't take it from you,' she said, but even as the words flew out they died on the ground; it wasn't true. 'He won't make you go.'

'Before this blew up I was already under orders, and do you know what the funny thing is, the really funny thing? There I was hoping this trip might iron things out; that maybe for once luck was on my side and whatever this was could help my situation.' He laughed joylessly. 'I can imagine most things but never in my life did I imagine this. The final twist in my and Cato's story, and I'm not hanging around for the curtain. I've had enough. It's over.'

He started walking. Olivia chased after him.

'Running away isn't the answer.'

'Isn't it? There's nothing to stay for.'

'I've seen your photographs,' she blurted. 'They're wonderful. You're talented, Charlie, really talented. You could do something with this.' Her thoughts ran away with her, anything to stop him leaving. 'We could speak to Sackville Grey—'

'Wasn't once enough?'

'What?'

'The first time you went through my stuff—wasn't that enough?'

'I didn't mean to pry,' she floundered, 'I was—'

'It's a stupid waste of time and I don't need you patronising me about it. You had no right. It isn't your business.'

He started walking, stopped and came back again.

'Come to think of it,' he flashed, 'none of this is any of your business. You must think you've hit the jackpot. Biggest scandal the cove has ever seen and here you are right at the heart of it. I'm sure it'll be a fine story to tell your friends.'

'You don't believe that of me.'

'What are you even doing here, Olivia? Why are you wasting your time? You should have gone back with the others. In fact you shouldn't have bothered coming in the first place, I never wanted you here.'

Her face torched. She wanted to slap him but she didn't want to hurt him. She never wanted to hurt him. Every word she choked on. What she was feeling was too big to express, too much and too different to make sense of.

'I wanted to stay for Decca,' she said. 'And…'

'And what?'

'And for you.' The words were thick, tied together with rope, a knotted cord being pulled from her throat one notch at a time. 'I wanted to stay for you.'

His expression flickered, open and closed too fast to catch hold of.

'That's a funny way of showing it, running off the minute your ex-boyfriend shows up.'

'It wasn't like that. And he isn't my ex-boyfriend.'

'Your boyfriend, then.'

'He isn't that either.'

'I'll tell you what he is. He's a spoiled, selfish kid who will never see you for what you are. He'll never see you like I do. You're a fool if you think he cares about you. You're blind to the person he is. So don't go telling me how I should run my affairs when you haven't got the first idea how to run yours.'

She was close to tears. 'I'll stay out of your business if you stay out of mine. Sound fair?'

He gripped her shoulders. The sky opened. Thick splashes sprinkled the sand with pockets of dark.

'Leave me alone.' She tried to tug free.

'What if I have something to say?'

'You couldn't say the right thing if you tried.'

'Just because I don't voice it doesn't mean it's not there. Why do you have to talk so much anyway? Why does talking have to be the beginning and the end of a thought, as if it can't exist by itself and you have to catch it and pin it to the wall, so you can examine it from every single angle till you're satisfied? If I have something to say to you then I'll say it; if I don't, I won't.'

His hair was wet. A raindrop gathered in his top lip.

'You said I hadn't got a clue,' she threw back. 'What if I do? What if I know what it's like to lose something, to face every day with a hole in my heart? You don't know a thing about my life so don't pretend to know me now.'

'I know I can't trust anyone, but I do trust you,' he said. 'I know you miss your dad, even though you never talk about him. I know that necklace you wear is a gift from your mother, and you keep them both inside it, and if you had to save one thing in your world that would be it. I know you love my dogs and you brought my garden back to life. I know that when you get a splinter you know how to take it out with a needle and hot water and you never make a fuss. I know you can ride a bike faster than most boys. I know when you pour a cup of tea you put the milk in first, which I find really irritating by the way. I know you made the dress you wore at my brother's party and I know I've never seen anyone look so beautiful. I know you know where the Lustell Cove treasure is buried because when you were small you drew a map that took us to it, and I know that for longer than you realise I've wanted to find it with you. I know I like your teeth, and your laugh, and your eyebrows. I know I want to take your picture, but at the same time I don't because you're the only person I can think of who should never be still, you should never be caught, you should always be free. I know I want to keep you from the cold. I know I don't want to be a stranger any more. I know I want to kiss you every day for the rest of your life; more, for all the days I've missed. I know you're the most amazing girl I've never known. And I know that might be all I'll ever know, because you'll go back to London and I'll move away and there won't be Usherwood between us any more. I know this whole thing's useless because I don't have anything left that I can give you, and I know, after this, it'll be easier on me if we don't see each other again.'

She searched his changed face, open for the very first time, at last without shadow or shade, without darkness, only light. Perfect.

'Usherwood releases you,' he finished. 'I don't need you any more.'

He walked away. The rain came down.

PART THREE

CHAPTER THIRTY-THREE

BAD WEATHER CHASED him all the way back to Cornwall.
Charlie left late at night, hailstones pounding the windscreen from a black and inscrutable sky, the motorway
an endless bleed of melting lights. Olivia had already
gone.

With the aftershock of Barnaby's news had settled a
kind of detachment, enabling him to make the journey
with a heart full of steel. By the time dawn broke across
a wide West Country sky, the sight of Usherwood didn't
rip him in two as he had thought it might. Instead he
regarded it steadily, as a bruised, beloved building that
never had and never would belong to him. They had
been guardians of each other for a while, that was all.
Usherwood was Cato's now, to do with as he pleased.

A removal van was parked outside, a man loading
crates in the pouring rain. The fountain wall had been
smashed on one side where Cato's car had reversed

into it—the Bentley's bumper confessed to a crumpled dent—and its bricks were dissolving.

'What's this?'

'Junk, according to 'im indoors.'

Charlie lifted the flap on one of the boxes. He recognised his own clothes, several books and his stash of journals. The picture of Penny from his bureau drawer.

'Have you taken anything away?'

'This is the first load. Plenty more to come, apparently.'

'Would you hold off a second?'

The man winced up at the glaring sky. 'I'm not hangin' about, mate.'

'Five minutes, that's all.'

With an unhappy grunt he hauled open the door to the cab and climbed inside. 'Whatever you say.' It slammed behind him.

Charlie faced the arched entrance, rain driving across his vision. The dogs bounded in before him, excited to reclaim their territory, making a beeline for the kitchen and their usual feeding spots, ensuring all was as they'd left it.

It wasn't. The hall was unrecognisable, piled high with cardboard. He checked another package and this time recognised his mother's belongings: her lilac dressing gown, a casket of hair pins, a framed picture of Cato and Charlie before they returned to Harrow. A handkerchief he remembered Barbara sewing, bearing her initials.

Cato wasn't just clearing his brother out, he was clearing out the attic and with it Usherwood's history: the totems of the past, all reminders of the mother who had soiled the Lomax name. For Charlie, it was harder to let go. Beatrice was all he had left, the only thing he had to hold on to. Without her he was rudderless.

Sigmund and Comet circled his legs, looking up for reassurance that he couldn't give. Outside, the downpour slashed furiously against the panes, whistles of chill needling through the stonework and down the chimneys.

'Mr Lomax?'

Barbara appeared at the foot of the stairs, a crumpled tissue in her hand. Her cheeks were red from crying. 'Please tell me it isn't true.'

He wrenched the words from his gut. 'It's true.'

'It can't be.' Her face was drained. 'I refuse to believe it. Her ladyship was… She would never have… There has to be some mistake, Mr Lomax, there has to be…'

'There isn't.'

Barbara came towards him, enveloping him in her arms. He stood rigid as a pole, her soft hair beneath his chin, scented like Parma Violets.

'I can't understand it.' Her voice was stifled against his jumper.

'Did you know?'

'No,' her answer was instant, 'and you must never doubt it. All those years I never thought, I never would have once suspected…' She drew back. 'I promise you.'

'You would tell me if you knew who he was…'

A tear slipped out of the corner of her eye. 'My loyalty is yours, Mr Lomax; it always has been. If I had so much as an inkling I swear I would not keep it to myself. I've been racking my brains trying to find a clue, something I might have missed; anything she might have said, anything to help you find your...' She swallowed. 'I wish I could help you, my darling. I wish I could make it better.'

He found it impossible to look at her. 'Cato's here?'

'Upstairs. It's been a dreadful week. They're planning to make the move quicker than we thought. Cato wants to be in by the end of the month. I tried to stop them clearing your things, but he won't listen...' Barbara averted her gaze. 'After all, what am I but the housekeeper, and after this who knows for how much longer... He'll let me go, I know he will. What with Arthur being at home I can't afford to lose this job. This house means so much to me.' Her voice cracked.

Charlie put a hand on her cheek. 'I won't let that happen.'

The storm grew louder as he mounted the stairs. Usherwood shook precariously on its higher levels, windows rattling and shuddering, and channels of cold ribboning through the vaults. He wondered how Cato would take care of the place. Electing not to do the work himself, he would hire in an army: one that spent a morning at most in the grounds, and whose creative direction would alter its character completely. Did Cato care about that? Would Charlie come to visit ten years from now, and find it had been bulldozed, or ransacked, or turned into a hotel, a spa resort, a theme park?

With Susanna in charge, anything could happen.

He heard her voice before he saw her.

'How about this one?'

She was at Beatrice's wardrobe, holding a sweeping gown to her chin and turning to appraise her reflection. Cato sat at the dressing table browsing through a jewellery box, and extracting bracelets with the exactitude of a surgeon.

'Was your mother terribly fat?' Susanna asked, bunching the material. 'If I keep this we're going to need to consult a *very* expensive tailor.'

'Depends if she got knocked up again,' Cato replied, holding a pair of cufflinks to the light to inspect their hallmark. 'It's always a possibility, I suppose...'

Charlie stepped in. 'Excuse me for interrupting.'

'Oh, look,' Cato said, not looking, 'a visitor. Good trip back, old bean?'

'Where do you get off chucking my things?'

'I'd rather assumed you'd be moving on.'

'Nothing like striking while the iron's hot, is there, Cato?'

'Don't be sensitive; there's a good chap. Forgive me if I thought you might find the process painful. It's like packing up a dead person's home, isn't it? Can't be easy at the best of times. Let me shoulder some of the responsibility.'

'There's a first time for everything.'

'Come now,' he drawled, twirling the links between his fingers, like the gem-encrusted knuckles of a tyrant king. 'I know this isn't easy. Why not stop with us for a few nights? I'm not heartless, Charles; I'm not turfing you out on the street. We can put you up in the servants' quarters, can't we? Mole will sort it out. Get a fan heater going in there and a spot of air freshener; it'll be as good as new.'

Susanna's eyes slid towards the brothers, pretending not to be interested.

'Don't trouble yourself,' said Charlie. 'I've made arrangements. And I'd appreciate looking after my own belongings. I'll organise them as and when I see fit.'

'As you wish.'

'Mother's too—her clothes, possessions, everything. There are things that are important to me; things I want to keep.'

'Where?' Cato couldn't resist. 'In your father's paddock?'

'You came this close.' Charlie pinched a slice of air. '*This close*, Cato. Consider that for a moment.'

His brother smirked. 'It's considered.'

'You're loving this, aren't you?'

'Whatever makes you say that?' A bracelet dripped from Cato's fingers. Slowly he released it, the chain pooling on to dark velvet.

'And another thing: you'll keep Barbara on.'

Cato snorted. 'Will I?'

'She has nowhere else.'

'And exactly how is that my problem?'

'If you don't make it your problem then I will.'

His brother shot him an alligator grin. 'So easily wound up, Charles. Don't you ever trust me to do the right thing?' He plucked a ring from the casket. 'There's a fortune in here if you find the right seller. Couldn't you have pawned some of it off? It might have helped your money troubles no end.'

'I've parted with enough, and not through choice. Everything you see, our mother held dear. That's her engagement ring right there.'

'A fine omen that turned out to be.' Cato chucked it back into the coffer, snapping it shut with a tight *click*.

'She wasn't all to blame.'

'My father was too good for her.'

'He made her life hell.'

'She castrated him.'

'He did the same.'

'Do you think she ended it?' Cato toyed with him as he had when they were children, planting an idea and watching with interest as its dark implications flourished. 'Don't tell me you haven't thought about it; you've questioned it as much as I have. She took herself down in the plane that day and she decided to take Daddy with her. Just like Barnaby said.'

'Just keep your fucking mouth shut.'

'Now, now, don't go overreacting. You always did take things to heart.'

'Watch what you say, or I swear to God I'll…'

'It must be why you insist upon keeping the remnants of a lying, conniving tart. Then again you're fond of a tart, aren't you? That ex-girlfriend of yours—'

Charlie punched him. With all the strength he had, with all the hate and all the pain and all the anger Cato had heaped his way, he launched a swing and smacked it straight back into his brother's jaw. The impact had been a long time coming and was delivered with a deep fierce smack that lifted Cato clean from his chair and sent him crashing like a rag doll against the window. It was the first time Charlie had struck him. At the end of his crunched fist his brother felt smaller and weaker than the giant he had made him. In the flesh Cato was just a man, and a slighter man than he was.

'Darling!' Susanna bolted to his side. She whirled on Charlie. 'Are you *insane*?' she shrieked. 'Have you lost your *mind*?'

'I've never been thinking so clearly.'

Cato's lip was bleeding. Deranged, he fronted to full height, squaring for a brawl, but the twitch by his eye betrayed a realisation. They were no longer boys, thumping each other on the lawns or in the back of Richmond's car. He was no longer ten, his brother no longer five. Gone were the days when he could attack without risk of retaliation. Charlie's muscular chest was concrete. Words were the safer bet.

'Don't you ever speak of Penny like that again,' said Charlie. 'Ever.'

Cato tasted the iron of his blood. 'Get out, Mole.'

'Why? Who's Penny?'

'Do it.' He didn't take his eyes from Charlie. 'I will not ask you again.'

Obediently she retreated.

'You killed her, Cato. Admit it.'

'Never,' he spat.

'Admit that you killed her. Admit that Penny didn't stand a chance. Admit that stealing her from me wasn't enough; that you had to steal the breath from her lungs before you were satisfied, and even then you didn't have the balls to look yourself in the mirror and confess to what you'd done.'

'She left you of her own accord.'

'She did. And your affair was something I could eventually have got my head around. Maybe I could even have come to terms with her death. But your denial... No, never that. Of all the debts you owe me, that one's the hardest to bear.'

'I owe you nothing.'

'If that's what you truly believe then you're more fucked up than I gave you credit for. You're so deluded you don't even know what day it is.'

'Oh, I do.' Cato's voice was smooth as a snake. 'Today's the day when you're not welcome here any more. Get out of my house, Charles, and never come back.'

'Do you know the one good thing to come out of this?' Charlie leaned in. 'I'll tell you. *I'm less your brother than I was before.*'

'Without me you're nothing. A farmer's bastard.'

'But an honest one.'

'You're going the right way for a rucking, old boy. Don't make me hurt you.'

'Go right ahead,' said Charlie, rising against him. 'Do your worst. After everything we've been through, whatever you do, however hard you fight, however you make me bleed, you can be sure of one thing: you can't touch me. You can't touch what's important, Cato, because I hid that from you so long ago that you wouldn't know where to start looking for it.'

Cato clenched his fists. He considered combat, asked what for. He had won. Charles had lost. That was all. 'You're not worth it,' he rasped, turning away.

Before he could, Charlie grabbed his collar. He pulled his brother up close. He could smell Cato's breath, sour with tobacco, and the sharp tang of fear.

'Wrong,' he said. '*You're* not worth it. You never were. You're a liar, Cato. A liar and a coward and a murderer, and when you lie in bed at night I hope to hell you know that one day everything you've done, all the hurt you've inflicted and all the damage you've caused, will be re-visited on you tenfold. And when it is, you had better pray you've got people around who care a damn about what happens to you—because I'm telling you now, I won't be one of them.'

CHAPTER THIRTY-FOUR

FLORENCE LARK'S CARAVAN roof shuddered in the howling wind. It had never been a structure adept in coping with the elements, and as Olivia lay on her bed, staring dazedly up at the ceiling and listening to the incessant lash of the rain, she pondered if it might not collapse in on her, and whether she'd much care if it did.

'Aren't you going to get up?' Florence put her head round the door and lifted a concerned eyebrow. 'It's gone eleven.'

'Mmm.'

'You don't look well, darling. Have you got a fever?'

'I'm fine.'

'Try to eat something… I could make you cheese on toast?'

'I'm just tired, Mum.' She turned to face the wall.

The mattress yielded with the weight of her mother's bottom.

'Come on, pumpkin,' Florence said. 'Spill the beans.'

'There are no beans.'

'Ever since you got back from Norfolk you've been casting about like the war-wounded. What's the matter? You can tell me.'

'I already have,' she replied flatly. 'I'm worried about Decca.'

'In that case let's invite her to stay. A change of scene might be just what she needs, and I'd be happy to show her round the cove.' Florence stroked her daughter's back. 'I think it's lovely you're so concerned, but Decca's got people around her and that's what matters most at a time like this.'

There was a pause before Flo continued carefully, 'And I know you've become involved in this Lomax affair, but darling, it isn't your responsibility.'

Various terms had been used around the town to describe the outrage: *affair*, *sensation*, *scandal*, *shocker*, the list went on. Doubtless there would be more to come with the nationals getting hold of the story. Soon it would be everywhere. With Cato's removal team charging up and down the Usherwood drive it had been about as subtle as a call to the editor's desk. Maybe he had done that as well, just to be sure.

'If you're worried about your job, I'm sure Charles will keep you on.'

'Charlie won't be living there any more.'

The stroking stopped. 'Ah.'

'He said he never wanted to see me again.'

There was a longer pause this time, and a longer, 'Aah.'

'We fell out.'

'I see.'

Olivia sat up, as if besieged by a startling idea. 'I don't know what to do about it, Mum. He's so difficult, and confusing, and he makes me so mad, and sometimes I absolutely can't stand him and other times I just have to be with him, and it's all so complicated and why can't things ever be easy? His whole life's imploded, every-thing he counted on, and he thinks I don't get it and maybe I don't, maybe I can't, but at least I could try, and I could try to be his friend. But he says he doesn't want that either, he says he doesn't want anyone and most of the time I believe him, but then some of the things he said to me I can't ever forget, not ever, and he must have meant them because I saw it in his eyes, I heard it and I felt it, and I wish he'd given me a chance because I never got to tell him; I never got to tell him that I feel it too...'

Her mother looked at her sideways. 'It?'

Olivia slumped back on to the pillow. The wind moaned. She dragged the blanket up under her chin.

'You know what it is.'

Florence slid her a glance. 'I do. So where does that leave you?'

'I have no idea.'

'Yes, you do. You're my daughter. You'll find a so-lution.'

She did. She called Beth.

The girls arranged to meet at the Anchor. They hadn't been in touch since the night of the party. Olivia was nervous about seeing her again. What if things were different? What if they couldn't get their friendship back on track? She couldn't consider it. She needed Beth now more than ever.

The pub was packed with beachgoers taking shelter from the weather, and the odour of ales, anoraks and warming smoke proved a welcome haven from the bluster. Olivia got drenched on the way over and spread her coat by the fire to dry it out. She bought them both drinks, found a tucked-away table, and sat anxiously watching the clock. When Beth arrived she was equally bedraggled, a blustered, chill-blown figure hurrying through the door and flapping out her umbrella.

Hesitant across the crowded room, the girls exchanged a cautious, regretful smile. When they hugged, Olivia wanted to cry with relief.

'I'm so sorry,' Beth told her. 'I've wanted to call you every day but I was too ashamed. I didn't think you'd pick up—I mean *I* wouldn't speak to me if I were you. I behaved so awfully. I should never have taken my problems out on you.'

'It's OK.'

'No, it isn't. I said some horrible things that night and I didn't mean any of them. You're my best friend, Oli, and I don't ever want that to change. I was upset and I lashed out at you and I regret it. Please forgive me.'

'Of course I forgive you. And anyway you were right—about Addy, at least.'

'I heard he followed you. What happened?'

'I told him where to go.'

'You did?'

'Yes. I said I wanted more from my life than what he could give me. I said I deserved better. That I'd felt that way about him once but that I didn't any more.'

'Wow.' Beth winced. 'What did he say?'

'His ego was wounded. I'm not sure if he was.'

'I'm proud of you. I really, really am.'

'Oh, he never liked me properly.' Olivia sipped her pint. 'I mean there I was, waiting my whole life for Addy to fall in love with me, and in the end it came down to that. It's like suddenly I opened my eyes. I saw the light. I realised it didn't have to be like that, pining after the same person just because that was what I got used to.'

'Hear hear.'

'And anyway, this whole acting bag—how can I take it seriously? Remember when Addy wanted to "sign up" to NASA? Like it was an after-school chess club or something. Or when he said he had to go find himself in Africa building shelters for refugees and teaching kids how to speak English—that never happened, did it? Or when he wanted to join the army but then he realised there wouldn't be anyone on camp to do his highlights every month, not that we're allowed to talk about that...'

Beth laughed. Olivia joined her. There was an easy, happy silence.

'Gossip's rife around town,' said Beth. 'D'you want to tell me what happened?'

Olivia filled her friend in on Norfolk and the boat, Decca and Barnaby, Susanna and Thorn, deliberately skirting the edges of the Lomax exposé because it felt disloyal to be jumping on the tabloid bandwagon. She had ignored the turning heads when she'd entered the pub, as if she had now been inducted into the clique.

'Is he OK?' Beth asked. 'How's he bearing up?'

'I haven't seen him since we got back.'

Impish, she narrowed her eyes. 'Something happened, didn't it?'

'No.'

'But you wanted it to. Shit, are you serious, *Charlie Lomax*?'

'Shh.' Olivia batted her down.

'Or should I say, Charlie whatever-his-name-is.'

'That's not funny.'

'I know it's not. It's totally awful. What a minx that Beatrice turned out to be.' Lightly she punched Olivia's arm. 'And what a minx *you* are—Addy showing up to whisk you off your feet on top of everything else. Did they fight over you?'

'It wasn't like that.'

'I know, I'm only messing.'

Olivia changed the subject. She didn't want to talk about Charlie any more. Her head was full of him. Her heart was full of him.

'What's happening with Archie?'

Beth grimaced. 'I've been doing all I can to raise the money. We're nowhere near.' She thought twice, before admitting, 'I even signed up for the Surfathon.'

Olivia nearly spat out her drink. 'You *what*?'

The Lustell Cove Surfathon was infamous. In just a few days the biggest wave of the season was tagged to hit their shores, a crazy anomaly of swell conditions and Atlantic tides, and the contest was on for who had the guts to ride it. She and Beth had toyed with the idea in previous years but had always ducked out last-minute: they were good but they weren't that good. This was the playground of the kamikaze.

'I know.' Beth smiled wryly. 'One of us finally did it.'

'Have you lost your mind? You'll kill yourself!'

'I had to do something, didn't I?' Beth bristled in defence. 'I wasn't going to sit about feeling sorry for myself, waiting for you to come home so I could moan about it some more—and only that if you were speaking to me, which I convinced myself you weren't. I had to raise funds somehow so this is what I did. I've had loads of sponsors already and it'll get me about a third of the way there—'

'You don't have to do it.'

'I'm not teetering on the ledge of a New York high rise, Oli, and there's no way I'm letting everyone down. They've already paid me. I can't back out. You know what? The cove's been brilliant. Fiona and Wilson pledged me two hundred quid! And Saffron on the Sea were really generous, too.' She paused, blushed a shade. '*And,*' she added shyly, 'you'll never guess who else has got involved…?'

Olivia raised her eyebrows.

'Sackville. Oh, my God I've been *dying* to tell you. I was so nervous going to see him but he was so sweet, he totally got it. He grew up with horses and he knows just what they mean. We've got tons in common. We talked for ages, and, well…'

'What? Come on!'

'He's taking me out for dinner this Friday!'

'Oh, Beth, that's wonderful.' She grinned. 'I'm so pleased for you.'

Her friend was shining. 'Thanks.'

'But look.' Olivia fumbled in her bag for a piece of paper, which she handed over, folded in half. 'I meant it when I said you didn't have to do the Surfathon.'

'What is this?'

'Open it.'

Beth did as instructed. She stared at the cheque for several seconds.

'Did you win the lottery or something?'

'No. I looked after a kid for a very rich woman who's too lazy to do it herself.'

She passed it back. 'I can't accept it.'

'Why not?'

'It's an insane amount of money. You're insane to give it to me.'

'No, I'm not. I can't think of a better thing to put it towards.'

'Oli, come on…'

'Don't you know it's rude to return a present?'

'What about the move back to town? A deposit on a flat in London, all the stuff you talked about?'

'I don't know if I want that any more. I need to figure a few things out.'

'There's no way. Please. It's too much.'

'It isn't.'

The cheque dangled forlornly between them. When Olivia thought of her time in Norfolk she ached, deep inside. 'Besides,' she said, 'I don't want it.'

'You make it sound like blood money.'

'In some ways it is.' Olivia put her hand over her friend's, the paper tucked inside. She remembered her reasons for agreeing to the trip and realised the truth. 'Take it, Beth. It'll make me happy. Pay the Feenys off and put this whole thing behind you. That's why I did it, that's why I went to Norfolk in the first place, because I wanted to do this for you and I want you to be OK. OK?'

Beth's eyes sprang with tears. 'I don't know what to say.'

'Thanks?'

'Thanks. And I love you.'

'I love you, too.'

'And if there's ever anything I can do in return, anything at all, you know you only have to ask.' She smiled. 'But you knew that anyway, right?'

Olivia leaned on the table, her chin in the palm of her hand.

'Actually,' she said, 'there is one thing. It's about Sackville's gallery...'

CHAPTER THIRTY-FIVE

COME THE END of the week, Susanna was settling into her new address nicely. Before Norfolk she had been a guest at Usherwood—an important one, yes, but still a guest—but since their return she had felt integral to Cato's life, his staunch companion where so much else blew away. Now it was starting to feel properly like home.

The added press attention cemented their golden couple status. People were referring to them as the new Wills and Kate, which was deeply agreeable; and studios were sniffing round her again. Jennifer called daily with news of a fresh opportunity: a make-up giant was pursuing her as the face of their age-defiance range; a TV channel wanted to film the relocation to England, maybe even live with the couple in Cornwall for a while; a major publisher had been in touch about her penning a book on traditional British interiors. It seemed she and Cato could do no wrong.

Once she signed on Howard Brice's dotted line,

Susanna would begin packing up her LA pad—she hadn't told Cato this yet, he had far too much else to think about—but she felt certain that his big proposal had to be just around the corner.

Descending the stairs on Friday night (Cato was indulging in a bath of Susanna's remedial lavender beads because his shoulders were tense), she stopped at a portrait of the former Lady Lomax, and put her hands on her hips.

'You naughty girl,' she chided it. 'What *were* you getting up to?'

The portrait returned her inquisition. In it Beatrice was seated, a sleek-snouted greyhound resting at her feet. Behind her spread a yawning forest, from which the twin spires of Usherwood could be seen breaking the surface, shapely as the peaks on a pronounced top lip. Her face was porcelain, the chin neat and the cheekbones sharp. Undeniably she was alluring, in a brittle, English way, and Susanna found herself wondering about this farmer of hers, someone she painted as rugged and thick with the hand span of a gorilla; a frantic love maker formed of fire while her husband cradled the dormouse coiled between his legs, as cold as an empty bed in winter.

Soon it would be Susanna's own likeness on the wall. The thought was a thrill. Perhaps she would replace this one, for its scrutiny made her uneasy. Would Cato commission it for their wedding day? To whom would they bestow the charge? She was keen to depart from these starchy formal studies, opt for a freer pose that heralded a new generation of Lomax women. Reclining on a chaise longue, draped in a sheet? In ardent embrace with her bare-chested beau? Riding an ivory stallion, her hair blowing in the wind, as Cato the rugged woodsman gazed on?

What a kick it would be.

She wafted downstairs, enjoying the peace. No more Charles, no more dogs, no more frumpy Baps letting down the image. Who knew, in a couple of years' time she and Cato might even have a family of their own. While Thorn was undeniably a darling he was still a boy, and in her heart of hearts Susanna craved a dolly-sweet daughter whose hair she could plait and who she would dress in frilly white ankle socks and who wouldn't cause any mess, or charge about like a torpedo, or adhere molluscs to the palm of her hand when she was trying to eat her breakfast.

Of course she pitied the housekeeper but there was nothing else for it. Dead weight had to be cut. If only Cato would see sense about that cook.

'We need *someone* to prepare meals for us, don't we?' Cato had argued when she'd complained about Caggie staying on. 'Who else is going to do it? You're hardly Michel Roux.' Admittedly Susanna was no maestro in the kitchen—the most she'd managed was emptying a bag of salad leaves into a bowl: that was what caterers were for—but wasn't there an alternative? She didn't even like Caggie's cuisine, it was so carb-heavy she felt as if she were a turkey being fattened up for Christmas, and she disliked the chef even more. Unfortunately Cato had a soft spot for his childhood nanny, and Susanna would have to play prudent if she were to get her way.

Trying her best to remain buoyant, she drifted into the scullery. Caggie was at the sink, brushing plates.

'I think I'll head to bed now,' Susanna trilled, 'it's been an awfully tiring day. Make me a camomile infusion and bring it up, would you?' She wanted a camomile infusion less than she wanted to give Caggie an order.

Caggie wiped her forehead with the back of her arm. 'All right.'

Pleased at her ability to pull rank, Susanna contemplated her theme. 'Cato'll be out of the tub by now, I wouldn't want to keep him waiting...'

'Certainly not.'

'I mean,' she sidled along the counter, 'when you're in a relationship as sensual as mine, it's impossible to keep your hands off each other. Cato's a tiger.'

'Is he really?'

'We're addicted to each other.'

'I'm sure.'

'He can't help himself, you know.' A thought popped into Susanna's head and she ran with it, like a blind person into a river. 'Sometimes he just wants to tear me right open and dive inside and wear my skin like a coat!' Ugh, that sounded horrible. It was less *Sleepless in Seattle* and more *The Silence of the Lambs*. She wished she'd never said it—Cato certainly hadn't. 'What I mean,' she clarified quickly, beneath the cook's astonished glare, 'is that ours is a very *physical* partnership.'

Caggie dried her hands on a towel and tossed it to one side. 'Believe it or not,' she said, 'I've no interest in the ins and outs of your sex life.'

'Of which there are *plenty*,' Susanna replied smugly. 'I guess you wouldn't know what that's like, being on your own and all.'

Caggie turned her back. 'No,' she mused, 'I don't suppose I would.'

There it was again—that tone!

Clearly Caggie imagined that she staked some claim to Usherwood, by virtue of her long service, and saw Susanna as a frittery amusement that would soon be cast to the wind. Logically she was jealous. What was she but an aged, frustrated spinster? Here Susanna was, passionately in love with the devilishly sexy Cato Lomax, and set to take her throne as Lady of Usherwood—probably what Caggie had always wanted.

If Cato refused to put Caggie in her place, then Susanna most certainly would.

She stormed upstairs, deciding she would refuse to drink the tea even if Caggie did bring it, on the possibility it could be laced with arsenic.

She passed the portrait of Beatrice, climbed a couple of steps, stopped, turned back and stood in front of it. Susanna lifted the frame from its moorings, spitting out dust, and propped it gently against the panelling.

She brushed off her hands. Something was still not right.

With a final heave she turned it to the wall.

* * *

The quality of night at Usherwood was profound. It was the inkiest black to wake to, close and thick as liquid. Into it and into it you could stare, watching for a shape in the cloak, waiting for an outline to surface, no detail decipherable in the absolute pitch.

Susanna fumbled for her cell and its green display light bathed the room in a sickly, incongruous hue. She groped for Cato but he wasn't there.

'Cato?' she whispered.

The emerald tinge made the room appear like some Gothic nightmare, or the bowels of a lunatic inventor's laboratory. She rooted for the switch and the space was flooded abruptly, painfully, with white light. Shielding her eyes, Susanna listened with acute concentration, sorting sounds like marbles from a jar as she tuned into a frequency beyond the moan of the gale.

Two a.m.: the ghost's hour! Susanna yanked the blankets to her chin. Panic filled her like oil. The wail swam at her with grim predictability, thin as a thread through a needle as it weaved between the hectic loops of the squall. She locked on to the door, counting the seconds before the handle turned, and imagined the gnarled hand on the other side, skin paper-thin, gripping with sinister intent…

Quick and brave as a ripped-off plaster, she flung herself from the bed. Throwing on her dressing gown she flew to the door and eased it a crack, pressing her ear to the gap. A cold mustiness assailed her. The wail was louder out here, and tinnier, but still so far away—that sad, sad song of exquisite agony.

Warily she peeled the door open. Moonlight flooded the hall, the floorboards a silver lake that swam around her naked feet. The gale was playing tricks, whistling close to her ear one second and flashing through a distant hollow the next.

And then, there it was.

Straight away she saw. A scream climbed from Susanna's stomach into her throat and she had to clamp a hand to her mouth to stop it winging free.

The portrait of Lady Lomax had turned.

She flattened herself against the wall, terror circling like a giant bird.

There the picture was, exactly where she had left it—only now it faced out, the wrong way round, a macabre switch whose subject eyed her beadily in the pearly glow, daring her to approach. It was...*alive*. In the melting dark the face of Beatrice Lomax morphed and dissolved, still one minute and animated the next.

The realisation hit her like a slap.

The ghost had been Beatrice all along! Wretched, cursed Beatrice with her lover and her forbidden son and the covetous husband who kept her chained to the marriage like a bear to a post. Of all the people to haunt Usherwood, of all the people with unfinished business, it made absolute sense that it should be her. Beatrice had been tethered to the estate in life and so she had in death. Somehow Susanna had pitched into that dread; perhaps Beatrice had known her secret wasn't long for the shadows, and pleaded with someone to hear her lonely cry? Susanna had. Only she had been privy to the calls in the night, the warning and the grief...

The howling grew intense, rising and falling and flipping like a paper bag on the wind. Susanna put her hands out, seizing pockets of dark as if the passage between them could be climbed on an invisible rope. She became convinced that any second the portrait would fold out of itself, Beatrice standing and dusting off her twenty-year-old clothes and stepping from the frame as if she were departing from her porch.

'Hello,' she'd say, in a clipped British tone. 'You received the invitation...'

Instead the whimpering gathered, incessant now, breaking into a continuous bawl, and it seemed to get louder and louder the closer she came to the landing. Spreading her palm on the banister Susanna gazed to the rafters, half assuming Beatrice would be floating up there in her white gossamer gown; a phantom made of bed-sheets, two holes cut for the eyes. Beatrice's yearning was everywhere, above, below, inside, throughout, and rising now to its familiar, dastardly crescendo. Susanna had never asked for this gift, yet here it was. She would be the vessel. She would help this creature if it were the last thing she did.

The sound travelled closer. In the grand hall the door was ajar, blown open by the gust. Susanna stepped outside, bracing herself against the cold.

A glow spilled on to the pebbles like a bucket of

slopped paint, thrown from the side of the building. She rounded the corner and detected the light.

It was coming from the stables.

Rain soaked her gown. Silk caught on thorn but she paid it no heed, not even when a coarse rip tore through her sleeve.

As she approached, the plates of Susanna's world shifted slightly, nothing seismic but a subtle manoeuvre that made her have to reach to steady herself, guided by the contours of the house, the bricks soaked and grainy beneath her fingertips.

She was itched by a niggling, horrible idea.

The stable gate was shut. As if in a dream she watched it swing open.

Cato's bright white ass was the first thing she saw. She would know that ass anywhere. If she crossed oceans and found it darting between the trees on a remote island paradise, if she visited a telescopic planet and witnessed it crouched on an alien rock, if she uncovered a time machine and encountered it on a thirteenth-century moat, it was the most famous ass in America, and it belonged to her.

But not tonight.

Susanna absorbed the scene a clip at a time, because the entirety of it was certain to crucify her. Cato's ass was earnestly clenching, pounding and releasing, and with every thrust eliciting those accustomed-to yelps of ecstasy that until this instant, this despicable, unimaginable instant had belonged to a nightmare no worse than this.

On top he wore a tailored blazer, his dark mane contained beneath a riding hat. His left hand was gripping a woman's thighs, his right brandished a crop.

Susanna knew, deep in her heart, long before she saw her.

Caggie Shaw.

They were splayed on a bed of hay. Cato was rutting from behind. In the cook's mouth she held a horse's bit, a leather brow band wedged round her head.

'Faster!' she was crying, roiling on the brink of ecstasy as the bit was pulled and her throat laid open like a lamb to the slaughter. 'Faster, ride me faster!'

'Little pony likes that, does she?' came the hoarse, guttural reply. 'Little pony wants some more?'

'Whip me again,' she begged, 'please!'

Cato did as directed, lashing Caggie's pink flesh and rearing her up on the reins. Above, the ramshackle roof let in the whine of the wind as fast as it set free that persistent female moan, winging her song across the lawn and to the house, tapping on the windows and seeping through the doors. Waking Susanna in the night.

At first her own scream was indistinguishable from the ones coming from the horse, but long after Caggie's shrieks abated her own continued to pour. Susanna screamed and screamed and screamed until there was nothing left.

'Jesus Christ!'

Cato's mouth fell open in a ragged O. Still he was bucking, looking Susanna squarely in the face while boning Caggie squarely from behind. She couldn't tell if he was coming or not. She turned and fled, blind with tears, suffocated with shock.

That was the ghost? *That was it?*

'Mole!'

Cato was stumbling after her. He caught her at the entrance to the house, the jacket and hat still in place, his dick flapping like a windsock, and tugged her round to face him. Incredibly he was unabashed. He was, dare she say it...*amused*.

'I fucking hate it when you call me that!'

Ravaged by tears she thumped his chest, battered him blue, struck his face but it would never be enough. Even if she killed him it would never be enough.

He grabbed her wrists.

'Pull yourself together. I can explain.'

Laughter broke out of her like a brick through a window.

'How can you *possibly* explain?' she raged. 'I hate you! *I fucking hate you!*'

'Come now, Mole, old habits die hard—'

She slapped him—once, twice, a third time. She shoved him with all her might but he didn't move. She kicked his shin and in the process stubbed her toe.

'How could you?' she bewailed. 'With that...that *slut*?'

'Caggie and I have a long-term arrangement.'

'More long-term than you and me?'

Cato sighed, as if the situation had nothing whatsoever to do with him and yet inexplicably it kept happening.

'I never promised to be faithful,' he said.

'You never promised to be an asshole but you're managing that just fine.'

She stalked indoors, wild with anger. There was no sign of Caggie. She hoped the woman had choked on her horse's bit. *The bitch!*

Cato sauntered in. 'You knew when you got with me that I had needs.'

'I thought I fulfilled them.'

'You do, as much as any one woman can.'

Red fury exploded. 'That's the best I'm going to get? That's the most you're going to give? What about marriage? Children? What about our future?'

Cato spread his hands, very reasonably for a man who was naked from the waist down. 'I'm content for you to be in my life, Mole, but I can't be content with just one companion. Let's talk about this, because I'm a modern man. I'm unconstrained by convention. There has to be more than one way of doing things—'

'And what exactly would that be?'

'Well,' he simpered, 'there's enough Lomax magic to go round—'

She slapped him again.

'Would you stop *doing* that?'

'You want me to *share* you?'

'If the cap fits.'

Stricken, Susanna rushed upstairs, stumbling in her haste, the landing fractured in her shivering vision. Thick, salty tears coursed down her cheeks; upset and fury and disappointment strangling her, burning like gasoline in her chest.

In the bedroom she began throwing things in a bag.

Cato was at the door. 'What are you doing?'

Already her PA was on speed dial. The instant the woman picked up, Susanna issued instructions. She was clear and concise about what she wanted: a car, a flight out of London, an upgrade to the finest digs the airline had available and a bottle of her preferred vodka on arrival—everything would be charged to Lord Lomax. Amazingly her voice held. She was frozen and exact in her anger.

The call finished, Cato stormed, 'Slow down a minute, Mole, would you? Let's get Caggie up here, see if we can't sort this out between ourselves—'

'Don't you dare even say that tramp's *name*! I swear to God if she so much as puts a toe over this threshold I will rip her fucking head off.'

He folded his arms. 'You're very sexy like this.'

She couldn't believe it. Didn't he care? Maybe he never had. She bet that ever since they had arrived at Usherwood he had been taking every opportunity to screw the ancient cook, choosing her gristly skirt beef over Susanna's fillet steak. The proposal she had longed for would never materialise. She had been a fool to invest that hope in him.

She zipped the bag, not caring what she'd packed or what she hadn't, just that she had to get as far away from this place as was humanly possible.

'Are you sure I can't persuade you to stay?'

That was what it came to—a question as flippant as

if he'd been enticing a dinner guest towards a nightcap. He had never loved her in the way she loved him.

'Goodbye, Cato.'

Susanna waltzed past, her cases behind her. She would wait at the gate for an hour if she had to—anything but look at him.

'Suit yourself.' His voice reached her from behind, a taunting, mocking scorn. 'I'm not sure you would have fitted in at Usherwood, after all, Mole. You're not from my stock. You could pretend all you liked but you'd still have been a fraud.'

She stopped. His words hit her like a wrecking ball.

'And I had to right that portrait of Mummy.' He waggled his finger. *'Tsk, tsk, tsk,'* he chided. 'This is her house, too, you know.'

Through the tangle of Susanna's despair, one rope pulled free: Cato Lomax would live to regret this if it were the last thing he did.

Without another word, she fled.

CHAPTER THIRTY-SIX

THE FOLLOWING MORNING Olivia drove her mother's sputtering car through the Usherwood gates, desperately trying to see through the rain. If anything the storm was worsening, daylight tinged with sombre grey as though the cove were in a state of post-apocalypse. The ocean darkened to green and purple and black, thrashing and heaving as it jumped and threw spray across the cliffs.

Shallow floods were pooled across the drive and she sloshed through them, tyres churning as spurting jets gushed up the flanks of the car. Round the giant oak a more serious overflow obstructed her route. The river's culvert had burst, soaking part of the lawn in feet-deep water, while the road itself was impassable.

She climbed out and slammed the door, holding her coat above her head as it flapped uselessly in the force of the gale. She hurried towards the house.

Usherwood's hall was a mess. Darkness enveloped her, the electricity gone. Mud was slashed across the flagstones, from which the rugs had been torn and kicked into a corner. The fire smouldered unhappily. Clusters of soggy towels were stuffed under doors and at window ledges, futile attempts to stem the weather's invasion. A heap of sandbags huddled uselessly at the foot of the stairs, one of whose casing had split and spewed grain across the ravaged floor. Empty plates and stained mugs littered what was left of the furniture. Everything was freezing and gloomy.

Cato burst out of the library. He was barking orders into the phone.

'Yes, yes, I understand that, but how soon can you get here?' He raised one finger when he saw her, an instruction to stay, as if she were a dog. 'For heaven's sake, man, this is a fucking Noah's Ark situation out here; we're about to get swept away—what part of the word "emergency" don't you understand? No, I will not hold. No, I will not bear with you. This is Cato Lomax and I *demand* a priority service, are you listening? I demand it. This is a fucking mockery. Are you being deliberately bone-headed? I find it impossible to believe you're managing it without at least a little bit of effort. What kind of a circus are you running over there? Hello?' He scraped a hand down his face, snatched a clump of his hair. 'Hello, are you still there? Hello?'

The phone was hurled across the hall. It struck a pillar and shattered to pieces.

'You're flooded,' said Olivia.

He launched his foot against one of the sandbags.

'Damn this heap of rubble to hell! What the fuck do you want? This had better be good.'

'I'm looking for Charlie. Where is he?'

'Search me,' said Cato acidly. 'Somewhere in town, I expect, feeling sorry for himself. Why? Hung up on him, are you? He hasn't got the best track record with girlfriends, I'll warn you.' He laughed meanly. 'The last one got killed. Took her out in his car drunk, he did, slammed her straight into a tree. Sexy, she was, too.'

He advanced, eyes flashing with lust. 'Like you.'

'Stay away from me.'

'Charles is dangerous.'

'I don't believe a word you say.'

Cato grabbed her, flattening his body against hers. 'Why not take an upgrade?' he snarled. 'From day one you've wanted that bastard brother of mine, it's been written all over your face. Why not set your sights a little higher, hmm? Why settle for the mongrel when you can have the pedigree?'

She shoved him hard but he was too quick, too strong, and he slammed her to the wall, clutching her face with his hand. All at once he was intolerably ugly, his skin too smooth, his hair too perfect, his teeth too straight. He was like a mint, white and blank and covered in a hard shell.

'Pretty little freckles,' he crooned, tightening his grip on her cheeks. 'Forget about Charles, it's me you want.'

'Never. You disgust me.'

'Quite a mouth, haven't you?' he leered, swooping in

like a raven from the rafters. 'Perhaps I ought to stuff it with something to keep you quiet.'

His touch skittered over her breasts. Filled with fury, she spat at him.

For a moment Cato was stunned, his lips parted, his expression glazed. Before he could act, she ducked and ran from the house, out into the pouring rain, toppling towards the shining green beacon of her mother's car.

Climbing in, she shook herself dry and flicked the choking engine. It failed to start and she twisted the key in desperation, again and again, her hands shaking.

Come on, come on, come on…

Not once did she take her eyes off the mouth of the house, fearing that Cato was about to fly from it, charge towards her, drag her from the vehicle and then…

Then what?

She realised she was afraid of him. Charlie wasn't dangerous; Cato was. All she had seen, all she had heard, all she knew of him led back to the same: a twisted nest of black and sinewy cords.

Come on!

The engine guzzled to life. She wrestled it into reverse and swung the car round, headlamps carving through the fog as she tore down the way she had come.

Emerging to the safety of the road she encountered a huddled figure, hurrying along the verge and picking a path through the wet. It was hunched in a coat, a small square bag held tight to its stomach. Barbara.

Olivia pulled up alongside, winding down the window. 'You're drenched—get in!'

Gratefully the woman accepted, slamming out the cold, her jacket prickled with raindrops. 'Arthur's collecting me at the cemetery,' she explained. 'The entrance was submerged when we arrived this morning—we couldn't pass the gates.'

'What are you doing?' Olivia indicated, putting on her hazards.

Barbara's face clenched. 'Gathering the last of my things.'

'You're leaving?' Cato really was getting rid of all the family assets.

'He fired me. I'm not the only one to go. Susanna left in the small hours; it seems she'd finally had enough.'

'What happened?'

Rain drummed on the roof. Barbara's voice leaked a shade of apology.

'I expect you knew about the Caggie affair.'

Just when Olivia had thought nothing else could shock her. *'Caggie?'*

'It's been going on for years. It started when Cato was still at school—I know, I know, but you had to be there; he wasn't your average sixteen-year-old, he wasn't your average *anything*—and as time went on, whenever he returned, it continued.' Wearily Barbara lifted her shoulders. 'We turned a blind eye, Charlie and I. Maybe this time, I thought, with Susanna here, Cato might refrain, but abstinence isn't a theme he gives much credit to. Last night they were discovered…in the stables.'

'The stables?'

'You can imagine it. Susanna saw everything.'

'God. I bet she did.'

Barbara put her hands on the dash, bowed her head between her arms.

'How did we get ourselves into such a dreadful situation? Usherwood used to be a safe place, a brilliant place, clean of this sordid mischief—and now look! Corrupt to the core. If Richmond and Beatrice could see what's become of us they'd be spinning in their watery graves.' Swiftly she crossed her chest.

'Do you know where Charlie is? I have to see him.'

'No. And I'm worried. He left the dogs with us, "for a few days", he said—the old Charlie would never have done that.'

Olivia was desperate. 'He can't be left hanging like this, Barbara. We have to do something. We have to find answers. He needs to know who his father is; he needs someone to tell him what happened, someone he can trust; someone who knows. There has to be *something* you remember—no matter how small, or how incidental it might seem. Did you ever suspect what was going on? Did Beatrice ever talk to you?'

The housekeeper shook her head. 'I wish she had, dear, and then perhaps we wouldn't be in this predicament. But no, she didn't—fond as I was of the couple there was always a line; they were on one side of it and I was on the other.'

'She must have confided in someone other than her brother, she *must* have…'

'There was one person.'

'Who?'

Barbara clutched her bag. 'Fiona Montgomery—they were the best of friends. I couldn't second guess any aspect of her ladyship's behaviour after this—but what I will tell you is that if anyone can shed light on your story, it's Fiona.'

Olivia put her foot down. The car lurched forward, grumbling towards the cemetery car park.

'What are you doing to do?' breathed Barbara.

'I'm going to discover the truth.'

The Quillets Vineyard had taken a mighty pounding, its clifftop position in perilous line of the elements. As Olivia climbed from the car she steeled herself against a raging wall of wind, attacking it on the diagonal. Leaves churned a tornado at her feet and spiralled up in a reeling, spinning flurry. Far below waves crested. White froth leapt and rolled. Churning eddies swirled around clusters of lethal rock.

Rain sliced against her as she forged her way to the stone cottage.

Fiona answered, wrapped in a cardigan, and immediately hauled her inside.

'What on earth are you doing? Get in here before you freeze to death!'

Inside the kitchen a fire was going. The table was scattered with newspapers, Fiona's reading glasses and a mug of tea. Knotted beams were black-cracked with age; the ceiling was low. Through the window Olivia watched the gale-thrashed vineyard dance in the deluge, grasses bent double, flattened in the onslaught. A black-

and-white puppy yawned at her feet. The kettle clicked on, quickly arriving at a boil.

Fiona brought the tea over. She sank down opposite and watched Olivia for several moments. 'This is about Charlie Lomax,' she said, 'isn't it?'

At Olivia's nod, she exhaled sharply.

'Oh, dear,' she shuddered, 'I feared it would come to this. I vowed to them I would keep the secret. God knows I've wrestled my conscience so many times over the years. I'm fond of Charlie. I love him. But I had to keep my promise.'

'Beatrice is dead,' Olivia said bluntly. 'If you knew about the affair, you should have said.'

'Beatrice is gone,' Fiona agreed, 'but he isn't. *He's* been at Lustell Cove all along. I couldn't betray his trust—it wasn't my place to do so. Lives would be affected, people changed for ever. That wasn't my decision to make. You've seen the damage it's done.' She put her head in her hands. '*Why* did Barnaby do it? When I heard you'd gone to Norfolk, I knew he planned to confess. What's the point in telling them now? All it's caused is hurt and heartache. Those poor, poor boys…'

'You knew Barnaby, all those years ago?'

'I did. I was with them through it all—not that Richmond knew the extent of what Bea and I had shared: if he had he'd have forbidden me from seeing her, too. Over the years she told me everything, all about her unhappiness, what kind of a husband Richmond was, and then…'

'The man she fell in love with.'

'Yes. Him.'

A howl of wind crashed against the building. The overhead light spluttered and flickered, immersing them in obscurity before righting itself.

'Deliberately I've kept my eyes off the papers, but Wilson told me yesterday that Charlie was moving on, leaving Usherwood for good.' Fiona's fingers trembled. 'I *vowed* to Beatrice I would never betray her trust and yet here we are. What choice do I have? Charlie is so dear to me. I still see the boy in him.'

'Then you must do the right thing. Keeping this to yourself might have been right once upon a time but it isn't any more. Put yourself in his shoes. Imagine finding out the man you thought was your father hated you. Imagine finding out that he didn't love you and he never had, and never could because of where you came from.'

Another smash of wind plunged them into darkness. Shadows seeped in from outside, remnants of a day that was thick with gloom.

'You don't understand,' came Fiona's voice from the darkness: strange, disembodied. 'You've got it wrong. Richmond didn't hate him.'

'Yes, he did. We found a letter.' She remembered Charlie handing it to her on the beach. He had shared it with her. He hadn't had to, but he did. 'In it Beatrice said that Charlie was the lesser loved. Those were the words she used.'

'Lesser loved by her,' Fiona said gently. 'Not by Richmond.'

She went to the cabinet for a torch. Finding one she

switched it several times, to no avail, before flicking the battery compartment and seeing it was empty. From a cupboard she extracted a slender candle and lit it, cradling it in its holder.

'Bea tried to love him as much as she loved Cato, but how could she? Charlie was born of an altogether different situation.'

Olivia fumbled to unravel it. 'What situation?'

'By the time Charlie arrived, things with Richmond had deteriorated. Bea was wretched. I don't know if she had ever been happy in that marriage, but by now each day was a grind. She couldn't leave. He was forcing her to stay. He demanded another son: she didn't want one. Charlie was the bandage baby, but the relationship was a wound that could never be healed.' The room sparked with a flare of lightning, a growl of thunder close behind. 'Richmond couldn't see why it took so long to conceive again—almost five years, it was. He wasn't to know that he'd had nothing to do with the first.'

The candle shimmered between them.

Olivia dared not move.

'The night Charlie was made…' Fiona's confession flew free, spreading its wings after years in captivity. 'There was a struggle. Bea didn't confirm it either way, but for my money it wasn't consensual. All that dread and fear and unhappiness…'

Charles can never know where he came from…

Fiona gazed up at her beseechingly.

'How *could* she love him as much? Cato was born of fire and passion, recklessness and desire, devotion and addiction, and my God she loved that boy's father. Of course she adored Cato all the more.'

'You mean...?'

'Yes.'

'The farmer—he's not...?'

'After Beatrice and Richmond disappeared, he came back to the cove. He's been here for twelve years. How could he approach Cato, even when Cato bothered to return home—for what would he have said? The international film star, the untouchable icon—you couldn't have made it up. This man didn't stand a chance. He would have been laughed out of town.'

Olivia's mouth was dry. 'Who is he?'

As the question emerged, she realised she already knew.

She had known the instant she'd seen that photograph on the way to Norfolk, the one of Cato at the party. How he had reminded her of...

'Ben Nancarrow,' Fiona said for her. 'He owns the land at the foot of Lustell Steep.'

The name drifted across Olivia's tongue, light as snow.

'Farmer Nancarrow.' She thought of his broad shoulders, his coal-dark hair and his heavy brow. How afraid they had been of him as children. How he had danced with her mother that spring at the barn dance while Olivia had hidden by the stage, thinking how handsome and frightening he was.

'Until Charlie's fifth birthday,' Fiona explained, 'Richmond believed both boys were his. When he discovered that Cato wasn't—the son he had raised in his own mould, the undisputed apple of his eye—well, naturally he started treating him differently. He shifted allegiances.'

'Charlie always said that Cato hankered after Richmond's attention.' It was beginning to make sense, the knot loosening in her hands. 'Cato was the fallen one. Suddenly all the affection he'd been lavished was going towards his brother.'

'That's right. And in my opinion that's precisely why Cato behaves as he does. Even now he's working to prove himself to the father who lost interest; who up until that point had been his best friend, his ally, the man who worshipped the ground he walked on, and then one day, just like that, he didn't want to know.'

'Cato's jealous. He always has been.'

Fiona blew out a stream of air, and with it the burden of a lifetime.

'And Charlie's a Lomax,' Olivia said quietly, as if speaking it too loud or too quick might frighten the truth away.

CHAPTER THIRTY-SEVEN

CHARLIE OPENED HIS EYES and had no idea where he was. There was a dull thump in his head. A rope of pain skewered between his ears. His mouth was dry and the sheets at his waist were tangled and knotted with fever.

Memories of the previous evening trickled through the fog. He had left his hotel early and checked into the pub. A familiar routine, though it had been different to normal, not the usual taverns with their ships in bottles and their ales on draught: this one was neon-lit and had a Perspex bar from which a trail of students bought one-pound shots. Empty glasses lined up, the froth of beer and the stick of brandy. Loneliness. The barman asking if he'd had enough, and did he need a cab home—*home*—and then a female voice, enticing him to buy another.

He rolled over. The woman was asleep, blonde hair trailed over her shoulder. Shamefully he couldn't remember her name. He caught flashes of the sex—hard, aching, essential—and her skin wrapped up in his, the needlessness and necessity of release. Quietly he slipped out of bed and hauled on his jeans.

From the bathroom window he was able to decipher his position. Drowsily he drew open the blinds and detected the line of grey water in the distant east—at a guess they were no more than half an hour from the cove. The sky was thick with clouds, a billowing cotton-wool bed that bulged like rising smoke. From it broke occasional shafts of uncertain light, to be swallowed seconds later. The rain had ceased and its aftermath was hauntingly quiet, the tentative first steps to recovery.

He went downstairs. His shoes were where he'd kicked them off by the kitchen door, his wallet thrown on the counter, two glasses on their sides in the sink. He found another and filled it with water, downing it thirstily.

'Hello,' came a voice from behind.

She was pink-cheeked and pretty—yes, he remembered her now—and the back of her hair was a sex-muddled nest. Late twenties, long legs, blue eyes that skimmed over his bare torso and down.

'How did you sleep?' The woman had a lilting American accent, and was wrapped in a sheet. 'You sure wore me out… Breakfast?'

He wished he could remember her name. His eyes drifted to the stash of mail.

'You weren't thinking of running out on me, were you?'

'Listen, Alex, last night was fun…'

'It's Natalie. I'm surprised you forgot—you were saying it enough times while you were fucking my brains out. Alex is my husband.'

He was glad of the get-out. 'Right,' he set down the glass, 'OK.'

'He's in Paris this weekend!' Natalie trailed him upstairs, where he pulled on his trainers, and a T-shirt that smelled of cigarette smoke.

'He won't be back for ages...' The sheet dropped to the floor.

Charlie turned away. He opened the door.

'Neither will I,' he told her.

His flight left tonight.

In the event the return to town took him longer than thirty minutes, but it was a welcome invigoration. In the storm's wake the fresh air was bitingly chill and crisp. Lustell air. He would miss it.

Charlie entered the cove from above, taking a path over the cliffs so that the sea spread out before him in all her glory. The waves were no longer spitting and thrashing; the beat they drove now was deeper, a steady, serious roll, the tide rising and falling and the crests metres high. Of the many faces of the ocean this was the one that seduced him most. It was a reminder of the sheer and supreme power of the sea, its mighty drumroll as it heaved and sank, its rhythm launched from miles down and miles out, and its fatal currents a warning to stay clear.

It surprised him, therefore, to see a crowd of surfers gathered on the beach in their wetsuits, tiny as ants against its daunting sweep. A gazebo had been set up, near levelled when the wind picked up, and a canvas banner danced against the sky. Trickling down the path to the sand was a bigger crowd, spectators to the event about to unfold, and a couple stopped to glance uneasily at the sea.

'Charlie?'

Sackville Grey was coming over the hill. He smiled and held out his hand, which Charlie shook. 'I was hoping I might bump into you. Are you heading down?'

'To what?'

'The surf tournament.' Sackville was sceptical. 'Beth's in the running so I said I'd go. They were ready to call the whole thing off what with the weather; seems like a death wish to me. I'm only showing up so I can talk her out of it.'

'I can't,' said Charlie. 'Sorry.'

'Is it true you're leaving the cove?'

'That can't be much of a surprise.'

'Even so I'm sad to hear it.' Sackville put his hands in his pockets. 'Especially as I've got an opening coming up at the Round House. I thought you might be interested.'

'Thanks, but no.'

'Why? You're good, Charlie. Scratch that, you're excellent. This is a fantastic opportunity—I'd want you to adopt the entire exhibition space as your own. The work you did with us before was outstanding; everyone said so.'

'That was a long time ago.'

'Not so long.'

'It is for me.'

'I never understood why you didn't pursue it. You could have really started something.'

'I had my reasons.'

'And do they still stand?'

Charlie could honestly say, for the very first time, that he had no other commitments, nothing else that warranted his time or attention.

'At least consider it,' Sackville persisted. 'Come on, you're bloody talented. Don't let it go to waste. Do it for me, and if you won't do it for me then do it for yourself.' There was a shiver of a pause. 'And if you won't do it for yourself… Well, then do it for Olivia Lark.'

Her name did something to him, deep inside, a rusted-shut window swinging open on a summer's day.

'She thinks a lot of you,' said Sackville. 'We all do.'

'I'm not a charity case.'

'I didn't think for a second you were.'

'I don't need your pity—or hers.'

'That's lucky,' Sackville didn't miss a beat, 'because you don't have it.'

Charlie held a hand up. 'I said no. Excuse me, I've got a flight to make.'

Sackville watched him go.

'We've got some faces from London coming down,' he yelled, as Charlie made off across the grassy bluff. 'It's high time you showcased!'

A hand was raised to bid him farewell.

'When you're back, then?'

The distant figure didn't stop. It carried on walking, and the wind continued to blow.

CHAPTER THIRTY-EIGHT

IT WAS WITH a feeling of dread that Olivia surveyed the pitching Atlantic. Above, the sky was just as choppy, cauliflower clouds breaking to white and grey and casting at speed across the glowering sky. She had never seen the sea so unpredictable.

The beach had been decked out as in previous years, a ballooning marquee under which bystanders huddled against the cold, clutching cups of tea and placing their bets on which contender had it bagged. Music thumped from speakers, the hip-hop playlist of one of Addy's wannabe-ghetto buddies, and a thread of bunting marked the start range. In minutes the surfers would line up and wait for the whistle.

Olivia craned to see Beth, and instead landed on Addy. Draped off him was Thomasina Feeny, who was shivering in a pair of sherbet-coloured cut-offs.

'How's the acting shaping up?' Olivia asked, going

over. 'I'd say you deserve an Oscar for all that crap you recited in Norfolk.'

'Do you mind not distracting him?' Thomasina snipped, as if Addy were a four-year-old who needed his nose wiped. 'He's trying to get in the zone.'

'He tried to get in my zone as well. Without success.'

'Oh, go away, Chopped Liver. Everyone knows you're refrigerated.'

'Everyone knows you're a slut.'

Thomasina's mouth dropped open. 'If you must stick your fat nose in,' she hissed, 'Addy's set for amazing things, no thanks to you. We've arranged for him to meet one of Daddy's producer friends in LA.'

'Sell your soul to the Feeny clan,' she told Addy, 'that's a great idea.'

'Try not to be *quite* so bitter.' Thomasina sneered. 'Just because the Lomaxes ditched you and now your life's gone back to the dung heap it was before.'

'Like you'd know the first thing about the Lomaxes.'

'I bet you thought you had it made. Turns out you were just a flash in the pan.'

'I think you're confusing me with someone else. I never exploited that connection. I never would.'

'And now it's over, and you're rank old gypsy Chopped Liver, just like you always were. Serves you right for stringing Addy along.'

'Me stringing him along?' Olivia laughed. 'That's funny.'

Lavender joined them. In devotion to the matching

principles of her twinhood she had attached herself to Dax Riley, another of the Blue Paradise boys.

'You guys are so *brave*,' she sighed, swathing herself across him.

'Sexy, isn't it, Lav?' Thomasina tossed a satisfied glance at Olivia.

'You ready for this?' Dax asked Addy, over the girls' heads.

'Of course he is,' chirruped Thomasina. 'It's going to be fun, isn't it, bunny?'

Addy appraised the water with a queasy expression. Strange to think that once Olivia had found him so perfect, everything about him god-like, and now he was just a regular guy. He was smaller than she'd made him in her mind, only a fraction taller than she was. His shoulders beneath his wetsuit were not as broad as she remembered.

'Sure is,' he said, with absolutely no conviction.

Thomasina stood on tiptoes to kiss his cheek. Olivia noticed the way he didn't quite angle to receive it, his eyes flitting instead across her.

'You look nervous,' she commented.

'Ha!' Thomasina couldn't resist. 'Says the girl who calls herself a surfer but chickens out of the only serious competition there is.'

'Yeah,' Lavender agreed, 'you always were a cow—I mean *coward*.'

The twins snickered.

Finally Addy spoke up. 'Leave it out, Tom,' he said.

'Defending her now, are you?'

'Just don't see why you have to be such a bitch the whole time.'

Thomasina's face turned puce.

'Today's a stupid idea,' said Olivia. 'The water's crazy. Addy knows it; that's why he's busy shitting himself.'

'I am not.'

'Bets on for Beth Merrill flaking at the last minute,' Thomasina trilled.

'Everyone knows she'll bail; she's only doing it to impress her new boyfriend.'

Behind them, Beth was sitting at the marquee. She was kitted out in her gear, bent forward with a hand on her ankle. Crouching next to her was Sackville Grey. 'Good luck,' Olivia told Addy. She couldn't resist throwing a dirty glance Thomasina's way. 'I think you're going to need it.'

As she got nearer to Beth, it was clear her friend was nursing a serious injury.

'What happened?' Olivia asked worriedly, kneeling on the sand.

'You won't believe it,' Beth groaned. 'Bloody twisted my ankle, didn't I, getting down to the beach.'

'There's no way she can do the challenge,' said Sackville, relieved.

Olivia was, too. 'Thank God for that.' She held her friend's ankle, apologising when Beth winced in pain. 'You need to get this looked at. It's sprained.'

'The whole town sponsored me; there's no way I can drop! Everyone's here!'

'So? They'll understand. Return the donations if you're that fussed, it's not like you need them any more.'

A shrill whistle sliced through the air. Olivia saw Dax bound towards the start, board under his arm, his sandy hair ruffled by the wind. Addy was disentangling himself from Thomasina. Finally breaking free of her clinging arms, and leaving her upturned lips waiting in limbo for a kiss, he straggled down after him.

Checking self-consciously that no one had seen, Thomasina's reptilian scowl fell on Olivia.

'Not joining in, after all, wimp?' she taunted. 'There's a surprise.'

Olivia thought: *Fuck it.*

She bottled the look on Thomasina's face for later enjoyment.

'As a matter of fact, we are,' she replied. 'Because I'm doing it.'

Seawater splashed into her lungs, harsh and salty. The water was foamy and hostile, khaki-green, and in deeper pockets toe-numbingly cold.

The boys paddled out at double her speed, boards clipping the waves, their arms scooping through the breakers as they hollered and shook their heads against the exploding spray. Addy sailed past and she saw the soles of his feet, wrinkled and pale as cabbage leaves. Cries of encouragement blew in from the shore, fainter and fainter the further they paddled. Olivia concentrated on the bobbing horizon, appearing and vanishing with each crest and descent, the blood burning in her arms.

At last the train of boards levelled out. They turned back to face the beach, now reduced to a faint, remote strip, and waited. Olivia tuned into that private, addictive beat. It was a subtle shift in the senses, the tingling approach of the frightening unseen: the same as she felt when she was out on her own but different somehow in the collective, heightened, honed, becoming its own force, like the wired, suspicious energy at a séance at the end of a dinner party. This was the ultimate ocean ride—and she had her ticket. There was no going back.

The wind dropped. Everything was quiet and still. In the distance she could make out Beth in the shallows, her arm in the air, waving encouragement.

At the other end of the beach, a man was standing apart. Against the powdery cliffs he was little more than a black thumbprint.

She held her breath.

And waited.

The wave approached like thunder. From the outset Olivia knew that she wouldn't be able to ride it, the surge was too great; chasing her, tipping her forwards, the breath whipped from her chest. In her peripheral she saw one of the guys topple, tipped before he'd begun the pursuit; a second attempted to get to his feet and went somersaulting into the deep; a third crouched before he was tossed. The swell was boundless, pushing and pushing with unerring, unending strength, and she counted down to the moment to jump but it never came. Dax leapt on to the board too soon and plunged off. Addy's was flipped before he was swallowed in an angry froth:

a brief flash of a panicking pale face swallowed by the rolling rush.

Cast out ahead of the line, she braced herself for the hurdle.

Not yet, not yet...

As far as she dared she hung back, and when the instant clicked she sprang to her feet, taller than the heavens, wider than the sun. The surf moved with her in perfect synergy, this unrivalled force of nature, carrying her, pulling her home.

I've done it, Olivia thought. *I'm flying.*

Too quickly, the rhythm changed.

She hadn't time to think about it, just felt it and in a whoosh the dome above her cartwheeled, the green below slipped away and she was under. Gurgling ocean churned in her ears. The sky folded into the sea. She kicked out to right herself and the board slammed against her head. Dizzily she groped for the surface, grappling for a wheeling arc of daylight as it foamed and heaved and the world turned to liquid. Momentarily it broke and she snatched at air before a briny wash engulfed her once more. She reached a hand to feel for something solid.

Oxygen was running out. Her lungs contracted.

The rush kept coming. She tried to touch down, had no idea how deep she was or even in what direction she had been thrown. She fought back panic, but with every thwarted gasp it flared, constricting her breath and filling her brain with fury. Salt and grit flooded her mouth, her nose, branding her eyes and scorching down her chest. The struggle became too much. She let go. Her limbs stopped flailing.

You have to go back in now...

She felt herself sinking, down, down, down into absolute darkness.

CHAPTER THIRTY-NINE

DON'T STRUGGLE, I've got you, I've got you...

Strong arms encircled her. The voice was carrying her across miles and miles of wide blue sea. She wanted to see who it was but the light was too painful, and she already knew because she recognised that voice. It had never left, it had always been there, and she was afraid that if she opened her eyes it would dissolve in the wind.

Flat, cool sand as it spread wide beneath her back. Muffled, hard-to-hear calls. A hand was cradling her head; it was hot and she was cold.

'Can you hear me?'

There it was again. Yes, she could hear.

A mouth was on hers, soft and warm, bringing her back to life.

CHAPTER FORTY

SHE COUGHED UP water, a salty cupful that splashed on to the sand. Charlie wrapped a blanket round her, rubbing her shoulders to bring up the rest.

The circle poured forward, frantic with concern.

Is she OK? What does she need?

Give her space. She'll be all right. She's in shock.

A dark-haired girl burst out of the crowd and fell to her knees, pulling Olivia into a hug. 'Thank God you're all right,' she cried. 'I thought you were dead.'

The rest of the surfers were clambering in from the water, rushing to see what had happened. The pretty boy led the charge, exclaiming when he saw her, 'Jesus Christ, Oli; what were you thinking?' He wedged his board in the sand, confidence restored, flicking his crop of blond. 'I knew this was way out of your league.'

'And I know she's way out of yours,' said Charlie menacingly. 'Back off before I make you.'

'All right, mate...' Addy scowled at the darkly sea-swept man before him, then realised who he was and with it the bluster dissolved.

'She was the only one who rode it,' put in Beth, scanning the ring. 'Notice how none of you boys stepped in to help.'

'It was quite the dramatic rescue,' supplied Thomasina Feeny, her face bloated with envy at the sight of handsome, heroic Charlie Lomax bounding into the sea, powering through a swell of currents and dragging out Chopped Liver. Why didn't that sort of thing ever happen to her? She was so much prettier, for God's sake!

'You didn't even *stand up* out there,' Thomasina muttered tightly to her boyfriend. 'How embarrassing! Couldn't you at least have made an effort?'

'You try doing it, then,' Addy retorted grimly.

Charlie guided Olivia's face round to his. 'Are you OK?'

Dazedly she nodded. 'Is it really you?'

He wiped a streak of sand with his thumb. 'Yes. It's me.'

Into her green eyes he fell without fear of the drop.

Olivia Lark. His Olivia.

He had never kissed nor been kissed quite so tenderly. She tasted sweet, of the deep, deep quiet of the sea.

'Done playing the hero yet, old bean?'

A familiar snarl broke them apart. Charlie stood. The circle around them split, and Cato could be seen through the rift, charging towards them. His brother's hair was wild, his expression more savage than Charlie had known it in twenty-six years of savagery. Close to, it was apparent he'd been drinking: his eyes were rimmed, the flesh sallow and flaccid.

In the distance, a raft of photographers was trickling down to the bay. Cato's emergence from Usherwood had brought them out like rats from a sinking ship.

Charlie opened his mouth to speak, to ask that they take this somewhere secluded, but before he could Cato pushed him. The thump was hard, and momentarily winded him. He fell backwards on to the sand.

'Happy now, *brother*?'

Their tide of onlookers shrank back. There was an unusual aura about Cato, one that at first Charlie couldn't put his finger on but then it fell into his hands, slippery as a fish. Cato was afraid. His defences were stripped. Vulnerable, not invincible: he could be broken, his armour melted, unveiling the skin beneath.

'I had a visit from Fiona Montgomery this morning,' Cato rasped, his face twisted and grey. 'Very enlightening, it was. She came looking for you, but with a little gentle persuasion I managed to squeeze it out of her.'

Charlie's eyes flicked to the advancing paparazzi.

'Go home, Cato,' he said. 'You're attracting attention.'

'She told you the truth…' Olivia spoke. 'Didn't she?'

Charlie turned to her. 'What truth?'

'It's not the truth, you fucking bunch of idiots.' There he was, the Cato they knew. 'That's what I've come to tell you, to save you the indignity of believing that trout's heap of total and utter fucking bullshit. You've been deceived enough, old boy; don't let them do it to you again. It's a lie; do you hear me? *A lie.*'

The cameras were having a field day. Images clicked and flashed, and a new declaration rose from the crowd, a man's voice, low and clear.

'No, it isn't.'

A ripple travelled through their audience. Cato's head twitched like a bird's, searching for the source of the treachery.

Slowly the man stepped forward, his arms held out. Charlie knew the man, and yet until this moment hadn't known him at all. His expression was sore with longing and apology. Cato stumbled in the sand, his face leached of colour.

'Stay away from me,' he hissed. 'You stay the *fuck* away from me.'

Charlie looked from one to the other. The man was close now, in spite of his brother's caution, and with each tread Cato seemed to flag, he seemed to mislay for whom or what he was fighting for, weakened in the shadow of this gentle approach.

In a last-ditch kick against the facts, Cato pitched a swing. It was ill-judged and drunkenly chaotic, but in any case his target was too fast.

The man caught Cato's fists in his own and held them. In that moment of locked, silent combat, the curtain lifted. There it was.

His brother's mouth, his brow, the bridge of his nose. The chin, the lips and the curve of his shoulders... Bright as day, there it was.

Cato had never come up against Richmond like this.

He had never been reduced by Richmond to his lesser self, rescued of all his nonsense and bravado.

With this man, his brother was a boy.

Charlie's past, his present, his future, spun before him on the roll of a dice.

In Ben Nancarrow's eyes blazed a fury that was years in the melding.

Cato buckled to the sand. His father caught him and held him up.

EPILOGUE

One month later

ITALY IN SEPTEMBER was beautiful.

Olivia opened her eyes to the warmth of unbroken sunshine. A gentle breeze drifted in through the shutters of their Tuscan *pensione*, scented like lemons and the sharp green of freshly cut grass. The day rolled out before them, endlessly perfect.

Standing, she slipped on one of Charlie's T-shirts and went to the veranda. Bountiful fields stretched before her, studded with slender Cypress trees. She stretched and caught his aroma on the material: the heat of his body.

On the table her sketchbook bulged with drawings. Since arriving she had captured everything her imagination had latched upon: the wide landscape aglow in the setting sun; an isolated church buried in the hillside; an elderly shopkeeper going about his daily business; a group of children playing football in the square…and Charlie, always Charlie, whom she could draw for ever.

She turned to the bed. His chest was golden, his dusky hair a mess. Not wanting to wake him, she crept outside and breathed the air.

The trip had been his idea. If they were going to start again—with the cove, with Usherwood, with everything—they had to do it right, and that meant putting some sliver of distance between now and the future. Over the summer Charlie's world had been thrown upside down, and while in some sense, with Fiona's input, it had been righted, they accepted that it would be for ever changed.

In the end, Cato had borne the brunt of their mother's deceit. Despite his behaviour Olivia couldn't help feeling pity. All his life Cato had sought to prove himself to a man who had turned out to be nothing to him, and the Lomax anchor nothing but a temporary float. Without his inheritance, Cato was lost.

He had returned to the States to live. The press had gone wild for the illegitimacy story, splashing the Lustell beach pictures across every tabloid, and a keen-eyed passer-by's phone footage making waves on YouTube. In it Cato could be seen on his knees, his father's arms around him. Fans embraced it as an emotional, long-lost reunion, testament to the happy ever afters peddled by the movie industry, but they would never know the journey that had led them to that point.

As far as his fledgling relationship with Ben Nancarrow went, that was anyone's guess. Reports had sailed over that Ben had been spotted with his son in an LA restaurant. Olivia hoped they were true, but common sense told her better. Thanks to Richmond Lomax's threat all those years ago, staying out of the spotlight was a skill Ben had perfected for life. Irrespective of the years he longed to make up for, he couldn't fit in with Cato's world. As men they were poles apart.

Since the revelations, Cato too had shied from the limelight. Charlie was confident this was a short-term arrangement, and that Cato would tend his wounds for a while before coming back fifty times stronger. Olivia searched for a tone when he spoke of his brother, some mean or uncharitable inflection, something that betrayed Charlie's own narrow escape, but there was none. He said that his past with Cato was behind them. It was over. He had said what he needed to say. Cato knew where he was if he wanted to see him: they still shared Beatrice, they were still brothers…

And Usherwood was still Cato's home.

So, it seemed, was Caggie Shaw, who was becoming something of a celebrity herself over in LA. Word had it she'd been offered her own cookery show on a top lifestyle network; a sexy British schoolmarm-type affair with a splash of *Nigella* finger licking. Her rumoured dalliance with the man himself, inflamed after a string of enigmatic comments given to the press by ex-girlfriend Susanna Denver, had Caggie pegged as the definitive cougar. Olivia remembered the cook making breakfast at Usherwood and was bemused by it. She'd never guessed her affection for Cato ran so deep. Then again, they had been sleeping together since he was a teenager—for both of them their longest, and probably most meaningful, relationship.

Once, Caggie had been a replacement for his mother; now she was a replacement for his past. Cato had to hold on to something.

Susanna, meanwhile, was set to embark on her first major film role in years. Her chick-flick days had limped on to bloody stumps, and this venture, her team promised, would mark a shift in audience perception. Directed by movie colossus Howard Brice, it was tagged for mega things. Olivia had been pleased to see her hook up with a British producer, and even more when Susanna had been snapped with her happily smiling six-year-old in a New York park. Thorn had now been officially unveiled as a part of her life, and was expected to spend his school holidays there. At last Susanna was facing up to her responsibilities, and with it had filled an absence that no man or movie role or ten-thousand-dollar gown could ever hope to.

Olivia leaned on the balcony. She closed her eyes and pictured the autumn approaching at home, her mother's caravan covered in leaves: her favourite time of year. Wherever she went in the world, Lustell Cove would always be the place she yearned for. They had only been gone three weeks, but she was excited to get back.

She couldn't wait to see Beth. For days after the Surfathon her friend had barely left her side, worried Olivia was about to develop post-event hypothermia or choke on some remnant of seaweed. Beth was in awe

of Charlie, and never got tired of relaying the story of
how he had bound unthinkingly into the ocean, tearing
off his shoes and shirt and ploughing into the waves.
'That sort of thing just doesn't *happen* in real life!' she'd
swooned, and Olivia had to admit it was kind of amazing. Beth wasn't short of a bit of romance herself, and
was blissfully loved-up with Sackville.

Olivia confessed to a twinge of smugness when she
pictured Thomasina and Lavender watching the rescue. All through school they had mocked and derided
her, and finally she'd had her moment. Bizarrely Addy
and Thomasina were still together, though according to
Beth they were constantly at war. He had sacked off his
acting plans and instead was pursuing a modelling career, in true Addy style making a beeline for Serendipity
Swain in case she could provide him with a useful in-
road. Apparently Thomasina felt threatened by the company he might be keeping and was attempting to get
her own foot on the fashion ladder, which automatically
meant that Lavender was doing the same. Daddy Feeny
was paying for the best portfolio money could buy.

She was pulled from her thoughts by a trail of kisses
being planted along her neck. Charlie's strong arms
looped round her waist.

Melting against him, she smiled.

The house would be waiting when they got back, it
and the dogs ably looked after by a reinstated Barbara.
For the first time he could look forward to Usherwood's
future. Days before they had left for Europe, an anony-
mous benefactor had donated an astonishing slug of

money to the estate, enough to cover everything that Charlie had been working for years to achieve. It could only have been Barnaby Cartwright.

'I could get used to this,' she said.

'Good.' The word was muffled against her shoulder. 'Now come back to bed.'

'What time is it?'

'Time you let me kiss you.'

She turned into his embrace. The kisses she had known before could never come close. Charlie Lomax's kiss was sublime.

As he led her back inside, she thought only of the promise of the days to come. They would take things slowly. Charlie had been persuaded to take up the offer of an exhibition (as it turned out, Sackville had approached him before Beth had a chance to put in a word), and as for Olivia's own artistic endeavours she had a tough call to make. A friend's museum had contacted her, suggesting to her a residency. It would mean relocation back to London, at least for a while. She hadn't told Charlie. Occasionally he would slip when he spoke of the estate, talking of 'we' and 'us' and catching himself and retracting it. To think of her life there was both exciting and terrifying. Even in her wildest dreams she could never have imagined it.

There would be a world to occupy and inspire her, the gardens and the house endless muses. A world to love in Charlie alone.

After the day of the rescue, he had taken her back to

Usherwood. In a case in the library, undiscovered by Cato in his clear-out, had been a wrapped parcel.

'This is for you,' he'd said, holding it out.

Olivia had unpacked it. It was the plate she had seen in Cley: the grey-green paint that had drawn her on the afternoon with Thorn and the crabs and the sunburn.

The movement on the waves and the lifting, invigorating spray, it was just the same: the same as the day they had laid her father to rest.

'I saw how much you fell in love with it,' Charlie had told her, looking deep into her eyes. *'And that was when I fell in love with you.'*

He kissed her now as fiercely as he had then. Olivia held him close, Charlie Lomax, her Charlie, her lover and her friend, and knew she had unlocked the secret.

* * * * *

Read on for an extract from Victoria's fabulous novel

WICKED AMBITION

available now

Prologue

IF NOT VICTORY, REVENGE!

It was printed in hot-pink marker on the back of the cubicle door, the lettering neat and precise. Ivy Sewell reached to touch it, her fingertips tentative, tender almost across its surface, as she might in another life have caressed a lover's cheek.

Her hard blue stare locked on to the affirmation. Ivy's was a malice years in the making, a shoot green in youth that had turned black through adolescence, insidious and strangling as a weed, so that tonight, here, at last, the instant of her retribution had arrived. In the wings, the truth gasped its final throttled breaths; the old order shrugged off a wilted coil. She was deadly. Lethal. Toxic. *Poison.* And the world prepared to feel her wrath.

There would be before tonight, and after tonight, and

nothing would ever be the same again. In the eleventh-floor washroom of LA's Palisades Grand Arena, on the most televised event in the entertainment world calendar, vengeance was their apocalypse.

Ivy carved a painted fingernail, danger red, into the print, gouging a nub of plaster.

IF NOT VICTORY, REVENGE!

Victory had never been hers. But revenge? Revenge was in her blood.

From inside the stadium she could hear the muted thrum of beats and the united roar of the fans. Ivy imagined the cries were for her, urging her on, baying for the carnage she was about to unleash. She released her breath, tasting salt and iron, her tongue flicking across the split in her lip where she had bitten too hard in anticipation.

Three women.

Each was here to claim the spotlight. Each was an international superstar, a glittering icon with the world at her feet. Robin Ryder, UK talent-show sensation, the rags-to-riches sweetheart rescued from oblivion. Kristin White, global pop phenomenon with the voice of an angel, who had ditched the princess act after tragedy struck. And Turquoise da Luca, America's number one female vocal artist and now tantalising toast of Tinseltown.

One of them was going to perish.

At the mega-event better known as the ETV Platinum Awards, Ivy Sewell was concerned with one target and one alone: her twin. The hated sister, born identical and torn towards an opposite fate, who had claimed everything Ivy herself should have been, who had snatched it all from her grasp, who had turned her back and slipped so seamlessly into a life of opulence and glamour, forgetting where she had come from or what had gone before.

Ivy shoved the bag into the trashcan, forcing it down with her fists. Later, when it was discovered, they would know how clever she had been. In it lurked the disguise she'd worn, the orange T-shirt with its Burger Delite! logo emblazoned across the front…a whole person, just like that, folded away in a sack. She stared indifferently at the hands that would carry out this great execution. Wrists pale and brittle, like branches in winter; the fingers thin.

Only when the bullet entered would it be over. Only when that flawless skin was ruptured, that smile erased, that heartbeat frozen, one and the same as hers and yet a universe apart, would it be finished: one life in exchange for another.

A rapturous cry exploded. The show was beginning, the stage lit up to welcome the players, the kings and queens of twenty-first-century music, the alphas and the studs and the bitches and the beauties with their diamonds and their hundred-thousand-dollar gowns.

Ivy closed her eyes. The letters were emblazoned on her lids, bright as fire.

IF NOT VICTORY, REVENGE!

The curtain was up. And now it was show time.

PART 1

One year earlier

Robin Ryder was seeing stars, weightless and electrified as she flew towards the raging sun of her orgasm. Fuck the wardrobe her stylist had spent hours perfecting; fuck the producer's countdown mere minutes away; fuck everything except this glorious, glittering fuck.

'Does that feel good?' the man breathed, gripping her waist and pulling in deeper. Robin, on top, ground against him; the slippery, yielding leather of the seat was soft and sticky beneath her knees, and she threw her head back to moan her reply.

Backstage in the VIP suite, ahead of a live Saturday night broadcast of *The Launch*, she was riding this guy like it was the last ride of her life. What she was doing was reckless, it was sinful, but Robin had never been able to play by the rules. She was a judge and he a contestant; it was all kinds of wrong and yet all kinds of right. RnB tunes filtered through the music system, and at the bar an empty magnum of Krug nestled on a bed of ice. As Robin held tight she decided she would definitely, oh *definitely*, be putting him through this week.

'I'm there,' she cried, 'don't stop, I'm there!'

'Me too,' the guy choked, driving in hard. 'My God, you're so fucking hot.'

The throne-like chair was a prop, used in the early audition stages: when a judge liked what they saw they hit a lever, prompting the seat to rush forward on a pair of rails. Thankfully for Robin the gimmick had been relegated backstage once the live nights began—she'd proved a hit during those first weeks where her inclination to back everybody had her getting motion sickness every ad break. After all, *The Launch* was where she herself had begun: now she was the nation's darling, drawn from obscurity, a rough diamond polished through song. Robin had risen to fame through the very show she was tonight judging.

The public loved Robin's voice, raw and sensuous, somewhere between pain and deliverance. They loved how she wore her heart on her sleeve. They loved her guts, and her honesty. They loved her story—loved that she'd been hurt and wanted to seize her dues. Over twelve months Robin had soared to a dizzying stratosphere, invited to every party, on to every red carpet, booked for every event. Her gift was undeniable and her smile lit up a room.

'Do you want it?' the contestant was panting, his sweat-slicked six-pack glistening in the half-glow. 'Right there, do you want it?' He was this year's favourite, tough guy with the voice of an angel—and a heavenly body to match.

She came in a crash, a bursting galaxy of dazzling confetti as she writhed on the brink of paradise. Sex was Robin's release. It enabled her to feel that warmth, that closeness, without risk of being wounded. You got what you came for and you left. She didn't get why people wanted to stick around afterwards anyway; she had never understood this sleeping-in-each-other's-arms thing. She'd got this far alone and she didn't need anyone else.

'That was amazing,' he groaned, cradling her, kissing her over and over as she gasped through the aftermath of her climax.

She had barely had time to fling a shirt over her nakedness when the door opened. Robin didn't know which happened first: the contestant's face dropping as fast as his pants had ten minutes earlier; or her attempt to dismount disastrously striking the switch that jolted the chair meteorquick towards their visitor like some sort of warped sacrificial offering.

'Oh,' said their caller, as Robin scrambled to conceal herself. Instead of a mortified exit (which would have been the polite thing), he stood there, an infuriating grin on his face.

Light flooded the room. 'Shit, man,' gabbled the contestant helpfully. 'Shit, shit, shit.'

'Do you mind?' she raged, so mortified she couldn't bear to turn round.

'Sure.' She could hear the smirk in his voice. 'Guess I'll come back later.'

It was a miracle she made it through the show without punching him.

Leon Sway, Olympic sprinter, was guesting on tonight's panel. Since the summer Games had decreed him a World Personality, the athlete was hotly in demand for every broadcast going. Leon was mixed race, with close-cut black hair, strong cheekbones and an all-over movie-star look: it was little wonder he had been gracing billboards across the globe with a ream of sponsorships and modelling contracts; and now here he was making a star appearance on the adjudicating *Launch* line-up—what the hell did he know about music?

'I've been a fan of yours from the start,' Robin told a quivering choirgirl after an impressive rendition of Adele. 'That was a brilliant performance; I really felt it. Well done.'

'Sure that's not all you felt?' came the murmur from her neighbour, just loud enough for her to hear. She tried not to scowl—either that or turn to Leon and chuck her glass of water in his face. It wasn't in Robin's nature to wish for the ground to open up and swallow her whole, but tonight had to be the exception. As the acts ran through their numbers and the board delivered their verdicts, she tried not to dwell on what parts of her anatomy might have been unveiled before they'd even been introduced—not easy with Leon's supercilious bulk to her left, interspersed with a hot flash of shame every time she recalled his untimely intrusion.

'Do you think she can win?' asked a producer mogul who had been tagged as her rival on the show. 'With those nerves I can't see her pulling off any live gigs.'

'This is a live gig, isn't it?' Robin snapped. She could sense Leon watching her. Why did he have to be such a smug, full-of-himself…? Ugh, she couldn't even think of the word.

'Well, yes…'

'I absolutely believe in her,' commented Robin, battling through her disgrace. 'This is where I got my break and it took me time to grow, of course it did. If she were cutthroat at this point you'd be tearing her apart for being difficult to work with. Which is it going to be?'

The arena shouted its approval. Robin's image filled the screens on either side of the stage, the people's champion: she was petite, her hair chopped short but with a trademark sweep still long enough to obscure her eyes, which were cat-like and aglow with dramatic make-up. Hers was a cautious demeanour that belied the tough, attitude-fuelled work that had made her name: Robin's music spoke of more years lived and more experiences earned, and had consequently secured her the first ever talent-show-spawned album to be nominated for—and win—a Brit Select Award. The victory had made Robin Ryder, at just nineteen, the hottest thing on the UK scene. She believed in putting everything into her art, the offering up of her heart and her soul, because for a long time she had imagined that both those things were damaged beyond being any use to anyone.

When the time came for *that* contestant to take the spotlight, she grimaced. Leon couldn't resist fixing her with a stare throughout the entire introductory VT.

'It wasn't for me,' he judged afterwards. 'It kinda felt like you were distracted.'

'I disagree,' put in Robin. 'For me it was a very focused, determined performance.'

Leon turned to her. 'Are you complimenting his performance?'

The blush threatened to engulf her. 'Sure,' she managed, the double entendre squatting resolutely between them. 'I am.'

'Focused *and* determined—that's how you like it, then?'

She returned his glare. 'Who doesn't?'

The host, confused, went to ask another panellist their view.

'It seemed like he had something else on his mind,' Leon steamed on before he could, 'something more interesting than being up on that stage. Don't you feel that's an issue?'

'Whatever drives him is fine by me,' she replied stiffly, knowing that every word she uttered was laced in innuendo. 'After all, what would a *sprinter* know about vocals?'

It was a cheap shot, she ought to know better, but humiliation had forced her into a corner. A blood-hungry cheer erupted and she could all but hear the producers salivating.

'Well, he is the bookies' favourite,' supplied the mogul.

'Not just the bookies'…right, Robin?' Leon joked, a crescent-moon dimple appearing on one side of his all too slappable face. His insinuation was obvious. There was a horrible silence. Robin's cheeks flamed. She tried to think of something to say and nothing came. She was so angry she could scream. This was *live TV*!

'Ex*cuse* me?' she spluttered.

But the presenter moved on, instructed to sever it at the point of maximum speculation.

Afterwards, everyone assured her that it hadn't sounded that bad. Robin wasn't stupid. It would be all over the papers tomorrow thanks to that insufferable bastard Leon Sway! The contestant looked hopefully at her as she fled: that was the end of him.

Her car took her straight to Soho's Hideaway Club, where she found scant solace in ordering the strongest concoction she could find. Her band met her there.

'I don't want to talk about it,' she said, before Polly, her bassist, had a chance.

Polly was American with a peroxide-blonde beehive. 'All right,' she said as they settled in a booth. 'But just to say—'

'Don't say anything.'

'It could have been worse.'

'Could it?'

'*Did* you screw him?'

Robin was aghast. 'Who, Leon?' she demanded, outraged at the thought.

'No!' Polly named the contestant. 'Although Mr Sway, well, you have to admit—'

'I'm warning you: don't even go there.' She downed the drink. 'Anyway, what difference does it make? Everyone thinks I did, so I did. Isn't that how it goes?'

Within minutes a tower of frosted glasses was deposited in front of them, together with several giant bottles of part-frozen vodka. An accompanying note read:

Want a winner on your team?

Her manager Barney signalled across the space. 'Hey, Robin, check out your secret admirers.' Close to the neon-bulb-strewn bar, just decipherable through the low-lit shadows that gave way to pockets of absolute dark, Olympian Jax Jackson, officially the fastest man in the world, was partying with a harem of lovelies. Two Olympians in one day? Some luck that was. Jax raised a glass and Robin prayed he wouldn't come over: thanks to Leon he probably thought it was a free-for-all.

'If we accept these you don't have to do anything in return, right?' Matt, her drummer, was already pouring. He winked at Robin when she raised her middle finger. 'What? Girls never buy me drinks; it's not like I know the rules!'

Robin tossed back a syrupy shot, then a second, then a

third. Polly threw her a glance and she matched it. What was wrong with having fun? She was young and free and famous, and didn't need anyone to tell her she deserved a break.

'What?' she countered. 'Aren't we partying?' Matt grabbed the second bottle and filled the glasses and everyone went in for a sticky collision before the liquid vanished.

'Sure,' said Polly, not sure at all. What Robin had gone through didn't go away; you had to deal with it before you could move on, not get trashed till you forgot. 'You earned it.'

'Nah, *we* earned it,' corrected Robin, putting one arm round Polly and one round her manager and pulling them close. 'We're family, aren't we?'

Family.

Even as she said the word she could hear how hollow it sounded.

If you've enjoyed this Mills & Boon® book.

We'd love to hear from you at

millsandboon.co.uk

Three superstars. Three secrets.
Who will fall first?

Some will do anything for fame.
Others will do anything to bring
the famous down.

For Robin, Turquoise and Kristin, the spotlight
shines brightly. They've reached the glittering
heights of stardom, but in the shadows lies the
truth... An exposé could be their end.

'It's 600 pages of sin'
Now magazine

Welcome to Paradise.

Only the rich are invited…only the strongest survive.

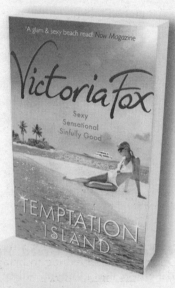

Three women drawn unwittingly to the shores of Temptation Island, all looking for their own truth, discover a secret so shocking there's no turning back. It's wicked, it's sensational. Are you ready to be told?

www.mirabooks.co.uk

*'A juicy tale of glamour,
corruption and ambition'*
—**Jo Rees**

Power. Revenge. Lust. Greed. Betrayal.

Scandal circles like a vulture—dirty secrets
are about to be exposed! For from the deepest
desires come the deadliest deeds...and these
Hollywood A-listers are about to pay for
their sins...

Sexy. Sensational... Sinfully good.
If you love Jackie Collins, then you'll devour
Victoria Fox!

M201_HS

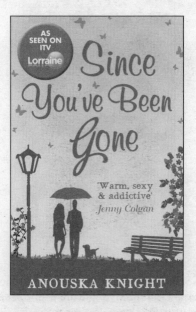

Remember that summer when everything changed?

Katy: Days away from marrying a man she doesn't love, Katy's shocked when fate throws her in the path of Jago Rodriguez—he may have left her years before, but now he's back...

Libby: Spirited, impulsive and independent, Libby has no interest in relationships, until she comes face to face with a man who won't give up and a date she can't turn down!

Alex: Wanted by every woman he's ever met, Alex is totally unprepared when a stranger appears on his doorstep with a baby in her arms.

www.millsandboon.co.uk

0713/MB425

WHAT DID YOU MISS OUT ON BECAUSE YOU FELL IN LOVE?

Kate Winters might just be 'that' girl. You know the one. The girl who, for no particular reason, doesn't get the guy, doesn't have children, doesn't get the romantic happy-ever-after. So she needs a plan.

What didn't she get to do because she fell in love?

What would she be happy spending the rest of her life doing if love never showed up again?

This is one girl's journey to take back what love stole.

M327_LIAT

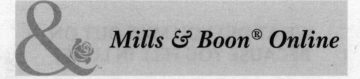